Praise for A

One More Chance

"This was an amazing book by Vali…complex and multi-layered (both characters and plot)."—*Danielle Kimerer, Librarian (Nevins Memorial Library, Massachusetts)*

Face the Music

"This is a typical Ali Vali romance with strong characters, a beautiful setting (Nashville, Tennessee), and an enemies-to-lovers style tale. The two main characters are beautiful, strong-willed, and easy to fall in love with. The romance between them is steamy, and so are the sex scenes."—*Rainbow Reflections*

The Inheritance

"I love a good story that makes me laugh and cry, and this one did that a lot for me. I would step back into this world any time."—*Kat Adams, Bookseller (QBD Books, Australia)*

Double-Crossed

"[T]here aren't too many lesfic books like *Double-Crossed* and it is refreshing to see an author like Vali continue to churn out books like these. Excellent crime thriller."—*Colleen Corgel, Librarian, Queens Borough Public Library*

"For all of us die-hard Ali Vali/Cain Casey fans, this is the beginning of a great new series…There is violence in this book, and lots of killing, but there is also romance, love, and the beginning of a great new reading adventure. I can't wait to read more of this intriguing story."
—*Rainbow Reflections*

Stormy Seas

Stormy Seas "is one book that adventure lovers must read."—*Rainbow Reflections*

Answering the Call

Answering the Call "is a brilliant cop-and-killer story…The crime story is tight and the love story is fantastic."—*Best Lesbian Erotica*

Lammy Finalist *Calling the Dead*

"So many writers set stories in New Orleans, but Ali Vali's mystery novels have the authenticity that only a real Big Easy resident could bring. Set six months after Hurricane Katrina has devastated the city, a lesbian detective is still battling demons when a body turns up behind one of the city's famous eateries. What follows makes for a classic lesbian murder yarn."—*Curve Magazine*

Beauty and the Boss

"The story gripped me from the first page…Vali's writing style is lovely—it's clean, sharp, no wasted words, and it flows beautifully as a result. Highly recommended!"—*Rainbow Book Reviews*

Balance of Forces: Toujours Ici

"A stunning addition to the vampire legend, *Balance of Forces: Toujours Ici* is one that stands apart from the rest."—*Bibliophilic Book Blog*

Beneath the Waves

"The premise…was brilliantly constructed…skillfully written and the imagination that went into it was fantastic…A wonderful passionate love story with a great mystery."—*Inked Rainbow Reads*

Second Season

"The issues are realistic and center around the universal factors of love, jealousy, betrayal, and doing the right thing and are constantly woven into the fabric of the story. We rated this well written social commentary through the use of fiction our max five hearts."—*Heartland Reviews*

Carly's Sound

"*Carly's Sound* is a great romance, with some wonderfully hot sex, but it is more than that. It is also the tale of a woman rising from the ashes of grief and finding new love and a new life. Vali has surrounded Julia and Poppy with a cast of great supporting characters, making this an extremely satisfying read."—*Just About Write*

Praise for the Cain Casey Saga

The Devil's Due

"A Night Owl Reviews Top Pick: Cain Casey is the kind of person you aspire to be even though some consider her a criminal. She's loyal, very protective of those she loves, honorable, big on preserving her family legacy and loves her family greatly. *The Devil's Due* is a book I highly recommend and well worth the wait we all suffered through. I cannot wait for the next book in the series to come out."
—*Night Owl Reviews*

The Devil Be Damned

"Ali Vali excels at creating strong, romantic characters along with her fast-paced, sophisticated plots. Her setting, New Orleans, provides just the right blend of immigrants from Mexico, South America, and Cuba, along with a city steeped in traditions."—*Just About Write*

Deal with the Devil

"Ali Vali has given her fans another thick, rich thriller...*Deal With the Devil* has wonderful love stories, great sex, and an ample supply of humor. It is an exciting, page-turning read that leaves her readers eagerly awaiting the next book in the series."—*Just About Write*

The Devil Unleashed

"Fast-paced action scenes, intriguing character revelations, and a refreshing approach to the romance thriller genre all make for an enjoyable reading experience in the Big Easy...*The Devil Unleashed* is an engrossing reading experience."—*Midwest Book Review*

The Devil Inside

"*The Devil Inside* is the first of what promises to be a very exciting series...While telling an exciting story that grips the reader, Vali has also fully fleshed out her heroes and villains. *The Devil Inside* is that rarity: a fascinating crime novel which includes a tender love story and leaves the reader with a cliffhanger ending."—*MegaScene*

By the Author

Carly's Sound

Second Season

Love Match

The Dragon Tree Legacy

The Romance Vote

Hell Fire Club
in Girls with Guns

Beauty and the Boss

Blue Skies

Stormy Seas

The Inheritance

Face the Music

On the Rocks
in Still Not Over You

A Woman to Treasure

Calumet

Writer's Block

One More Chance

A Good Chance

The Cain Casey Saga

The Devil Inside

The Devil Unleashed

Deal with the Devil

The Devil Be Damned

The Devil's Orchard

The Devil's Due

Heart of the Devil

The Devil Incarnate

Call Series

Calling the Dead

Answering the Call

Waves Series

Beneath the Waves

Turbulent Waves

Forces Series

Balance of Forces: Toujours Ici

Battle of Forces: Sera Toujours

Force of Fire: Toujours a Vous

Vegas Nights

Double-Crossed

Visit us at www.boldstrokesbooks.com

NEVER KISS
A COWGIRL

by
Ali Vali

2023

ISBN 13: 978-1-63679-106-7

THIS TRADE PAPERBACK ORIGINAL IS PUBLISHED BY
BOLD STROKES BOOKS, INC.
P.O. BOX 249
VALLEY FALLS, NY 12185

FIRST EDITION: MAY 2023

CREDITS
EDITOR: RUTH STERNGLANTZ
PRODUCTION DESIGN: STACIA SEAMAN
COVER DESIGN BY TAMMY SEIDICK

Acknowledgments

Thank you, Radclyffe, for your friendship and support—I treasure both. Thank you, Sandy, for the tweak to my story idea. Now I know more about cows than the average person, but it was a fun experience. You're the best. I value your friendship as well as your ability to pick great titles. When it comes to my BSB family, know that I value the family and friendship you have given me. It's a gift to have such rock-solid support.

Thank you to my awesome editor, Ruth Sternglantz. Ruth, you were one of the first people I met with BSB, and it's been one of the best friendships of my life through the years. Working with you has only made that so much better. I'm looking forward to many more years of fun and work. I'd also like to thank Tammy Seidick for the great cover.

A huge thank you to my beta dream team: Kim Rieff, Cris Perez-Soria, and Lenore Beniot. You guys make the process fun, and I'm glad you take the time to read these and give such great feedback. We've made it through thirty-four, so hopefully there'll be plenty more to come.

Thank you to you the reader. I appreciate all the posts on social media, the reviews you write, and the feedback you send. It's been a while since we've seen each other in person, but your notes and emails have kept me sane and laughing. I appreciate you all.

It's been nice getting back to normal with all my house repairs behind me and getting back to writing. I'm ready for new adventures with my navigator in all things, C. Verdad!

For C
Always

Chapter One

B o the Third!" The announcer said the name as if Bo needed to last a full thirty seconds, and the people in the stands should be awed to be in his presence. Asher Evans couldn't blame the old guy, considering the bull kicking the shit out of the chute he was locked in was an impressive beast. He was big, strong, and angry at the world.

Asher sat on the top rail waiting as the crowd stomped their boots on the old metal stands. The noise seemed to enrage the bull she'd drawn to ride, and she laughed at his building frantic behavior. Bo kicked both legs back, rattling the structure hard enough to make her momentarily lose her balance. She was grateful for all the upper body work she did, since her arm strength kept her upright. The crowd started chanting the bull's name, and even through the din, she had no problem hearing Bo snorting as he started to paw the ground as if readying himself for blood—hers specifically.

"Trying to make your great-great-granddaddy proud, big man." She laughed when he shook his head and kicked back again as if he'd understood every word and found them insulting. With his light yellow coat, short downturned horns, and mean disposition, Bo really was the spitting image of the famous Bodacious, a bull that had been inducted into the ProRodeo Hall of Fame. Some bulls were more famous than the fools who voluntarily climbed on their backs to ride them.

Bodacious had been one of those bulls, and his grandson a few generations removed was trying to surpass his fame. The problem was, Asher wasn't intimidated by his shenanigans, as her mentor would've said. And this time around, his rider had more name recognition than him, since there was only one woman ranked in the top ten of professional rodeo, and it was Bo's bad luck that's who was about to meet his rage with her own. Bo was the most dangerous bull to ride on the circuit at the moment, and she wasn't about to fall before she was ready to get off.

The thrill of eight seconds on a bucking bull had cost her plenty in scars, both mental and physical, but there was no quitting. There was no giving up until she was the best, with the belt buckle to prove it. She owed her success to the man who'd voluntarily taken on the task of raising her and taught her everything he knew about rodeo, ranching, and—basically—life.

"There's your opening, Asher." The rodeo worker yelled even though he was right beside her. "This is one mean son of a bitch, so careful."

She threw one leg over Bo's back, and that move made the animal lose his shit, but she had the guy working the chute pull the rope around the bull's chest taut as she moved into position. Once the rope lost the slack, she ran her gloved hand up and down its length her customary ten times, tightening as she went. All the while she paid attention to Bo since any unexpected move on his part would smash her legs into the sides of the chute. With an animal this big, that would be an invitation to the emergency room with a season-ending injury.

She tightened her thighs to keep herself in place and put her hand into the grip of the rope, going with Bo when he kicked back again. Her last step was sliding forward so her hand was even with her crotch and her legs were in front of the rope. The chute guy pushed her hat down to keep it in place, and she nodded her thanks. Her anticipation built like rising water behind a weak dam. When the chute door opened, that's exactly what it would feel like—millions of gallons of water bursting out with the intent to destroy everything in its path, her included, and taking her on the wildest ride she could ever conceive of.

"Ready, rider?"

Asher took a deep breath, nodded, and the chute door opened. The first buck came close to giving her whiplash, but she tightened her legs, threw her free hand up, and hung on. She gave the judges and the crowd what they'd come to see. Bull riding was way more than just staying on the bull's back. It was the art of how you kept your body in control and your free arm in the air never touching the rope or animal, and the rhythm you got into with the bull you were riding. She always thought of it as a violent ballet of sorts.

All that accounted for a possible fifty points, but the bull's performance accounted for the other fifty points. So to get the high scores it was important to draw a bull that moved with speed and with a talent for unseating anyone who dared ride them. She'd lucked out with Bo since he never stopped whipping from one side to the other, trying to get her the hell off him.

This would be her last ride for four months, and she had to make it count. Winning tonight with ninety points or more would move her into second place, giving her a cushion in the standings for the rest of the season. So far the judges hadn't given anything higher than eighty-two.

There was a moment where the adrenaline zapped the sound out of her head and all she could feel was the thrumming of her blood rushing through her veins. This was a test of wills, and she thrilled at it every single time. The clarity triggered by exhilaration brought every lesson Silas Wilson taught her to the forefront of her mind, and she paid attention to her form as she moved with the bull.

The buzzer was what brought her back to the present, and the cheering along with Bo's indignant snorting cut through the bubble in an instant. All she needed now was to get clear and wait. She loosened her grip and leaned to the left, waiting on Bo.

This was the point when you upped your chance to get hurt, Silas always said, so she'd been extra careful from her first ride. The bull reacted, and she jumped clear, lifting her fist to the crowd when her boots were back on the dirt of the arena. She took off her hat and bumped her leg with it once Bo had been lured away by the rodeo clowns. The Texas heat was making her sweat enough that the dust was sticking to her skin, so she was ready for a shower.

Asher accepted Wade Wilson's hug when she made it out of the arena. This event was small and out of the way, but it counted when it came to the national standings. Lajitas, Texas, wasn't on a lot of radars, but it's where Asher had first competed, with Silas screaming pointers from the sidelines. The arena had remained unchanged from the time it'd been built nearly seventy years before. It was steeped in tradition like no other place in the country and supported by crowds that loved the sport.

"Good job, kid," Wade said. She'd scored ninety-seven, tying her highest score ever. "Do you want a beer?"

"Let me get my buckle and a shower, and we'll go get a few. We good for tomorrow?" She sat across from him, glad her night was almost over. Wade, like his brother Silas and her father, loved the barren landscape of Lajitas since they'd spent years of their younger lives here, riding the rocky terrain as they learned the ranching business.

She'd spent years listening to Wade and Silas tell the stories of the three of them and the adventures they'd had. They'd been three cowboys who'd grown up riding herds and dreaming of what their futures would be, with Big Bend National Park as their backyard. Silas had gone the rodeo route, and her dad and Wade had run the ranching part of their businesses. The three friends had eventually moved to Louisiana because of the women they'd married, and they'd ended up with equal acreage southeast of New Orleans.

Asher's mom died in childbirth, and when her father, Dustin, died in the saddle when she was twelve, she was alone in the world—her dad's parents were dead, and her mom's didn't want her. But Silas stepped up.

She loved Silas for the time he'd put in to raising her to be the person she'd become even though he had a child of his own to worry about. He'd assured her from the day she moved in with them that she'd never be alone. Silas had been so proud that she'd followed in his footsteps in almost every aspect of life, from ranching to the rodeo.

"We're set for tomorrow," Wade said, "and I'll send Gavin down after we're done. More than fifty head, and railing them down will make the most sense." Wade stretched his legs out and crossed his feet at the ankles. He wasn't a tall guy, but like his brother, he owned every room he was in. "Frida told you the news?" The question was hesitant and softly spoken.

"Reagan's coming home. That news?" She did her best to bleed the emotion out of her voice.

"Yep." He slapped her back, squeezing her shoulder. "Remember, Buck"—he used the nickname her dad had given her—"shit has a way of working out. All you need to know is I'm proud of you just like your daddy and Silas were, and I got your back."

She was about to comment on his sentimentality when the announcer called her name as the winner. All she needed to do before that beer was pick up a check and the belt buckle to go with the dozens she'd already won. Hopefully Wade was right, but sometimes... sometimes shit didn't work out. She'd learned that, one painful lesson at a time, all of them ending with the loss of someone or something she loved.

❖

The crowd inside Cat's Meow in the French Quarter was starting to become unhinged as the time hit one in the morning. Reagan Wilson grimaced at the bad karaoke, but her coworkers had already threatened her twice for trying to sneak out early. They were all crammed around the table, and the size of the crowd was making her sweat.

Coming home had been a whim, and she still couldn't explain it to herself since she'd enjoyed the life she'd carefully constructed for herself in Seattle. That was as far as she could go to get away from her upbringing and the memories of this place. It had been four months since the move back, and she'd been able to keep it from her family. It was petty, that she knew, but when she'd landed in New Orleans it was as if the landscape was filled with landmines and she had no key to where they were.

Slowly easing back into the familiar was the only way to survive. So far her best move had been finding a job with a large sports medicine practice where she wasn't getting too attached to anyone. As soon as her Uncle Wade knew she was close, though, that's exactly what he and the folks on the ranch would expect—attachment. They'd want her to rekindle the relationships she'd not only outgrown but wasn't interested in.

She loved her work as a physical therapist and helping patients find a way to heal, but that was all the human interaction she was interested in at the moment. Being a loner was something she was used to. The people she worked with, of course, had other ideas. Someone reached over her shoulder and slammed a fresh drink down. It made her flinch until she realized it was Kendra Taylor, her boss.

"Take your head out of your ass, girl." Kendra was acting more like a bartender than their supervisor that night, but they'd had a long week. School sports teams had started their practices, and there'd been an influx of patients with a myriad of problems. Everyone was ready to blow off the stress and have a good time. "Go pick a song, or I'll choose one for you."

"Can I remind you this wasn't my idea? A night of bad singing isn't my definition of a way to spend an evening." She laughed despite that being the truth.

"Drink a little more, and it'll start to sound like you're at an Adele concert." Kendra pushed her drink closer. "Only pick something more upbeat than one of those ballads Adele is known for. We're supposed to be having fun, not getting over heartbreak."

She finally gave in and sang an old Elvis song her father had loved to hum. It wasn't until she'd started high school and told him the humming was driving her up a wall that he told her the song had been playing the night he met her mother. Both their lives would've been much happier if he'd kept walking and found a different girl to impress with his charming personality.

All she'd learned from her parents' relationship was that some people were rotten to their souls. Her mother hadn't been the staying kind, but leaving your child was vastly different than leaving your spouse. She was someone her mother should've taken responsibility for since she had no say in being brought into the world. That's not how Christine Wilson had seen it and had left without a backward glance. Christine had come for a visit when she was in Seattle, but it was more about asking for money than any interest in her.

"I'll see you guys Monday," she said to the group when they couldn't convince her to stay another minute. Her car was parked a block away at the Hotel Monteleone, and stepping outside instantly made her breathing even out. Bourbon Street was crowded with locals and tourists all intent on having fun, yet it wasn't like the crowded bar she'd left where everyone seemed pressed up against her.

But when she stepped inside the Monteleone, one glance into the Carousel Bar made up her mind to go home. She'd bought a place in the Garden District—a condo in an old home cut up into six nice-sized places. It had all the old charm she'd been searching for, with the homeowner's association taking care of everything she had no interest in. It was the best of both worlds.

Her phone rang as she waited for her car, and she thought it might be Kendra trying to talk her into coming back. *Uncle.* It was simply the title with no picture. Uncle Wade had been the second person in her life, growing up, who had never disappointed her. Both her father and uncle had been like oaks in a storm. They'd both swayed a little, but they'd been there every day until she'd run to Seattle. Her father's death had made it impossible for her to stay.

"Hey," she said, hating that she sounded concerned and out of breath. "It's really late, are you okay?"

"I'm surprised you picked up. I was going to leave a message, so I hope I'm not taking you away from anything." When the universe created family, or the idea of one, they'd modeled it after Silas and Wade Wilson. They loved like it was something they needed to prove daily, so you'd never question their devotion.

"My work friends talked me into going out, but I'm headed home. What are *you* doing up so late?" She pressed money into the valet's hand and slammed the door.

"I'm in Lajitas glancing up at the sky full of stars, and it reminded me of you. Sorry if it's too late. Last thing I want to do is bother you."

"How was the rodeo?" She could name the event if you gave her the date. The goddamn rodeo that had broken so many of her father's bones, then eventually had been the reason for his death was something she hated with a passion. It was the most asinine sport ever thought of, and it still amazed her how many fools signed up at a chance to get maimed or, worse, killed.

"Not in the mood to argue with you tonight, Reagan. Just wanted to check on you." Her uncle sounded tired. It was a weariness that she'd noticed the last couple of times they'd talked, and it worried her. "Why don't you come for dinner this week? And before you tell me a story, I know you're in town. Why you didn't want our help isn't something I'm going to ask you, but don't pile on by lying."

"Uncle Wade, we talked about this." Wade had visited her in Washington State when the thought of coming home was like facing a firing squad. There was no way she could face going home, knowing her father wasn't on that big porch to greet her and never would be. That's what she kept telling herself anyway. "I'll let you know when I'm ready to come, so I'd appreciate you not mentioning I just arrived." That wasn't really the truth. She didn't want one particular person to know she was back. Making that announcement was admitting defeat and that she couldn't stay away.

Until the day she left for college, she'd known in that one place everyone had that housed the truth of who they were that her father would always be waiting with a hug and an encouraging word, and Asher Evans was the one person made for her. When it came to Asher, she had a plan—they both had the same dreams and ambitions. They'd live, love, and build a relationship that revolved around devotion and commitment. Asher was as easy to love as her father, and their relationship had been so easy to rely on because Asher was the truest definition of loyalty, kindness, and partner she could ever hope to find.

The difficulty came when she realized she'd again come in second to the thrill of the arena. Her father had raised Asher to be all the things Reagan could love in a person, but also to love all the things he did. Bull riding was at the top of that list, and when she couldn't change Asher's mind, it changed *her* mind about Asher.

"I know you said not to mention you were coming back, but it wasn't fair to her to have it sprung on her. You have your reasons, and no one is going to try to change your mind, starting with Asher. She promised she wouldn't be a bother—put that out of your head."

Of course her uncle and Asher would've talked about how to handle her. Why should she have a say? "I'm not a cow, Uncle Wade."

"And we aren't feudal lords." Her uncle laughed. "I think that's what you called your father and me one Christmas, along with chauvinist pigs. Asher doesn't need to be beat in the head to understand what you want or, more importantly, what you don't. Besides, she's made her own life, and she's done well. Asher got your message loud and clear even if it took her a bit to get there. I'll never judge you for your choices, honey, but your leaving cut deep."

"I know that, and you know why that was. There was no way in hell I was going through that again." She'd run to protect what was left of her heart. Asher hadn't made it easy, though. She'd tried her best to keep Reagan's mind on her and what they'd shared, but there was no changing what Reagan wanted or what she wouldn't accept. She'd ended their relationship before she left for school, but decreed they could still be friends.

The first letter arrived two days after she moved into her dorm. Asher hadn't been interested in college, but she had a talent when it came to the written word. Her schedule and campus life didn't leave much time to write back, but Asher's letters came like clockwork every week until her junior year. Asher never pushed or begged, that wasn't her style, but her letters described life on the ranch, the night sky they'd loved to lie under, and the way the river looked during her rides.

The ones Reagan wrote in return were short in comparison. She gave brief descriptions of the campus and what she was doing, until that last letter arrived from Asher at the beginning of her junior year. Reagan had no trouble sensing her excitement. Her father had previously entered Asher in some junior competitions, but Uncle Wade had decreed that at twenty, Asher was ready for true competition. She was entering the professional ranks and was getting ready for her first big competition.

Reagan had skipped the return letter and picked up the phone. Asher had been happy to hear from her until Reagan had screamed until her throat felt like she'd set it on fire. An argument wasn't really a good description for what happened since Asher didn't fight back, but that hadn't stopped her tirade.

Asher, she knew, still held out hope Reagan would change her mind about resuming their relationship, and Reagan had used that to her advantage. She'd thrown out an ultimatum—it was either the bulls or her. Her mistake was not giving Asher the chance to make the decision—her word had been final, with no room for compromise. Asher hadn't said a word for a long while before quietly saying good-bye. It was the last time they'd spoken.

"You should think about apologizing one of these days, pretty girl," Uncle Wade said. "Sometimes you have to admit you were wrong to get back everything you lost." This was the most they'd talked about Asher in years, her uncle understanding she was too proud to bring it up. Not even her desperation to know how Asher was doing could make her bend her pride. "I'm not going to live forever, and I won't be around to look out for you."

"Uncle Wade, I love you, but I don't need anyone looking out for me. This isn't the wilderness, and Asher isn't Wyatt Earp." She'd tried to explain often how she'd outgrown what her clueless teenage self wanted a lifetime ago. It wasn't her fault Uncle Wade didn't want to hear it. "I'm sorry I haven't called before now, and I'll come when I'm ready. Just know I'm okay. I started a good job at a sports-centric clinic, and I'm making friends with people I have stuff in common with. Asher's only ever going to be interested in cows and riding fences. That's not what I want anymore."

"Not educated enough for you, huh?" The tinge of disappointment seemed to slice through his tiredness. It was so much like her father's tone, the one that her mother blamed as one of her reasons for leaving.

Christine had never taken any blame for running since her father made such an enticing target, but it was life on the ranch she didn't want, and she left for bigger and more exciting places. That's the only thing Reagan had in common with the woman who'd given birth to her. "That's not what I meant, and you know it."

"We might not have a lot left between us, but there's no reason not to be honest."

"You're right, and I don't want to argue with you. What we both have to face is we're happy where we are. You on the ranch, and me living in the city. We're worlds apart, and there's nothing wrong with that. The upside is I'm much closer, so we can see each other more often."

"Nothing at all wrong with that." Uncle Wade sighed as if realizing this was a losing argument. "Listen, I'm buying cows tomorrow, and I'll be home by Wednesday. If you could swing it, I'd love to see you. I'll have all your favorites waiting."

"I'm sure Frida still remembers each thing." Their housekeeper had been with them for years and had been the one who held her when her mother left, when her father died, and through every bad thing that had happened to her.

"Frida's not the only one who remembers. With a little practice I've become pretty good in the kitchen to give her a break every so often. Let me know if you can make it."

The phone went silent after that, and she didn't need the expensive education she was proud of to know she'd hurt his feelings. She wasn't proud of that, but she wasn't going to spend her life on her family's ranch along the river south of the city, talking about cows. There was no way in hell she'd do that even if it did hurt her uncle's feelings.

"Shit." All she could hope for now was her uncle keeping his promise not to try to play matchmaker for his favorite person in the world. It had been years since she'd seen Asher, and she wanted to keep it that way. The distance didn't keep Asher with her black hair, hazel eyes, and broad shoulders from haunting her dreams, but she wouldn't backslide now. "No way in hell."

Chapter Two

The last lot of twelve calves, four bulls in the lot, will start at fifteen thousand." That was as slow as the auctioneer would speak until the bidding was done.

Asher tapped her program against her thigh. Her business was mostly beef cows, but in the last three years she'd come to this auction in search of Lakenvelder or Dutch Belted dairy cows. The breed reminded her of walking Oreo cookies with a white belt around the middle while the rest was dark. They were a docile breed, and their milk had a high protein-to-fat ratio, so it got a higher price on the market.

She raised her hand, and the auctioneer called her number. Wade chuckled next to her, but he wouldn't try to stop her. He'd seen her books, and the numbers had made a believer out of him. Louisiana wasn't known as a dairy hub, but she was set on changing that with the herd she was building on the land she'd acquired to make this work.

"Thirty-six in the back." Asher glanced behind her and noticed the rancher who was bidding against her. They were closing in on his limit.

"Forty," she said to speed up the process. The number got her competition to shake his head and make a slashing motion at his throat. "Let's go buy these guys and finish up."

The ranchers in this area went about their businesses like she and Wade did, with respect and care for their animals, so the auction was one they both bid at with confidence. Between the two of them they had four hundred and eighteen thousand dollars' worth of livestock, most of it hers. Wade had dealt with some of the locals for years, but he was starting to cut back his herd. Moon Touch Ranch was still making money, but Wade was finding new ways to spend time in the afternoons, and she couldn't blame him. He'd been at this for years.

Wade had moved to Louisiana a few years after Silas and her father Dustin purchased what was at the time pretty worthless land that flooded in the spring. It wasn't protected by any barrier islands, so hurricanes that headed their way beat the crap out of the barns, but the flat grassy land stretches were the perfect home for cattle.

Once the business turned a profit, they purchased more land, and after Dustin died, first Silas and then Wade managed Dustin's land, until Asher was old enough to take over. Their stewardship over her ranch had given her a good foundation to build on, and after careful planning and using her rodeo winnings, she'd purchased additional large tracts of land to accommodate the cattle she needed to make all the expansion she had planned work.

"How many of those cookie cows you got now?" Wade followed her to the truck once they'd handed over their checks.

"Eight hundred head or so." She waited for him to close his door before starting the engine, glad it was still early. "I need a few more breeders to let go of some of their stock, so I'll have a good cross section to start breeding in earnest for myself."

"Your father's smiling down on you for the rancher you've become, Buck."

"I'm sure Silas is doing the same when it comes to you, Uncle Wade. You ready for your surprise?" She turned left out of the stockyard, loving the landscape that was completely foreign when compared to home. It wasn't hard to imagine her father, Silas, and Wade playing on the red rocks that lined the road for as far as she could see to the horizon.

She loved the trips here every year for more than the rodeo that hadn't changed much from Silas's time in the spotlight. They made a stop at the cemetery where Wade's parents were buried, their graves mixed in with those that had been there for years. Even those old graves topped with piles of rocks and crude wood crosses had flowers on them. This ancient land surprised her at times, but she took comfort in knowing that the people who lived here honored their history.

"What are you cooking up?" Wade relaxed back into his seat and rubbed his knee. He'd injured it in a riding accident, and he joked it was held together with rubber bands and prayers.

"You'll see."

They drove for an hour until she spotted one of her ranch hands, Austin Theriot, taking two horses out of the air-conditioned horse trailer she'd splurged on last year. "Hey, boss."

"Thanks for getting them ready." She shook her head when Wade got out and checked the tack on his horse as if Austin had no idea how to do it. "Y'all got everything else done?"

"Connor's got you covered. He'll hang around until you're close. I'll help him in the morning." Austin handed over her reins and stepped back. "Congratulations, boss. That arena is a little rough, but that bull was something."

"My teeth feel a little looser this morning, so I agree with you."

The afternoon had warmed enough for her to take her jacket off and tie it to her saddle. She waved to Austin, glad to see a big smile on Wade's face. The ride she'd planned would take them along the Rio Grande, and twelve miles down, another of her ranch hands had set up camp. She pushed her hat back on her head a little and studied the high rock wall on the other side of the river. Mexico was close enough to touch, and the waterway that separated them was shallow enough to walk over the border with no problem.

"Places like this make you feel the years," Wade said.

"What do you mean?"

"This land is ancient, hell, all land is ancient, but this place makes you think it's seen its fair share of history. When you consider that, it makes me think I'm insignificant in the realm of it all."

She chuckled at his insight. "That's damn deep, old man, but you've got plenty of history behind and in front of you. Don't worry, you won't be forgotten."

"I'm not going anywhere, Buck." He laughed along with her. "But you need to start thinking about your future. Cows and horses aren't going to make you happy forever."

"Says who?" She sighed, knowing this was going to lead back to Reagan somehow. "And before you drop any words of wisdom on me—I'm not the one who called it quits. Your niece knows her mind, and none of her choices included me. I doubt that's changed, and if I'm right, she's forgotten all about me."

The bitterness of the hurt Reagan had caused her was still like road rash on her heart. They'd grown up together, shared their first kiss with each other, they were each other's first love, and then…Asher wasn't enough. Reagan needed more, or really less of Asher in her life. She wasn't cut out for ranch life and for someone who'd be happy with such a simple way of living. Reagan had tossed her aside as easily as if she'd been expired milk, and that was the last time she'd let anyone in that deeply.

"She's back, and you're going to have to deal with that." Wade was like one of those burrs that stuck to your pants, intent on not letting go.

"We did deal with it when I turned twenty-four. The ranches are completely separate business entities now, but you're still my family. I'm not going to stop helping you run Moon Touch because Reagan thinks I'm a simpleton." She'd been twelve when she'd moved to Moon Touch with Silas, Reagan, and Wade. Life had been easy after she'd grieved the death of her father and accepted that the Wilson brothers weren't going to put her out. That had taken some time to truly believe, but she trusted both men with her life. "Don't worry. I'll call before I come over from now on. I think that'll avoid any awkwardness."

"You don't need to call to come home, dammit." Wade was a natural in the saddle, and he seemed to be enjoying the rough terrain. "I know you don't want to talk about it, so enough about all that…for now. Let's talk about your cookie cows."

She was grateful for the reprieve. Reagan was a wound that was always on the verge of festering. It never really healed, and it pissed her off that she wasn't strong enough to forget. No one was meant to be alone, and she hoped the woman she would eventually find would be understanding enough to accept even those broken parts of her.

"The cookie cows are worth their weight in milk, and if you keep making fun of them, I'm not going to help you with your morning cereal or nighttime cookies."

They laughed together again, and she was glad to be making new memories with him. Today was the anniversary of Silas's very unexpected death, and her goal was to take his mind to better times.

"Think tonight we'll see Silas and Dustin in a sky full of stars?" Wade sounded almost childlike when he uttered the question.

"There's no doubt."

❖

"Daddy, please." Reagan hated that she was begging, but she'd do what she needed to get her father to reconsider. "You're not back to full strength, so you could really get hurt."

"I'm feeling good, Peanut, so stop worrying." He had a coiled rope in one hand and his hat in the other. "I need this one if I'm going to make it to the finals in Vegas again."

"Don't you understand? I need you more than the standings in bull riding."

He leaned over and kissed her cheek as he put his arms around her. "I love you, sweet girl, and I promise I'll be careful." Her dad glanced behind her at Asher and smiled. "I love you both, so wait for me. This shouldn't take long."

"Yes, sir, and good luck." Asher held her as they watched him walk off. "He should've sat this one out, but you know how he is."

The admission had prompted her to turn around and put her arms around Asher's shoulders. At least someone understood her fears, but then again, Asher understood her like no other person alive. It was a blessing she never wanted to take for granted. They'd grown up together, and Asher had always done everything in her power to put her needs first and always listened to her fears. She was young but knew instinctively that no one would love her as fiercely as Asher.

"Do you agree with me that it's a mistake?" The silence that stretched out wasn't comforting at all. "Asher?"

"Honey," Asher said, leading her to a hay bale. "Your dad knows his mind, and he's been teaching me how to ride. He thinks I'm good. I stayed on the damn bull during the junior competitions he encouraged me to enter. I was going to tell you," Asher said, talking fast.

"Tell me you're not serious."

"I'm not saying I want to go pro like your dad, but he's taught me some stuff. And I don't think he would compete now if he wasn't ready."

Asher sounded so goddamn reasonable, something she'd learned from her father along with bull riding apparently. They were so close to graduation, and she still held out hope that Asher would change her mind and join her in going away to school.

"You were there in the hospital, day after day. It's taken months of hard work and therapy to get him to this point, and he's not strong enough yet for ranch work, much less bull riding. All three of you," she

*said of her father, Uncle Wade, and Asher, "are soft in the head if you
think this is a good idea."*

*"Lajitas isn't going to draw the best bulls, so it's a good way for
him to ease back into competition."*

She'd stormed off, not wanting to have a screaming match with
Asher when neither of them would bend on the subject. Less than four
hours later the call had come, and she barely understood Uncle Wade
when he told her that her father had collapsed and was unconscious.

*"They're running tests, but that's all I know, honey," Uncle Wade
said through his sobs. "I need you and Asher to get here. The doctors
aren't real talkative, but I got a bad feeling about this."*

Reagan woke with a start. She hated that dream. The words *I
got a bad feeling about this* rattled in her head, and they had been so
prophetic. That day was so ingrained in her memory that she could
testify to every second of it. Hearing Asher say *He's gone* two days
later was like someone removing her guts with a hot spoon. It was
excruciating, and the pain of their last moments together would make it
impossible to forget the guilt.

The way she'd talked to him and the way he'd displayed the same
patience he'd always shown her made her burn with the realization
she'd never be able to change those last minutes with him. He'd never
woken up, so she'd never told him she loved him, that she was only
mad because she loved him, and that he was the best father she could've
hoped for.

She went out on her small deck with a small bit of bourbon and
stared up at a violet sky. There weren't many stars in the city, but no
matter where she was, she liked being outside on this day every year.
It'd been seven years since she'd received word her father had died.
He'd been there one minute trying to reassure her, and then he'd never
come home. Death had come like an unwanted visitor he'd had no idea
was on its way.

"It was those fucking bulls," she whispered up to the heavens.
"You went when I asked you not to, and it cost us everything, including
our future."

She held up the heavy crystal glass and tried to smile through her tears. "I hope you can still see me, Daddy. If you can, you probably know I'm still pissed." The liquor went down with a slight burn, but it had been her dad's favorite. "Dying the way you did wasn't supposed to happen. You were supposed to walk me down the aisle, teach my kids how to ride, and tell me all those tales you loved, one more time."

"Are you ever going to tell me that story?" an unexpected voice asked.

Her shoulders hitched so much at Steph Delmonico's voice that a little of the brown liquid spilled on her thumb.

"I've always believed that's the main reason why you left me," Steph continued.

"I left you because you're a cheating asshole."

"Not exactly the forgiving kind, are you?"

"I thought you promised to leave your keys when you left. I'm sure the woman you started sleeping with while you were living here wouldn't be happy that you're returning to the scene of the crime." She didn't turn around, not because of a broken heart, but because she didn't care, not really. "Make sure you leave them on your way out."

"Come on, babe. Just because we didn't work out doesn't mean we can't be friends." Steph sat in the other chair, and Reagan could feel her eyes on her.

Steph had bought her a drink a year ago in Seattle and after a short conversation informed her that *coincidentally* she was planning a move to New Orleans around the time Reagan had planned hers. That she'd agreed to let Steph move in with her had been a surprise even to her, and that it'd turned into a mistake was not.

Sleeping with other people wasn't something Steph was willing to give up to be in a committed relationship. They were doomed to failure. She'd asked Steph to get lost three weeks after she moved in.

"I've never seen you as the friend type." She took the last sip of her drink, seeing Steph had poured one for herself.

"I'll keep apologizing, but we both know I was never going to be the love of your life. We both know that's true, yet I'd still love to hear the story of your father." Steph sat next to her, but Reagan's attention was on the small yard and garden.

"Why's it important to you?" They'd never talked about their families, and it'd be weird to start now. "And why exactly are you here?"

"I left a file I need later this week, and I really want to be your friend, so I was checking in on you. Your dad seems an important part of your life since you talk about him even when you might not realize it." Steph shrugged as she put her feet on the railing. "Your dad sneaks into conversations, especially when it comes to comparing his character against someone else's."

"My father was the greatest man I've ever known. That's a line a lot of people say because it's expected, but he really was bigger than life." And maybe she did compare other people to her father, but it was a way of not having to commit. That's what her therapist had said after talking about it until even she was sick of the subject. Never mind that only one person had ever lived up to the memory of the great Silas Wilson. That was a bridge she'd not only burned, but blown up and chopped into small pieces that were then scattered in a hell of her own making.

"Why are you so angry at him, then?" Steph sounded almost compassionate, which wasn't her norm. She was more calculating than caring, a trait that made her a great attorney. It wasn't that she was cold, because she wasn't, but Steph had a talent for compartmentalizing her emotions for the best possible outcome in every situation. "He died, so you might feel better if you let your rage go."

"Did you become a therapist since I last saw you?" She laughed, but Steph didn't join in. "I have my reasons, and while I loved him, I'm entitled to my feelings."

"I know you do, sweetheart, and I'm the last person who'll discount what's in your heart. We're never going to be a thing"—Steph waved between them—"and that's my fault. That doesn't mean I don't care about you."

"Don't think this is me being bitchy, but why are you being so nice?" The question was, of course, bitchy. "That isn't you."

"Good to know you think I have no redeemable qualities." Steph didn't appear upset, but she also didn't seem as open. "Look, I'm sorry I bothered you. I'll leave the key on the counter. Call if you need anything else."

"Steph, wait." She didn't reach out, but there was no reason to take her bad mood out on her ex.

"It's late, and I know I lost the right to ask you anything." Steph laughed but it wasn't a happy sound. "The thing is, I don't think I ever had that right, and I was a fool for thinking it didn't matter."

"I'm sorry. Don't go." It wasn't often she felt alone, but tonight the ghosts who'd kept her company in her thoughts and dreams grated against her skin like sandpaper. "My uncle called last night and invited me to dinner. It's not like I wasn't expecting it, but it threw me."

"Do you not get along? You seldom talk about your family." Both their glasses were empty, so Steph went in for the bottle. This was the only time since they'd met that they didn't argue. Sharing a glass was their way to call a truce. "I don't know why, but I've always been curious."

"Only I could've gone all the way to Seattle and found the one rodeo fan in the whole state of Washington." Steph had always been fascinated with bull riding. Reagan had laughed the day Steph found out she was Silas Wilson's daughter. Her father had won the national championship with the highest score ever recorded. It was a score that hadn't been achieved since.

"I can't imagine being related to someone in love with the sport. It's exciting because it's dangerous. That had to have been hard to watch."

"The hardest thing about growing up with my father was knowing he loved those eight seconds more than me. That was a bitch to know, much less accept."

"You're most likely going to get mad at me for what I'm about to say, but that's our norm." Steph had a way of stating the truth but making her laugh. "Your consistency makes it easy to be truthful."

"What great insight are you getting ready to lay on me?" She absolutely loved it when people told her how to feel, especially when it came to a man Steph had only seen on YouTube.

"It's like me being an attorney. You don't approve of, much less understand some of the clients I defend."

"You're like the devil's advocate, but if you're okay with it, there's not much I can do about it." She knew how to push Steph's buttons as well as Steph did hers.

"Not having that argument with you again, snookums. What I mean is, you love what you do. The satisfaction you get from helping people is something I love hearing you talk about."

It wasn't what she expected to hear. "I didn't think you were paying attention."

"It wasn't hard to hear the passion, my friend." Steph poured another small splash in their glasses.

"Why would I get mad at you for that?"

"Because in your view, you're the only one entitled to do what you love. I can't tell you how to feel about your father, no one can, but aside from you his love was bull riding. He was so passionate about the sport that he became the best in the world." Steph wasn't a winner in court because of her good looks. She had a freakish talent, a way of weaving words that got to the truth of every situation—at least, what she thought was the truth—and got twelve jurors to believe it. "As far as the score he posted to win it, he's still the best. Not many people can say that."

"Your argument is compelling, counselor, but you have to remember one crucial thing." It wasn't Steph's fault. Everyone including Uncle Wade forgot that not all situations had happy endings. "He did become the best in the world, then it killed him. I asked him to stop, and he didn't. What about that is hard to understand?" Her voice started to rise, and she had to stop to regroup. "He didn't die in front of a crowd, but what happened to him was caused by that last injury. No one can convince me otherwise."

"Tell me I'm all wrong, but I think it's more than that." It was a guess on Steph's part that was dead-on. She wasn't about to let her know that, though. Her secrets were hers, and she shared them with no one.

"Remember to leave your key, and I'd appreciate it if you called before you drop in again." That's all it took to make Steph disappear as if she had the power to open a black hole and drop her in it. "You still have your fans, Daddy. That should make you happy even if you never took my happiness into account."

Chapter Three

The cattle from the auction arrived, and Asher was taking care of getting both Wade's and hers from the railyard. She'd tried to take over the jobs that had the possibility of injuring Wade, without wounding his pride. That had been accomplished by leasing the trucks needed for the job before he had the opportunity. The cattle bolted for the chute set up to guide them into the transport, and all of them seemed skittish after the long train ride.

She shook her head, thinking this was at times more dangerous than riding an angry bull. Cows were in no way as happy or docile as portrayed in commercials. Most of the time their mood meter was stuck on tantrum.

"We got a new pasture cordoned off, boss," Owen Cormier said. Owen had been with Asher since she'd taken over the ranch and was an encyclopedia when it came to cattle. "There's enough grass to keep them happy, and they'll be in eyesight of the main herd."

"Good." The cows ran by her as she leaned against the bars. She never liked the spooked expression they all had as they came off the railcars. It took forever for them to calm down after the trauma of travel. "The contractor's coming by in a few days to talk about the new barn."

She'd negotiated a deal with Orchard Dairy—they'd underwrite the construction of a new barn that would be their milking center in exchange for a five-year contract on seventy-five percent of the milk she could produce. Orchard was a new star in the organic dairy world and had helped her get her certifications. She'd been ranching organically from day one. Animals jacked up on steroids and God knew what weren't her idea of how to conduct business.

"I heard from Gia already, and the boys staked the site out to get the surveyors going. You headed into town?" Owen lifted his hat and wiped his forehead on his sleeve.

Gia Faulkner was their architect on the project and an old friend. They'd met years before in a night class on marketing. Gia had been new to her profession and was searching for ways to attract clients, and Asher had been expanding the business and wanted to do it correctly. It hadn't been hard to accept Gia's invitation to dinner and then to be study partners. That they did most of their studying naked only made the class more entertaining.

"I've got a meeting with Keegan and Mackie to review the new line and the numbers, but I have to shower and change. Did you get my order?" Up to now she'd mostly sold to the fine dining restaurants in Louisiana, Mississippi, and Alabama that could afford her prices. The ranch was now large enough to expand their sales to higher end groceries and butcher shops that specialized in prime cuts of meat.

"It's in your fridge waiting for Mackie's magic touch." Owen tapped his hat against his leg. "I wasn't sure about the new breeds you've been introducing, but you were right."

She smiled at Owen's admission. Old cowboys like Owen believed in the tried-and-true Angus cows, so when the first Pinzgauer cattle came off the boat from Austria, he'd mumbled under his breath for a week. Like with the Dutch Belted cows, he'd taken one look at the animals, and his expression said he thought she'd lost her mind. It had been a gamble to mortgage what she owned to triple the size of her ranch, but her plans had paid off. And the Pinzgauer was by far the best beef cattle in the world. Their first breeding season had been highly successful with only two calves lost. They were now in their second year, so she was introducing the beef to the market, starting with her favorite customers. One steak would prove why it was worth four times the cost. It was like Wagyu without the cruel breeding practices.

"Good to know you don't think I've totally lost it." She laughed louder when he tapped the brim of her hat down over her eyes. "You and the hands all right with getting these guys home?"

"Go, and we'll get it done."

She watched a few more running through, knowing the next two cars belonged to Uncle Wade. Her guys loved Wade as much as she did, so they'd take care of his stock like they were hers. This was one of her favorite days, but the business side of things was taking more of her time, and that responsibility was solely hers and necessary if she wanted to keep growing. There was only one final step to complete.

Wade was slowing down, and Reagan had no desire to run Moon Touch Ranch—that was the truth as everyone saw it. Asher had invested all her rodeo winnings into land acquisition, and those investments were starting to earn enough for the one thing that meant the most to her. When Wade was ready, she wanted to buy him and Reagan out. That was the best way she could think to honor the three men who had given her so much.

Her father, Silas, and now Uncle Wade had spent their lives building the land into a world-class spread, and those dreams shouldn't die with them. Wade would eventually come to see this was the best solution, and Reagan certainly wasn't interested. Combining both places into one large ranch would give her the acreage to honor Silas's and her father's legacies while cornering the beef market in four states.

She took a shower and put on a suit before Rickie Rodriguez handed her a bag with *Pemberley Ranch* printed on the side and a bull's head underneath. Rickie's mother Frida worked for Uncle Wade and had for years. When Asher moved to her place, Rickie had asked to come with her, and Asher had built her a cabin, so Rickie could have her own space.

"There's six rib eye and ten filets in there. That's what you asked for, right?" Rickie went back to cutting up a pile of vegetables in front of her.

"If they eat more than that, they're going to be miserable. Do you need anything before I go?" She picked up the keys to the Land Rover since the truck was a bear to park in the French Quarter.

"Leave before you're late, and don't waste that suit and great bow tie. If you see a pretty girl, try your charm offensive."

She laughed as she threw her jacket on the back seat and headed for the gate. The house was three miles from the road, so she put on Beethoven's Symphony no. 6 and exhaled. The music relaxed her and made the voices from the past find someone else to bother. Really there were only Wade and Reagan left, and only Wade gave a damn, so she needed to stop thinking about a woman who'd left without an ounce of remorse.

Once she was on the interstate, she made it to Mackie's place in thirty minutes. She parked by the river, wanting to walk the couple of blocks now that the heat had broken. It wasn't cool by any stretch, but the summer's oppressiveness was gone. The hostess smiled when she stepped in.

"They're waiting in the kitchen for you, Asher. Would you like a drink?"

"Any recommendations?" She headed down the stairs to the main dining room. Mackie Blanchard prided himself on the steaks he served as well as his wine and liquor selections. This was one of the best places in town to have a drink. "If not, surprise me."

"You got it. I'll make it good." The hostess pointed toward the kitchen.

She nodded to a few people she recognized and could've sworn she spotted Reagan, but it had to be wishful thinking on her part. Whoever the woman was, she had a menu in front of her face, and the woman with her was saying something rather animatedly. Asher's attention went to the kitchen door and the beautiful woman standing there with her arms open.

"This must mean luck is on my side." She handed the bag off to one of the kitchen staff and put her arms around Jacqueline Blanchard, lifting her off the ground a few inches when she kissed her. "Are you hungry?"

"Always, and Keegan was swamped at the restaurant, so you're stuck with me. She did, though, make me promise to save her some steaks, so I hope you brought plenty." The Blanchard restaurant empire was ruled by its grande dame Della Blanchard, and she and her family owned most of the five-star places in New Orleans. Della's granddaughters Keegan and Jacqueline ran the crown jewel—Blanchard's in the Garden District—with Keegan in the kitchen and Jacqueline in the business office.

"Do you think that's a hardship?" She got Jacqueline to laugh before Jacqueline kissed her again. "I've missed you," she said as Jacqueline placed her hand in the bend of Asher's elbow. "How's Vegas?" Jacqueline had been gone for months as she worked to open the family's sister restaurant on the Strip.

"It's getting there, and I expect you and Wade to be my guests when you make it to the championships." Jacqueline led her to Mackie's office and put her hands behind her neck. "Are you rushing back home tonight?"

"It's been a while, so how about I take you out for a drink?" Jacqueline didn't cook, unlike her sister Keegan, but she did have a way about her that made you want to give her whatever she asked for. Spending time together was something she'd enjoyed from the day they'd met. "I can stay in town if you like."

"I have a better idea, cowpoke." Jacqueline moved her hands down to her shoulders and squeezed. "Let's have some dinner, then you take me home for an overnight bag and then take me to your place. Tomorrow I can go riding with you. I want to see these cows you're charging exorbitant prices for."

"You two come flirt at the chef's table while I cook the treat you brought us. Let's see if they live up to the hype." Mackie held up the bag of steaks before starting his seasoning process.

"How are Keegan and Sept doing?" The whole Blanchard family were so much more than customers to Asher, and she'd developed friendships with all of them, including Della.

"Blissful is the best way to describe it. They're sickeningly happy, at least that's how Gran likes to put it." Jacqueline sat so their thighs touched. "How'd you do in Lajitas?"

"I won it and moved into second. That gives me a few months off while keeping my chances alive before the final stretch of events." She tried not to move as Jacqueline ran her foot up her pants leg. "I've been looking forward to the break."

They clinked their glasses together when the waiter delivered drinks and talked some more about nothing important until Mackie delivered dinner. She sat back and stayed quiet after that. This family went about food like she did bull riding—with an intensity and enjoyment most people never felt about anything ever.

"Okay, how much can you get us on a weekly basis?" Mackie asked. "You can deliver here if you want, and I'll split up the order depending on what the rest of the family is interested in."

"You know I don't mind a few stops." She smiled when Jacqueline fed her a bite of filet. "And we've done enough business together that we can make this an exclusive deal until I'm ready to really ramp up production."

"We're planning to hold you to that offer, no matter how much you produce," Mackie said. "Keegan, Jacqueline, and I are in the final process of renovating two older groceries, one Uptown and one in Metairie. There's Wagyu, and then there's this." He held up a piece of steak on his fork. "And this, my friend, is divine."

"I think everyone's happy," Jacqueline said. "How about some desserts to go?"

"Sounds good. I'll call you this week, Mackie." She hugged him and took Jacqueline's hand.

"I want the same deal Jacqueline's getting, minus the overnight bag and the hand-holding." He slapped her shoulder and chuckled. "I'm not a great rider, but I like going out with you, and I want to see the new herd, too."

"Call me when you're off, and we'll set something up."

She led Jacqueline out, and that part of her heart that experienced loneliness like a very real physical pain wished Jacqueline would come to love her. Jacqueline had been honest from the beginning, though. She liked men too and thought she'd eventually end up with one. Her sister Keegan, though, had opened her eyes to the enjoyment of women. Jacqueline had come to like Asher's strength and her butchness, as she put it. What they shared was uncomplicated, and maybe that was for the best. Friends with pleasurable benefits had its place. She'd had enough drama to last five lifetimes.

❖

"Who is that?" Reagan asked the waiter when she spotted Asher again with the same beautiful woman who'd kissed her and was now hanging on to her. This was the last place she expected to see Asher again. When she'd come in, the sight of her had tightened Reagan's chest, and there was a flicker of equal recognition on that handsome tanned face, but Asher hadn't stopped. The nice suit with the equally nice cowboy boots didn't really compute with the mental image she carried of Asher, and the reality of her was so much better.

"Which one?" the waiter asked.

"The woman in the navy dress?" There was no way she wouldn't recognize Asher even if it would be better if she didn't. Sudden onset amnesia when it came to Asher Evans was the only way possible to purge her from her memories.

"That's Jacqueline Blanchard. Her cousin Mackie owns the restaurant. The other woman is Asher Evans." The waiter was like an action reporter as he cleared the dishes. "Do you know Jacqueline? I can call her over if you like."

"No, but thank you." She ignored Steph's curious stare as Asher disappeared up the stairs.

The last time they'd seen each other was two Christmases after her father died when she'd come home to sign some papers having to do with his estate. Her first instinct had been to let Wade have the whole thing to do with as he pleased. Wade had never married, and she was his only family—well, except for Asher. She wasn't the only one in her family who loved Asher.

During those first two years that she'd been incommunicado, Asher had lost all traces of adolescence, but she was still that tall skinny kid who loved to ride and was thinking of following Reagan's father's path to the rodeo and the bulls ready to take their pound of flesh. Asher had greeted her, made as much awkward small talk as she needed to, then left. Not once did those beautiful eyes soften like they always had at the sight of her. Her tirade and ultimatums had worked, and her wish for Asher to leave her the hell alone had been granted.

"I take it you know Asher Evans." Steph wore a great suit, which meant it'd been a court day. The expensive clothes were the armor that helped her slay dragons.

"Yes." There was no reason to expand on her answer. She already was a fool for accepting Steph's dinner invitation, considering Steph was still seeing the woman she'd cheated on her with when they were still together. Perhaps Steph was working up to making her the mistress this time around.

"She's second in the national standings right now," Steph said. "Barring anything messing her up, she should be the first woman to win it all." Steph went back to sipping her scotch like they'd been talking about the weather.

"Asher was my father's protégé. She idolized him, and he repaid her by teaching her everything he knew. The ranking doesn't surprise me. Asher has been a hard-focused worker all her life."

"She grew up around you, then?" The way Steph went about gathering information tried her last shred of patience.

"Spit it out before it kills you." She signaled for another glass of wine to have something to do with her hands, but she really just wanted to go home and sulk. How did cowpoke Asher know Jacqueline Blanchard, and who the hell was dressing her these days? The years had totally transformed Asher in both manners and physique. At eighteen she'd rather have been dragged behind her horse than wear a pink bow tie with little flamingos on it.

"I'm not pushing you, so there's nothing to spit out. I learned my lesson the other night, that you don't like talking about your family. That's not another mistake I'm going to make with you." Steph finished her drink as a waiter brought the check. "You don't have to tell me if you don't want to, but talking sometimes lets you release all that stuff that makes you miserable."

"I'm pretty content when it comes to my life," Reagan replied, "like I said before. The short of it is, if you're that curious—Asher's mother died in childbirth and her father died when she was twelve. So my dad took her in since he'd promised his best friend his daughter would be okay." The memories of their childhood made her smile even if she didn't want to show too much emotion. "Asher was sort of the son my dad always wanted—someone he could teach to love ranch life and the rodeo that took so much from us."

"You loved her." That was no question but a firm statement of fact. "And I doubt your dad was disappointed in the child he had."

"I did. And she was easy to love until she wasn't. There was no way in hell I was going to stay and watch someone else I loved lose to that barbaric sport." She swiped at her face, feeling like her tears betrayed her. "Thanks for dinner, but I'm tired. I'll grab a cab so you don't have to go out of your way."

She stood and turned abruptly after picking her purse off the floor. Steph stopped her and put her arms around her, acting like they were the only two people in the room. Reagan held her breath when Steph pressed her hand to the side of her cheek. If Steph kissed her, she was seriously going to lose her shit. It was the very feminine laughter that made her turn her head to find Jacqueline and Asher descending the stairs again. Asher's hands clenched into fists when she spotted her, but Jacqueline didn't seem to notice her discomfort, while Reagan couldn't notice anything but.

"I promise it will just take a minute," Jacqueline Blanchard said, kissing Asher's lips and patting her on the chest. She walked away toward the kitchen but glanced back, so perhaps she wasn't completely oblivious to Asher's unease.

"Asher," Reagan said softly. She shrugged out of Steph's hold and faced her past. She'd loved this woman as passionately as an eighteen-year-old could, and she carried the scars of pain from letting her go. Asher was the same but entirely different. Her eyes were still that hazel that made you want to fall into their depths, but the long skinny body had transformed into the type of bulk that radiated strength.

"Reagan." Asher said her name as if she couldn't find anything else to say. It was Asher's expression that prompted her to take a step forward.

"You ready?" Jacqueline came back out with a beautiful handbag and paused. "Friends of yours, honey?"

"No," Asher said, giving no leeway with the one-word answer and putting a bullet into any touching reunion she'd thought would happen. "Have a good night." The last words were a testament to Asher's kindness, like she couldn't help but be polite even when it hurt to do so. From the set of her jaw, it had hurt.

She watched Asher go and couldn't blame her anger. "Wait." The request didn't really matter since Asher was gone.

"Come on, babe." Steph put her arm around her shoulders and led her out. "Let me take you home."

The fight had left her, and she allowed Steph to take her hand. Thomas Wolfe was right—you can't go home again. At least, you couldn't and expect it to remain the same. New Orleans wasn't home, St. Bernard was, but even that place steeped in history and tradition was a vastly different landscape. One glance at Asher was the bellwether that she'd been away too long to make any meaningful amends.

"Are you okay?" Steph asked after buckling her in. She was too numb to care.

"I'll be fine. She was a surprise."

"It was more like a shock to the system." Steph ignored her phone when it rang. "I see what you mean, though. Asher Evans is a different animal in person."

"If we'd run into her four years ago, Asher would've been everything you imaged and more. The suit, white shirt, and dress boots are definitely new. The bow tie was mind-blowing." That had to be Blanchard's influence. A member of New Orleans restaurant royalty probably wasn't a fan of plaid shirts, jeans, and work boots.

"That's not what I meant." Steph kept her eyes on the road. "She seems solid, intense, and…"

"And what?" she asked when Steph's voice faded away. "Asher's all those things and more." What the hell was she doing? Asher Evans didn't need her to defend her character. There would be no picking up where they'd been headed before her meltdown. She'd moved on— Asher had more than moved on and had plenty more to show for herself.

"I figured that intensity was something reserved for the arena is all I meant. She's hard to read."

"Not at all." Reagan exhaled and took another breath. That wasn't working to curb the panic running through her. "What you saw tonight wasn't intensity. It was anger, perhaps rage, and all of it aimed at me. I can't blame her at all, so forget about it."

"You're hard to stay mad at, so I wouldn't worry about it."

Reagan laughed. "There are certain things you can't take back. Words you can't unsay. You want to know about me—here's the truth." Another deep breath was a wasted effort. "I grew up with Asher, and she was so like my father, but in truth, Asher is a lot like her dad, Dustin, as well. He had ranching in his heart, and even though we raised cattle as a business, Dustin treated all animals as well as people with respect. That's the thing I remember most about him."

"Dustin and your dad were partners, then?" Steph followed her upstairs as if not wanting to miss out on her tale like the fangirl she was. At one time she might've found it adorable. Tonight, Steph was nothing but a cattle prod to her psyche.

"They grew up together like Asher and I did, and they married best friends from Louisiana. When they wanted a spread of their own, they bought one big parcel everyone thought was wasteland and split it in two. All this was before I was born, and my dad credited Uncle Dustin for the success they had." She remembered Uncle Dustin's face since it was so much like Asher's. His loss had been so much more painful than her mother leaving them. "Uncle Dustin was the one who took care of us when Daddy was away chasing belt buckles."

"What happened to him?" Steph asked.

"Right after Asher turned twelve, a week after actually, Uncle

Dustin had a massive heart attack that killed him before he hit the ground." Asher's sobs when they brought her dad back haunted her dreams sometimes. "Uncle Dustin's parents had been gone for years and Asher's mom's parents weren't interested, so my dad and uncle raised her. Asher's spent her life working hard, and…" She let her voice fade away, knowing she was sharing too much. Giving away Asher's secrets didn't sit right.

"Trying to outrun the loss," Steph guessed.

"That's only part of it." They sat outside again, only this time, Steph opened two bottles of water.

"Remember what I said," Steph said. "Don't tell me if you don't want to."

"Asher reminded me of one of the yearlings on the ranch before they're trained to be ridden. Young horses are skittish, untrusting, and high-strung." She smiled, thinking of how the young horses were also playful and full of energy. That's how she liked to think of Asher.

"She doesn't seem high-strung."

Reagan nodded. "She's not. I was talking about horses, but Asher experienced so much loss so young, and it changed her. It was like she was always waiting for the next thing that would be snatched from her with no real explanation. I think that's why my father and Uncle Wade spent so much time with her. Daddy wanted Asher to know she always had a home and family with us."

"How'd he feel when Asher fell in love with his little girl?" It was like Steph was reading a script of her life. "That's what happened, right?"

"Daddy was as happy about that as I was. Asher to him was the perfect choice—the only acceptable choice when it came to his only child. He wanted someone to leave the ranch to who wouldn't take advantage and would make taking care of me their priority." She could still see him clapping his hands with his big smile plastered on his face when he'd caught them kissing in the barn like a scene from a Lifetime movie.

"Only you weren't interested, but that's another guess on my part." Steph shrugged as if waiting to be reprimanded again.

"You're wrong. I did want that. I got interested in physical therapy when my dad got really hurt right before his death. It was my goal to help put him back together and keep him home. The PT who came to the house encouraged me to learn and assist her. That was my wish, and I certainly got it. He's home permanently." She stopped talking, surprised Steph didn't push.

"He died," Steph said, "and you've been angry ever since because he left you. The only target for that anger was the one person who not only understood the loss but loved you." Steph put it much more succinctly than her, but the facts were correct.

"Right before he died, he told Asher she was ready to go pro if that's what she wanted. His go-ahead was all she needed to start a career I would never accept. I didn't want to be a rodeo widow, sitting at home waiting for the call that she'd been trampled to death." She let her tears fall, not caring if Steph saw them. It's not like they were new.

"You can stop."

Reagan stared at Steph, feeling like this was the first time she ever saw her. "Why?"

"Because the end to that chapter will be too painful for you to finish. You made her worst fears come true. She loved you and would've eventually come to terms if she'd lost you like her father, but you voluntarily hurt her."

"Yes," she whispered. The reality of what she'd done came back to slap her in the face when she saw Asher. It was plain that heartbreak had given way to anger and resentment.

It was a shock to see tears on Steph's cheeks, but they fell as quickly as hers did. "My parents did the same thing when I came out," Steph said. "I expected the worst, and they didn't disappoint. That's why I've always found it better to have no expectations of people. It protects you, but it does make for some lonely days."

"I regret what I did, but I also wanted to protect myself. I still do."

"I get it. Is she why you came back?"

"I came home because this is, well, home. I also didn't want Uncle Wade to be alone any longer."

"But you bought this place months ago and haven't been out to see him yet."

"I'm still processing—"

"Seeing her tonight blew that to shit." Steph laughed after her insightfulness.

"No wonder you're so successful. Such a way with words." She couldn't help but laugh too. "I agree with you. She wasn't what I expected, either."

"You were expecting hay in her hair and manure on her boots, huh?"

She shoved Steph on the shoulder, making her laugh harder. "I'm not that bitchy, but the dapper butch from tonight was not the girl I left behind."

"Maybe you were wrong about her."

"She's the number two bull rider in the world, Steph. That makes me *not* so wrong."

CHAPTER FOUR

Do you promise to invite me out here even if you get married and have a dozen kids?" Jacqueline sat behind Asher and pressed her cheek to her naked shoulder.

Asher had driven them to the small cabin at the southeasternmost point of her land. There were only a small number of cows sharing the pasture with a dozen or so horses, but no houses or people in sight. Jacqueline loved the quiet of this place, better than the main house, and it was nice to share the space with her. She'd built the cabin to make it easy to keep an eye on the horses and cows when they were in birthing season.

"What the heck am I going to do with twelve kids?" She turned from the first hints of the rising sun and put her arms around Jacqueline. They were wrapped in a sheet on the porch swing, naked and sated.

"I can see a herd of ponies with gorgeous kids on them, following behind you, all complaining because they don't want to go to school." Jacqueline straddled her lap and combed her hair back. "They'll all know more about animals than that Dr. Pol show you watch sometimes."

"That's crazy talk." She had a hard time concentrating on Jacqueline's face when her gorgeous body came into view. Jacqueline pulled her hair when she kissed her left nipple. "I'm more about practicing the baby-making than the doing."

"Are you sure? The girl from last night seemed ready to bring little bronco-busting Ashers into the world." Jacqueline guided her lips to the other breast.

"That's such a dead subject even God can't breathe life into it, and I'd rather talk about what's right in front of me." She ran her hands up Jacqueline's sides before reversing course and pulling her closer by the hips. "You do make me glad I'm alive and have an appreciation for beautiful women."

"And I like the way you string words together." Jacqueline inhaled deeply when she sucked on her nipple. "But like you said, I'm interested in a different conversation."

"What do you want to talk about?" She kissed Jacqueline when she pulled her head back by the hair.

"If you can't guess, I might give you the silent treatment and talk to myself."

She kissed Jacqueline again, and she reached down and dragged her fingers through her wet sex. Jacqueline was a good friend, but she did enjoy the fact that she got to touch her. She probably wouldn't have tried anything until Jacqueline made the first move. It would never become more, but they were safe with each other.

"Stop daydreaming, cowpoke," Jacqueline pulled her hair in a clear effort to make her focus. It was all the hint she needed as she reached down and positioned her fingers for Jacqueline to come down on.

Their pace was as slow as the sunrise, and she felt her clit harden at the way Jacqueline squeezed her fingers. The way Jacqueline moved did make her want to savor this. There was nothing better in life than to see a woman claim what she wanted with genuine need in her eyes.

"You feel so good." Jacqueline picked up her pace and dropped the sheet as if wanting Asher to look at her. "Harder, baby, harder."

She pushed her thumb against Jacqueline's clit and enjoyed the way Jacqueline squeezed her shoulders. Her grip was hard enough to leave bruises and reminded her that not only was she alive, but there was so much pleasure left to have. She moved them so she was on top, making it easier to move her hand. Slow would make it last longer, but Jacqueline had a way of making her greedy and impatient.

"Yes," Jacqueline said, loud enough to startle young horses if the neighing was any indication. "Jesus H. Christ, don't fucking stop."

She used her hips to put more force behind her hand, and Jacqueline moaned as she wrapped her feet around her ass and clawed up her back. "Let go for me."

"Fuck, Ash, it's so…so good." Jacqueline lifted her hips twice more before she tightened around her like a constrictor. "You make me feel good and beautiful. Is it weird that you make me feel more feminine than some of the men I've dated?"

"Maybe you've been dating people who don't appreciate you for the smart, funny, gorgeous woman you are. You are beautiful." She moved to the side so they could reverse positions, and Jacqueline covered them both with the sheet. "Doubly so when you're naked."

"You make me understand why my sister and her fiancée never want to leave the bedroom. The way you touch me makes me crave you." Jacqueline laid her head on her shoulder and seemed content to drift as the wind moved the swing.

"That's not a bad thing, is it, Jac?" She tried never to sound vulnerable, but the question might've been a spectacular fail.

"No, it isn't. It's just that I'm heading back to Vegas soon, and the distance wouldn't be fair to you." Jacqueline paused but as always was honest. "It wouldn't be fair to either of us."

This line of conversation seemed to be more about Jacqueline and what she wanted and didn't want, than her. It didn't make her ecstatically happy, but it didn't shock her. "No worries. Uncomplicated, remember?"

"That doesn't make it easier, does it?" Jacqueline kissed the side of her neck and sighed. "Can I tell you something and not make you think I'm a hypocrite?"

She smiled as she turned her head and kissed Jacqueline's forehead. "After everything you did to me last night, you're free to tell me anything you'd like no matter the subject."

"You make it sound like it's something bad." Jacqueline lifted up on her elbow and gazed down on her. "I just don't want you to think I'm telling you something simply to make you think I'm leading you on."

"You're no poser, sweetheart. I might not be who you picture in your head, but that doesn't mean you're not present when you're with me." Maybe this was a conversation best had at some other time. If Jacqueline was about to tell her it was fun but now it was over, it could wait.

"That woman from last night, she's a fool." Jacqueline kissed her the way anyone dreamed about being kissed. "She hurt you, didn't she? Made you this skittish sometimes?"

"Could be I was an asshole once upon a time."

"Were you?" Jacqueline's question was warm against her ear.

"No, but I could've been."

"Didn't think so, and if you don't interrupt me, I'll tell you my deep thoughts on the subject of Asher Evans." Jacqueline put her head back on her shoulder, and Asher could feel the press of her sex on her lower abdomen. "You're the first person I think about a lot when I'm not with you. I'm not a daydreamer—it's the reason Keegan swears I can't cook. A good chef needs a mixture of romanticism and imagination. The imagination I have, but I've never been overly romantic."

"I think about you too if you're worried that it's all one-sided." She'd learned early on not to expect too much from any situation, except animals or Wade. They were the only ones in her life that weren't a disappointment. Silas and her dad had been true too, but they were gone.

"That's not what I'm worried about, and you're wrong. You're so much more than what I ever imagined." Jacqueline combed her hair back and appeared to be studying her. "It's going to take five more months minimum before the restaurant is open."

"Should be perfect, then, for the championship. I'll either treat you to a celebratory dinner, or I'll use the good food to get over the loss." She closed her eyes at another great kiss.

"Stop doubting yourself—you are going to win. You're also interrupting me again. Let's make a deal, you and me. How about we give it until the championships in Vegas? If we're still single, we give this a try. Maybe an us is something we need to explore. I'm not saying I'm actively looking for someone else, but sometimes it's beyond our control. The last thing I want is to hold you back."

"I don't want to hold you back either. I don't want you to settle on me if you don't think I can make you happy."

"Asher, you've made me happier than you can possibly know."

"You'd be happy with ranch life?" She and Jacqueline were from as different worlds as ever existed.

"If this is how I get to start my days on the ranch, my answer is yes." Jacqueline really did have the best laugh. "If you're doubting that I'd be happy here, listen to me—my answer is yes, but only if you agree to city life every so often. The simplest way to think about it is we're kind of in the same business, only you're more on the front end of the operation. If we try, you'll need a nice suit every so often when I have a work event."

"It's a deal." She returned Jacqueline's hug when she squeezed at her answer.

"Really?"

"Sure, but you have to promise to enjoy yourself in Vegas, and don't forget to be happy." She was willing to try but really didn't want Jacqueline to settle. No one, especially her, wanted to be a consolation prize because another person was tired of searching for the one who'd fit better than anyone else.

"Are you ordering me to play the field?" There was a tinge of incredulity in Jacqueline's tone.

"I'm asking you to be sure. We've known each other long enough that you have to know I care about you. I care enough to let you be happy if there's someone else who's a better fit and already has more than one nice suit." They'd had too many conversations about how they wouldn't commit, shouldn't really, to change trajectory so fast. "You've always told me about who you thought you'd end up with."

"Give me a break, cowpoke. I've seen you on ESPN, and the Discovery Channel did a piece on all these exotic cows you have. I've also taken you shopping, so I know exactly how many nice suits you have. You even agreed to the pink flamingo bow tie, which I think sucker punched the woman you refuse to talk about right where it hits me whenever I look at you. I'll give you a hint and tell you it's not in the gut."

"If the bulls ever saw me in that pink flamingo bow tie, I'll lose all credibility. As for the girl—she's Wade's niece, and we grew up together. She made a bunch of promises she wasn't going to keep, and I was the chump who hung on way past the expiration date." She stopped when Jacqueline ran her tongue up her neck until she bit her earlobe. "She moved back four months ago and thinks no one knows that, which means she really doesn't want to be here. Once Uncle Wade figures that one out, it'll end up hurting him that much more."

"How about you, honey?" Jacqueline tightened her hold on her and rubbed her stomach as she spoke. "How much is it hurting you?"

"My father told me once that there's things you can't control, change, or wish away. The sooner I learned that, he said, the easier life would be. All I had to remember was that it wasn't my fault—well, maybe sometimes it would be, but those big painful things that happen to you were best put behind me." Her dad had gone way too soon, but she loved all the memories of riding with him, shoeing horses, feeding animals, and just talking on the back porch after a long day.

"And is *she* one of those hurtful things you couldn't control, change, or wish away?" Jacqueline bit her chin softly as if to soften the question.

"Nope." She ran her hand down Jacqueline's back to the slope of her butt. "This time I went in fully knowing the consequences. Reagan loved her dad, me, and this place. What she didn't love was bull riding, the rodeo, and the truth of the fact that Uncle Silas and I did. She wanted us both off the circuit."

"Threw down a gauntlet, did she?"

That made her laugh. "She did, but I thought love would win out. I wrote and called for two years like some kind of fucking lovesick fool, but she expanded her horizons when she left for school." That last meeting with Reagan when she'd come home, and the short letters, like she had no time for her any longer, were like a slap to the face.

"Like I said, her loss. Does she have any idea of what you've accomplished?" Jacqueline sat up, seeming truly insulted on her behalf. "You're almost the best at what you do in the arena, you run a highly successful ranch, and you graduated top of your class from Tulane. You're no bumpkin, Asher, and you wouldn't be even without all those accolades. I love you for you, not all this. I may not be the greatest at commitment, but I do love you."

"I love you too, sweetheart." She said it and meant it, even if right at that moment she knew it was more about friendship than romance.

"I'm sorry, but that makes me mad. Whoever gets to be with you should first and foremost understand what a catch you are." Jacqueline took her hand and shook it. "That you're not with me because of *my* money is what makes it so easy to be with you."

"I'm with you because you're beautiful and understand the importance of a good steak."

"Shut up"—Jacqueline pinched her and laughed—"I want you to understand how important to me you are, so I'm not going to be actively looking for anyone else no matter how long we're apart."

"Neither will I, but if I fall in love with my horse, I'll be sure to send you a wedding invitation."

"If that happens, I demand to be the flower girl."

"That's a deal, but Albert isn't as good a kisser as you, so I wouldn't worry about it." Albert wasn't a common horse name, but the horse was highly intelligent and she'd trained him herself, so Albert Einstein Evans seemed like a good choice. She stood with Jacqueline and carried her inside. "All I'll be doing the next couple of months is training, for the next few events before Vegas."

"You don't sound like you're all in if you're asking me to date while I'm away from you." Jacqueline hung on as Asher headed for the bathroom.

"I meant what I said. Your happiness is important to me. Let's table that talk for now and take a shower. I texted and asked the guys to bring a couple horses out here. We'll go riding, and I can show you all the new stuff going on. The new cattle should be getting comfortable in their new home and on the way to making friends. The Pinzgauer isn't like the other cows you've seen around here."

After coffee they rode along the fence line. That would take them by not only the beef cows but the dairy herd as well. The markets the Blanchards had planned would be a good place not only for her beef, but also for their dairy products once they started production. Jacqueline enjoyed the tour and talked her into a race in the open empty pasture. To make it sporting, Asher held back and laughed when Jacqueline stuck her tongue out at her.

"No fair, you let me win," Jacqueline accused.

"I was being chivalrous."

"The name of the ranch is all the proof I need when it comes to chivalry, baby."

They slowed and Jacqueline held her hand out. She took it and leaned over to kiss her knuckles. Yes, this was someone she could come to love passionately. Jacqueline was fun, sexy, and driven. Having someone like that would make every day something new, and Asher was ready for all that and more. Way ready.

CHAPTER FIVE

Reagan's bedroom needed some light filtering blinds or curtains since she was awake way too early again. It was time to get dressed and make the drive to see Uncle Wade even if she'd rather shop for new window treatments and perhaps schedule a root canal. Facing the music wasn't one of her favorite things, but the overwhelming urge to go home had come after seeing Asher. That wasn't something she was willing to unpack at the moment. Denial, though, was something that got easier the more she did it.

She threw on jeans and a sweater and drove to the coffee shop she loved on Magazine Street. The latte and scone kept her company as she made the trek to the east. Once the fishing camps started to thin, the familiar pastures started, and the grass her dad and Uncle Dustin planted years before came into view, instantly relaxing her.

Everything about both ranches had been planned to assure success. Grass was sometimes just something green to brighten people's yards, but it wasn't when it came to grazing cattle. Rye grass wasn't popular in Louisiana, but Uncle Dustin had kept at it until all the acres they owned were covered with the energy-packed grazing grass. It was beautiful when the seed heads were blowing in the breeze. Memories of Asher tickling her with the stalks made her smile as she slowed.

She stopped and pulled over to watch two riders racing along. It wasn't hard to recognize Asher from the way she sat in the saddle, but she hadn't seen that carefree expression in a long while. Asher was laughing, and when she stopped and kissed the hand of the woman riding with her, it gripped something inside Reagan, and it left her hurting.

"You're the one who threw her away. Don't get sentimental now." She drove off, wondering who Asher had taken on an early morning ride. The woman had to be either understanding or stupid to put up with Asher's irresponsible side because that's what bull riding was—irresponsible.

She pulled in behind the big truck with the large Moon Touch Ranch decal on the back window and knocked. Frida studied her with that disarming mom stare for an eternity when she opened the door. While everyone knew Wade ran the ranch, the house was Frida's domain, and it was an unwritten rule that you didn't mess with her. When Reagan had gone and stayed away, Frida had not held back when she told her what a mistake she was making. It had been one of their bigger blowups when she hadn't backed down, so sure that she was in the right.

"Since when do you knock in your own home?" Frida, despite the question, stood blocking the door.

"It's been a while, and I didn't want to be presumptuous." She stepped forward and hugged the only mother figure she'd ever known, overcome with a sense of shame. How many people had she hurt by running?

"It's okay, sweetheart," Frida said, holding her. She still smelled the same, which made Reagan cry harder. The scent of lavender from Frida's perfume and of cinnamon from the baking she did every weekend were the definitions of permanence, a sign there was a place where she belonged.

"I'm sorry." She leaned away and wiped her face. Big emotional displays weren't her norm.

"You haven't changed a bit, which means you're still making yourself miserable." There was tough love, and then there was a mallet to the head kind of love. Frida swung her mallet with pinpoint precision.

"Let's not fight right away. Is Uncle Wade around?"

Frida finally let her in, and Reagan followed her to the kitchen. "He left an hour ago to open the west pastures and move some of the steers there to graze. I say that, but he mostly sits on the horse looking pretty and supervises now." The sticky buns Frida took out of the oven smelled delicious, but instead of offering her one, she placed them in a box and opened the back door. It had been a few years, but

Reagan recognized Rickie, Frida's daughter. She was all grown-up and beautiful.

"Hey, Miss Reagan." Rickie still had a wide smile. "Good to see you. Talk to you later."

Rickie left with the box as if talking to her any more than that would somehow taint her. The speed, though, might've had something to do with the box and what it contained. Rickie, she was sure, was meeting Asher.

"Is she headed for the old cabin?" The small structure had been the only thing standing on the property when her father bought it, and Asher had fixed it up a million years ago as a way of giving them some privacy. In Asher's letters, when she still got them, she'd mentioned moving out there.

"That shack burned down three years ago. No, Asher went home. It took some hard work, but she got it fixed up. That old house hasn't been lived in since Dustin, but it's been waiting for her." Frida took another pan from the oven and served her a pastry with a cup of coffee.

"What do you mean?" The damn sticky bun was delicious, and she closed her eyes at the first bite. These could seriously be her last meal.

"Just that she got started on what was hers. I hate that I don't see her as often, but Rickie left with her, saying she needed to be taken care of." Frida fell silent after that as if she'd already said too much. "Finish that, and I'll have one of the hands saddle a horse for you. Booker isn't ridden too often, so it'll be good for both of you."

"That'll be nice. Is Asher out there helping Uncle Wade?" The only thing more childish would be to pass Frida a note. "I don't want to get in their way."

"Don't worry about Asher." Frida phoned and ordered her horse for her before picking up her dishes. "Get going and tell the old man to be careful."

The gray mare one of the hands led toward the porch was as beautiful as the day her father had gifted her to Reagan. Booker had been better than a car, and she'd spent most of her afternoons riding with Asher. She walked down and ran her hand down Booker's nose.

"Hey, girl." She put her arms around the thick neck and fought the urge to cry. "I missed you."

"Do you need a hand up, Miss Reagan?" the ranch hand asked.

"Let's see if I still remember how." She put her foot in the stirrup and took a minute to find her balance in the saddle. When she did, she spurred Booker into a run with a flick of the reins and headed toward the pasture Frida mentioned.

It was like waking up after sleeping a lifetime and finding she missed all the joy in the world—the wind in her hair, the green that rolled for miles that made the sky that much bluer, and the familiar clomp of Booker's hooves hitting the ground. Her memories were safe on this land because they were forever tied to it.

She slowed at the family cemetery her father had built a few miles from the house. There hadn't been a plan for one, but he'd wanted Dustin close for Asher's sake. It was a place she could ride to and visit when she had a need to. There was no way for her to know what Asher's thoughts were now, but when she was younger, she did come and talk to her father often.

She dismounted and opened the wrought iron gate. There was a bench in front of the only three graves in the whole plot. Dustin Evans and Silas Wilson had been best friends from the age of three, so it made sense for them to spend eternity side by side so they could share stories for as long as the sun rose. Alongside them, Maya Evans was also buried there—her dad had reinterred her after Dustin's death. Reagan placed her hand on each tomb over their names and glanced up.

"Hey, Daddy and Uncle Dustin. Sorry it's been so long, but as you both would've said, I had my head up my ass." The day was starting to become uncomfortably warm, but the marble was cool to the touch. "I need you both to watch out for me. I'm home to stay, but it's hard coming back here, knowing I'll never see you again, Daddy."

The bench was in the shade of the large oak tree, and she enjoyed the quiet of this place. It was so peaceful—she could see why her father had chosen it. A grove of ancient oaks were the perfect sentinels to watch over her family. There was only bone and ash to guard now, but no matter. They were still precious to her.

"Put in a good word for me."

She headed out and smiled when she saw Uncle Wade herding cows toward a gated pasture. He appeared to be an excited small boy, which made her happy, considering how long he'd been doing the same job. The ranch hands with him shouted to get the stragglers back in line, and one of them pointed in her direction.

Wade turned his horse and moved to the end of the line and waved her on toward the river. It'd been a long time since her last ride, but he obviously still remembered her love of horses and the places she liked to ride. They took the long circuit back to the house but stopped at the levee. The river was high, and the current made hundreds of small whirlpools as if in a hurry to get to the Gulf.

"It's good to have you home." It's all he said, and it was like spending time with her father again. They both had infinite patience when it came to waiting her out.

"It's interesting to be back." It was still too early to decide if it was a good move on her part. She'd been unhappy in Seattle, but would she be more miserable here?

"You've always had a home here, but only if you want one." Wade tipped his hat back and sighed. "It's not a total surprise you're back, but I've been curious as to when you'd come home and why."

"You shouldn't be alone anymore," she said before he could utter anything else. That'd been her reasoning, and she'd repeated it in her head until she believed it.

"Your father and I raised you to be independent and strong. Don't waste your time on an old man set in his ways." He laughed in a way that shook his belly, identical to her father's laugh. "I was hoping you'd come home eventually because you'd become interested in ranching. That's not going to happen, is it?"

"You have Asher, Uncle Wade. She knows this land better than anyone, and she'd fall on her sword before she let you down." Except on days when Asher was riding around with a beautiful woman—then she forgot about the cows. And that was the last thing Reagan should be thinking about.

"Asher isn't in charge here, and she doesn't own the land—we do. Eventually you're going to have to make some decisions about how we go forward." He straightened his hat and tapped his fist on the horn of his saddle. "Doesn't have to be anytime soon, so don't think there's a rush. I would, though, like for you to come and have a meal every so often."

"I just got here, and with the move and work..." There was only so much lying she could do, especially when she could see he didn't believe her.

"If that's how it is." He stopped and glanced at the river as if fishing for the right thing to say. "I'm glad you're enjoying your job, and it's good that you're busy."

"Uncle Wade…"

He waved his hand. "You've made something of yourself, sweet pea, so you don't owe anyone any explanations, least of all me. Just as long as you're happy." He handed her the gift of not having to come up with any more stories, and she loved him for it.

They rode back in silence, and Frida had lunch ready. "Thanks, Frida." The fried chicken and carrot soufflé were some of her favorites, but she'd lost her appetite on the levee. Frida's intense stare was a pointed dare to her not to eat, so she found a way to bring her interest in food out of hibernation.

The phone rang, and her uncle got up, waving Frida to stay put. "Moon Touch Ranch."

Whoever was on the other end talked for a few minutes straight. All her uncle did was say *yes* a few times before he came back to the table. The call seemed to get his good mood back, so she didn't need three guesses as to who it was.

When he and her father gave their word to Dustin to watch over Asher, they'd truly meant it. Hell, it had been Asher who'd been with her father when he died. Reagan had gone to the hotel from the hospital to take a shower, and that's when he picked to go, with only Asher at his side, probably what he'd wanted.

"Everything okay?" she asked when he sat back down.

"We have three cows getting ready to drop calves, so I'll go and check on that when we're done here. That'll make this one of our best years." He put his head down and finished eating. "I'm glad you came out today. I've missed you, so remember we love you, and we'd love if you weren't a stranger." He hugged her when she stood up, clearly being dismissed.

"I know, Uncle Wade, and I love you too. If you're not busy next week, I'll come back and go riding with you again." She took his hand and he smiled. "You take care of yourself."

"You do the same, Buckaroo."

Ah, the nicknames he and her dad had given her and Asher a lifetime ago.

Buck was Asher at her most genuine. She'd been young and impressionable once upon a time, that was true, but Asher really had been easy to fall for. What they shared wasn't something she'd ever replicate. Asher loved her in a way that was pure, all encompassing, and that didn't exist in the world any longer. She'd found that out with people like Steph. Honor had to be ingrained from an early age and taken as an oath to live by.

That was something Asher prided herself in. She had not only honor, but devotion to those she loved, and she'd loved like she'd never be hurt. That had changed. Reagan didn't need to be told—she'd seen it the night before. The walls she'd seen in the way Asher looked at her were not only high, but thick. Nothing would penetrate them, and she'd done that to Asher.

"It was good to see you both, and promise you'll call if you need anything. Thanks for today."

"There's no need for thanks," Frida said. "You're family. You're the slow, dimwitted part of the family with a tendency to self-sabotage, but we love you anyway."

"Then call me the next time you make the chicken. Eventually I'll have to learn how to make it, so I can make stuff up about you when I feed it to my kids." She kissed their cheeks and waved when she got in the car.

The spot where she'd seen Asher earlier held only cows now, and they were massive. She pulled over and walked to the black border fence to get a better look. One of the cows moved slowly toward her as if it was used to dealing with people, which was unusual in beef cattle. The brown and white coat and the large head were like nothing they'd raised before, and her uncle hadn't mentioned introducing a new breed. Granted, her being MIA hadn't helped on the communication front, but he usually loved telling her about stuff happening on the ranch during their sporadic phone calls.

"Where'd you come from?" She scratched the cow's snout and got a head shake. "You make me think maybe I should get more involved. All we need is for Uncle Wade to lose everything because he waited until now to get adventurous and gamble on new untried breeds."

Her conscience told her it was his ranch to do with as he pleased, but she still worried. She didn't want to run the ranch, but its permanence was her talisman. It was her truth, the North Star that guided her life. But there was plenty now that was different than before. Maybe she needed more than four months of adjustment to wrap her head around all that had happened in her absence.

CHAPTER SIX

The next morning, Asher woke up to a text from Jacqueline. She was back in Vegas, glad the project was still on schedule, and there hadn't been much cleanup to do because of her absence. Jacqueline had ended the text with an emoji blowing a kiss, and she had to laugh. Neither of them was the emoji type, but the real kisses from the day before had been nice.

It was back to work for her as well, and while she had a break in the rodeo circuit, she couldn't simply stop. Close to the main barn she pastured ten bulls raised for their orneriness, and some came from the family lines of the bulls Silas had raised. They bucked like monsters and were fresher than the circuit bulls, since they were mostly unridden. First, though, she put on workout clothes and shoes for a run to start her morning.

Bull riding was dangerous. She'd never lost her healthy respect for the bulls she faced, but to be successful only took leg strength, upper-body strength, and letting go of your fear. That's what got her out here on days when all she really wanted to do was sleep in. This was the year, though. She'd either win or she wouldn't—either way, once the championships were over, she was retiring. With or without the buckle she was missing, she'd had a stellar career she could be proud of.

All she had to do was end up in the top three, and the purse along with her sponsorships would bankroll whatever she wanted to do for as long she wanted to do it. In the six years she'd been competing, she'd made close to ten million dollars, and she'd been smart in her investments like Silas had taught her to be. She'd mortgaged the ranch to expand only because she didn't want to dip into those investments, but she'd never been in danger of losing what she had.

No one, especially Wade, would try to talk her out of quitting, and for that she was grateful. She was closing in on thirty, and maintaining what it took to be at the physical level she needed to be would become that much harder if she hung on too long.

There'd be no way she'd ever admit it to Reagan or anyone else, but she wanted to walk away from the sport way before Silas had. She'd loved him as much as she did her father, but he'd stayed in the dance way past what was smart. It's what had caused his last accident, and she hated that the short remaining weeks of his life had been spent in physical therapy and not riding the land he loved.

The music in her ears stopped, and her phone announced Gia Faulkner on the line. "Hey."

"Are you doing something physical or is the heavy breathing because you're thinking of me?" Gia made kissing noises into the phone.

"I'm jogging so my ass will look good for you," she joked back.

"Did I forget a meeting? I apologize if I did."

"No worries, you're not getting forgetful. I had time this morning and wanted to finalize the specs for the new barn. I can be there in forty-five minutes."

"Sounds good, and have Rickie set you up with breakfast if I'm running late." She turned around and laughed when Albert fell into step with her and bumped her off stride with his head. "See you soon."

Albert bumped her again, and she stopped to give him what he wanted, which was her attention and a good head scratch between his ears on the only white patch on his shiny black coat. He was prancing around her when Helki Jaci rode up and had trouble controlling the young horse she was riding. Helki had been working her way up the ranks at a horse ranch in Kentucky when Asher met her at a horse auction. It wasn't like she needed to add other livestock to worry about, like thoroughbreds, but the chance to buy more than the normal ranch horse was hard to pass up.

Albert had been in that lot, and she was as happy with him as she was with the others she'd purchased. Her explanation for the purchase had interested Helki, so when Asher offered her the job of running the horse end of things, Pemberley gained a horse whisperer who'd worked wonders to turn their horse operation into something others envied. She didn't have many horses, but they were starting to sell off some of the foals for a lot more than she'd imagined.

"Good morning," she said, watching her feet around the slightly nervous animal. "Did he have a bowl of Wheaties this morning?"

"It's more like Albert told him his daddy was Secretariat or something. He's definitely full of oats and energy this morning. Do you need me for anything today?" Helki laughed when the horse turned in a circle a couple of times as if trying to entice Albert to play.

"I have Gia coming by, and when we're done, I'm heading to the barn. Wade should be here this afternoon to help me work out and give me some pointers." She stood with her back to the sun and laughed when Albert rested his heavy head on her shoulder. "Need the day off?"

"I'm thinking you're at the point where you could give Wade some pointers if he loses his mind and takes up bull riding." Helki patted the young stallion on the neck to calm him down. "And not a day off. There's a horse in Luling that just came on the market, and I want to take a look. It's a gray mare that should be good for at least four more years of breeding. Matched with either of these guys, she should throw some beautiful foals."

"Give Gavin a heads-up so he'll be ready with the horse trailer." She trusted Helki and had given her a budget to buy stock as she pleased. "If you're looking at gray mares, though, give Wade a call and ask about Booker. She's a beautiful animal, and I haven't seen her much except along the fence line when I'm out in the mornings. She'll be a good mama if Wade agrees."

"What kind of deal do you want to make?"

"If Booker's available, offer him the first foal if we get the next two. Make sure to mention we'll be breeding her to one of the new stallions we picked up in Kentucky." She grabbed Albert's mane for leverage to get on his back. "Call if you need anything."

"Thanks, boss."

She rode to the fence, giving Albert some more love before running up the drive to take a shower. Mentioning Booker made her think of Reagan as she stood under the hot spray, and there was no shaking the memories once they started. Now, though, she thought about the woman Reagan had been with. The suit, her stare, and the way she held

Reagan made her think they were together. Whoever the woman was, she was no rancher, that was plain.

If she had one guess, she'd have to say the woman was an attorney, and that meant Reagan's personality transplant was complete. In a way she had to thank Reagan for her rejection. Not being good enough had driven her to take a chance on what she wanted her legacy to be after people forgot her name as the only woman professional bull rider in the top ten. When her life was done, she'd leave the family she hoped to have a home they could be proud of, complete with the history of who'd come before her.

"Hey, Gia," she said, kissing her friend's cheek. She'd opted for an old pair of jeans, work boots, and white T-shirt since the weather was starting to get warm, and the protective jacket she'd have to put on later for practice would be hot. "I'm sorry for keeping you." Gia had gone directly to the site and had a set of plans open on the hood of her Jeep. Asher spotted another truck coming and waved when she saw Wade behind the wheel.

"Good morning," Wade said kissing Gia's other cheek. They'd met when Gia had offered him some design improvements on his barn that had worked out well. "Hope you don't mind me being here, Buck, but I thought I'd see what you had in mind."

"No problem at all, Uncle Wade. You know you're always welcome." She adjusted her hat to shield her eyes from the sun and watched as her ranch manager Owen and a few of the guys moved dirt with tractors. Owen was spreading new soil in some lower areas to start planting rye grass that would be cut in early fall for hay. The pad she'd put down to elevate the barn was twice as big as she needed it to be.

"Are you married to this area?" Gia asked. She was staring at the pad as if she had plenty on her mind.

"This puts the barn in the middle of my new acreage. Any farther to the west and you run into a little traffic, which won't be good for mellow cows, and too far to the east and it's the boundary for the Pinzgauer herd." The tract of land was large and marshy in some areas, but a little dirt work every year would take care of that. Right now, it was like standing in the middle of nowhere. "You see a problem?"

"No, just making sure before we break ground. It's perfect for the solar array that's going in, and it gives us room for the digester bladder.

Once we have that up and running you can start to convert all your farming equipment to methane gas. This operation will be so green it'll put us both on the cover of *Architectural Digest*."

"What the hell is a digester bladder?" Wade asked, laughing.

"All the waste runoff from all these dairy cows will be collected in a big bladder that will hold it, so eventually you can collect the methane," Gia explained. The costs of the sustainable items she was putting in the design were more than Asher wanted to spend, but Orchard Dairy was picking up the tab, so she was on board.

They went over all the plans again before Gia put them in the leather tube with the ranch's name stamped on the side and kissed them both good-bye. The construction would begin in a few weeks, and Asher was looking forward to it since the pasture work would be complete before that—which meant she could move the dairy herd to this spot, freeing up the majority of the land for the Pinzgauer herd.

"Want to take a ride before we head to the barn?" Wade asked.

"Sure."

She hopped in his truck, and they headed to the levee at the end of the property. The Mississippi was at its widest here and they weren't far from the buoy that marked the mouth of the river. The width was so great that it actually slowed the current enough that there were months you could walk out a ways and not feel the pull of the water around your legs. This was a spot she'd come to with her dad often to talk about whatever was on their minds.

"Must be serious if this is where you want to talk," she said, smiling.

He lowered the tailgate and hopped up. "Saw Reagan yesterday. She came out for a ride, then had lunch at the house."

"I saw Reagan too…her and her date." She told him about what happened, and it wasn't until then that she knew she could've handled the situation better. "It's good she's back. She's the only family you have, and I'm sure you've missed her."

"I helped raise you, kid, so that's not exactly true. You're my family just as much as she is, and I told her it's time for us to talk. I think, though, we need to have a conversation before that." His eyes were on the water, and he seemed like there was plenty on his mind.

"Can I be honest with you?"

"Buck, I'd think you're always honest with me." He put his hand on her shoulder and squeezed. "There's no way in hell I want you to stop now."

She nodded and took a deep breath. "Reagan is your family, and I love you more than any person alive. I love you like I did my dad and your brother, but there's no way in hell *I'm* ever going to forget what happened." It was all water under the bridge, or whatever other bullshit clichéd thing people said about what went down, but the anger was always there. Sometimes she forgot about it for months at a time, but it'd never be erased from her soul. "I'll never do anything to jeopardize your relationship with her, I mean that. I'd also like a heads-up if she's going to be there, so I can avoid a repeat of the other night."

"I know, and you have my word. What she did? I can't forgive that either, so I know where your head is with all that." He sighed again. "That's not what I wanted to talk to you about anyway. I was hoping she came home to do what you did and start to take some responsibility for what we're leaving her."

"I'm guessing here, but I doubt Reagan is interested in ranching." The woman Reagan was with would never have anything to do with this life.

"You're right about that, so I wanted to talk to you about the future of Moon Touch. I'm not going to live forever, and I want all that hard work not to have been done in vain." He looked at her and smiled. "This is a crappy way of asking, but I'm legally tied to Reagan, so I can't do what I'd like to do without her approval."

"If it's buying Moon Touch from you, I've been thinking of a way to ask you myself." She bumped shoulders with him and joined him in the kind of laughter that came from deep in her belly and spoke of friendship, caring, and belonging. "Was that not what was on your mind?"

"I don't want you to buy what I think is rightfully yours, Buck. All this stuff you're doing makes me sure that Moon Touch should go to you. It's the right thing, and the right thing is me giving you what I think you should have."

"The last thing I want is to cause problems for you, so you meet with someone who knows what Moon Touch is worth and we'll come up with a plan. There's another hundred and fifty acres on the other side of you that would complete what I need. I haven't made an offer yet because I'd have to drive around you to get there." She swung her legs like she had when she was little in an effort to bleed off some raw energy. "Reagan agreed to this?"

"I haven't talked to her about it yet, but she's not coming back here to live on the ranch. She got a place in town and found a job at a sports-centered clinic. Sounds like she's set, so all she needs is the money from the sale to set her future." He rubbed his chin before offering her his hand. "This is what I want and the right thing for the ranch. Silas would agree with me if he was here, so I've made up my mind."

"I'll go at your speed, Uncle Wade, and whether it's tomorrow or five years from now, nothing but the name on the deed is going to change about Moon Touch. The house, the stock, and everything else will be yours until you want to completely retire. Even then, you're going to live out your years at home like Dad and Uncle Silas." She shook his hand, sealing their verbal agreement. "I don't say it often enough, but I love you. I have from the day you guys took me in and gave me a home."

"You made me proud even before that, Buck. Once the rodeo stuff is over maybe you'll think of making me a grandpa so I can teach the next generation how to ride." He laughed and slapped her on the back. "That's a pretty girl I saw this morning, and she looks good in the saddle. Is there a story there?"

"We're tentatively talking about it, but don't get your hopes up. Jacqueline Blanchard isn't someone you just move onto a ranch, so I want her to be sure. Della Blanchard's granddaughter is used to five star restaurants, not cow shit and ranch hands."

"Like I keep telling you, Buck. Shit has a way of working out. Now get in and let's go rile up them bulls of yours."

CHAPTER SEVEN

A sher strapped on the practice helmet and zipped up the flak jacket that would protect her torso if one of the bulls got his hooves on her. She had two ranch hands on bull duty, Connor Young on chute duty, and Austin Theriot in the practice arena to lure the bull back to the holding pen when she jumped clear. As always Wade was sitting in the spot she'd constructed for him that was an approximation of where the judges sat in competition.

"Ready, boss?" Connor asked when she got the rope around the big black bull with the short horns.

"Open it up," she said with a nod of her head. It was a struggle to stay on the entire time since the damn bull seemed to be on steroids. She didn't need Wade shaking his head when she headed back to the chute to let her know that was a piss-poor ride.

"Were you trying to rile him up, kicking your legs up like that?" Wade asked. "You haven't done that since you were eighteen."

"I think Connor shocked him with a prod before I climbed on," she said, making a rude hand gesture. Wade laughed it off. "Let's try that again, and put Bub back in the lineup after a few rides. He's worse than Bo the Third, and my teeth still hurt from that son of a bitch."

Connor laughed and gave her a thumbs-up. By the time she got five good rides in, she was exhausted but ready to do it again the next day. "Thanks, guys. You can line up the others for tomorrow around the same time. We have a little over four months to get ready for a month's worth of back-to-back competitions before the championships."

"You got it, and we'll run the skimmer around the arena and take all those divots out. If you don't need us for anything, we'll head out to the new pasture and get some more dirt work done," Austin said.

The phone rang loud from the speaker it was connected to. Wade waved her off as he headed into the barn to answer it. Whoever it was didn't stay on the line very long, and Wade crooked his finger at her. She took off all the safety equipment and handed it over to Connor to place in the barn. Whatever this was, she hoped he remembered his promise to keep some distance between him and Reagan.

"Who was that?" she asked, accepting her hat back.

"That was Red," Wade said, scratching the side of his head.

Henry Bird—Red—was the biggest promoter on the rodeo circuit responsible for the larger events around the country and was slowly introducing the sport in Europe. You didn't get very far if you made an enemy of him, but the old guy was so charming it was hard to find someone who didn't like him. He'd been a big fan of hers from the time Silas introduced them, and he'd been encouraging her from the sidelines for years.

"If he's calling now, there has to be something he wants." Red was famous for the small favors he asked, at times reminding her of a real-life Tom Sawyer. You'd end up paying to paint Red's house, thinking it was your idea by the time you were finished with the second coat.

"He said Louisiana is one of his last frontiers as far as a premier event, so he's been working on something for the last eight months. It wasn't until the advertisements started to go out that he realized you weren't on the roster." Wade put both his hands up. "And don't shoot the messenger."

"I didn't put my name on the roster because I wanted to take some time off."

The way Wade was frowning was starting to give her a headache. "You might not have a choice, Buck. The only way to make this a success was to make it count toward the rankings. If you skip it, it could knock you out of contention, depending on the scores the big hitters post."

"Say what you will about Red, he's a sly bastard. I don't have much of a choice, do I?" She had four days to get ready to face the guys who'd love to knock her down quite a few pegs, putting the championship out of her reach.

"Think of how big your cheering section will be for this one. I doubt Frida, Rickie, and all your guys and mine will sit this one out." He put his arm around her shoulders and smiled. "Come on, I'll put some steaks on the grill and have Frida bake you a chocolate cake to soften the blow of missing out on your vacation time."

She took a shower and put on a pair of shorts and a clean T-shirt, and drove with Rickie over to Moon Touch. The dinner was nice, reminding her of old times, but after chocolate cake she excused herself with a kiss to Frida's cheek. The drive to the same spot Wade took her to earlier didn't take long, and she headed to the top of the levee so she could sit on the truck bed and watch the boats pass by.

One of the things she used to do with her father was to make up stories about where the big freighters were going and what treasures they carried. She could hear the soft mooing and the crickets, and it was like nothing much had changed in all the years she'd lived and loved this land. There were four large ships heading out of the New Orleans port, and from their drafts, they were loaded down. The sight made her think of Jaqueline and how far away she was.

"The West Coast is different but beautiful. Even though that's true, I still missed this spot."

It was strange to recognize Reagan's voice right off even if she hadn't heard it in years. It didn't affect her like it once did, but in a strange way she couldn't be upset with the intrusion because Reagan belonged here. That was probably the last thing Reagan thought— Reagan had outgrown them all but especially her.

"I'm not sure that's true." She didn't raise her voice and didn't turn around. "You haven't been interested in your uncle or anyone else here. Or did you only miss the ranch?"

"Asher." Reagan said her name like she had the night before, and her tone held something she couldn't figure out. "I can understand you're mad, but we were friends. I'd like to be that again."

"You're right." The urge to leave was strong, but she was tired of being accommodating to this woman. She'd gone out of her way to make Reagan a priority, giving her what she wanted and needed, and all that got her was a kick in the teeth. "We were friends."

"That sounds like past tense," Reagan said as she sat next to her. It was odd that Asher hadn't heard a car. This was a ways to get to by foot. "I can't blame you for being mad."

"I'm not angry, and nothing has changed. You weren't hard to understand, and I know what you wanted." She glanced at Reagan and she was still beautiful. "If you think I'm going to punish you for that, you still don't know me well." It was a dig at how Reagan had punished her for the things Asher wanted and Reagan couldn't accept.

"Still riding, huh?" Reagan said and laughed.

"Still riding, so I'm still brainless." She hopped down and faced Reagan. "Can I drop you somewhere? It's not safe to walk around here at night."

"The nearest person for ten miles is you." Reagan jumped down as well and brushed off her jeans.

"True, but the bulls are grazing around here somewhere. Walking across their path is riskier than riding them." She opened the door to the passenger side and waited. Her begging days were over.

"I'm parked by the road," Reagan said. "I didn't want to bother everyone, and I didn't call ahead."

"Uh-huh." She knew she sounded like a fool, at least to Reagan, but she couldn't help it. "Is that you?"

The small SUV sat in the dark, and she tapped her finger on the steering wheel of the truck to keep from saying anything else as she stared straight ahead at the Washington State license plate. In a way it was like a gigantic billboard that said *I left your butt behind and along the way I outgrew your country bumpkin ass.* The damn thing didn't even have to be spelled out in neon for her to get the message.

"Thanks for the ride."

"See you around." She started driving before Reagan had the chance to close the door. Forgiveness might be good for the soul, but Reagan had damaged hers. Damaged things didn't work the way they were supposed to, but she still wasn't proud of her behavior. Frida had taught her that no one could be forced to love another person. It was the best answer she had when she'd asked herself why she hadn't been enough.

Her ringing phone stopped her spiral down the snake hole of her thoughts. "Hi, pretty lady."

"Are you sure you aren't interested in the restaurant business? You could come out here and we could do naked bookkeeping." Jacqueline had a talent for making her laugh. "You know I don't do over-the-top sappy, but I miss you and thought you should know that."

"I keep telling you—it's not sappy if it's mutual. I miss you too, and the cows did look a little down when I rode out there by myself this morning." She went along the long road back to the house, wanting

Jacqueline's voice in her ear and the cloak of darkness. "Tell me you're not still working."

"Afraid so, cowpoke. The only good news so far is the steaks were a hit. I didn't freeze them, but packing them tight with ice on the top and bottom got a little messy. You were right about the frozen packs." Jacqueline obviously had a small threshold of sap in her and it was back to business.

"I'll think of something so you don't spend a fortune overnighting every package." She stopped at the fence line leading up to the house and studied the area. They were isolated out here, but there was a lot of gang activity less than twenty miles from them, so they took turns riding the property at night.

"Enough about that. Why are you riding around this late?"

She dropped her head back and closed her eyes. "I had dinner with Wade, Frida, and Rickie. I stopped at the levee on the way home and ran straight into my past. Got clobbered over the head with it, and you weren't there to run interference for me."

"Darling, you have to remember one important thing." Jacqueline sounded soft, sincere, and so very far away.

"What's that?"

"Sometimes the past is a road you have to finish walking before you can head into the future. Della is a big fan of unburdening the heart so there's only room for the one person you're meant to be with." Jacqueline laughed and it brightened her mood. "You should listen to my grandmother—she's a wise woman."

"Della is wise, and she's also scary when she wants to be. You know I hate talking about my past, but I think I owe you a conversation about it." She stared at the house and the section the construction crew was working on now.

The small house her father had built had needed work after sitting empty so long, and she'd expanded on the original footprint. She'd decided on an Acadian-style house with a wraparound porch and the same green additions she'd put in the barn. Gia had done a great job on all the projects she'd taken on.

"I've got time now, so tell me whatever you want to."

She tried to bleed the emotion out of the story she told, like she had with Wade. The arguments she'd had with Reagan about the way she wanted to live her life, the things she wanted to try, and the rodeo.

She'd been a kid who wanted to run a ranch and had learned plenty about how to go about it. Bull riding and the rodeo had been the ticket to getting it done.

"So she blamed the rodeo for killing her father," Jacqueline said. "Then you tell her you want the same thing."

"I did, and that was that. She left for school, came home two years later, then disappeared again." She stopped, not wanting to sound whiny. "All I want now is for Uncle Wade to build a relationship with her, and for her to be open to that. He deserves that and so much more."

"Listen to me, okay," Jacqueline said softly. "Everyone does what they can to survive. How you go about it doesn't always make sense to another person, but you can't prosecute their actions because they don't fit the scenario you want."

"Forgive and forget, huh?"

"Don't ever forget, honey, but maybe think about it from her perspective. I'm selfishly not telling you to start over from where you left off, but letting all that go will make you enjoy the distance you've come since then."

"You might not believe me, but I have let that go." She got that great laugh out of Jacqueline again, and it was like winning something big. "I know you can't make it, but tell Della if she wants some rodeo action, Red put something together for next week in the Dome. I'll get her and Mackie some tickets if they're interested."

"Who says I can't make it?"

"Don't leave work, and trust me, if I could skip it, I would. The old bastard made it mandatory for everyone by making it count toward the final scores. It's one more I'll have to add to my list, but at least after that I'll still have almost four months off." She pulled under the open carport and walked out to the barn. There was a bucket of carrots by the large open doors, and she grabbed a handful and walked the stalls. Albert the piglet had his head out before she reached him.

"What if I want to?" Jacqueline sounded like a woman you didn't want to disagree with. "I need a break from this place every so often. When people tell me how hard it is to open a place in New Orleans, I'm going to call bullshit when you compare it to the Vegas Strip. Plus a rodeo event gives me the excuse to wear jeans."

"I'll send you some VIP tickets, so let me know who's coming." She tapped her phone against her chin when she hung up, happy

Jacqueline could maybe make it, but her mind hadn't completely cleared of Reagan. "Forgetting her should be as easy as jumping off a bull." All she had to do was take care that she was clear of danger before she made the leap.

❖

Kendra helped Reagan with the elderly man with the pain threshold of an infant who'd had a hip replacement. Getting him to stand and walk had become a major undertaking. He really wasn't the usual client they got, but he thought that since it was a sports clinic, he'd get to talk to all the Saints players. There was plenty the team was doing wrong, and he was dying to tell them how to fix it.

"Okay, Mr. Fletcher, up we go," Reagan said as she pulled on the assistance strap around his chest. "Remember to find your balance before you start walking."

"Girl, I've been walking a hundred years before you were born. You think I don't know how to do it?" He yanked away from her, fell into his wheelchair, and started a streak of cursing. "You pushed me down. What kind of animal are you? I demand you get the team out here so I can tell them about the mistreatment I've had to experience."

"Mr. Fletcher," she said with as patient a voice as she could muster. "Sir, if you could calm down, we can get through this." Reagan laughed and shook her head, then said to Kendra, "You're doing this to me because I keep leaving early when we go out, aren't you."

"You're the newbie, so you get some of our more problem children," Kendra said softly.

"Is there anyone more problematic than Mr. Fletcher?"

"No, he's the truest pain in the ass we have, so you're lucky that way." Kendra pulled Mr. Fletcher back up and put his walker within reach. "Once we're done with Mr. Fletcher, I need to talk to you."

"Anything wrong?" She'd been lucky there'd been an opening when she applied since the Riverbend Sports Clinic was exactly what she was looking for in a job.

"No, you're doing a great job even if Mr. Fletcher doesn't agree. It's just an opportunity I think you'd be great for."

They worked together to finish with Mr. Fletcher, who kept insisting they produce the football players who were obviously hiding in the office. Once the assisted living center came and got him, she and Kendra went to her office with their last coffees of the day. The clinic closed in thirty minutes, and she was due to drive out to Moon Touch and have dinner with Frida and Uncle Wade again. It'd been a week since their last awkward meal, so they'd all agreed to try again. She'd made a deal with herself to try to relax around her family, and to stay away from Asher if she spotted her again.

"The owners started a program a year ago for certain high-profile clients. Instead of them coming to us, we go to them. Usually, clients like that have home gyms and do better in the environment they feel comfortable in, especially if it means they can avoid people like Mr. Fletcher. Cindy Eastman usually takes these cases, but she's on an extended maternity leave, so I thought you might want to give it a shot."

"When you say high-profile, what exactly do you mean?" Like Mr. Fletcher, she wouldn't mind working with the town's professional teams. The right connection could land her a full-time job with the team, patrolling the sidelines. That's not what she'd wanted when her career path started out, but a little taste of it in Seattle changed her mind about that.

"Pro athletes, college players, and some high school standouts. There's plenty of business to go around, and I think those clients are the best clients to deal with, since they put in the work, minus all the whining." Kendra pulled out a few files to make some notes. "So can I count on you?"

"Definitely," she said, smiling. "Do you mind if I cut out a little early? I'm having dinner with Uncle Wade and Frida tonight and wanted to stop and get dessert."

"After Mr. Fletcher you deserve to come in late tomorrow as well, but don't push it."

Reagan drove to Whole Foods and picked up an Italian cream cake before heading home to change. Uncle Wade had called her a few times after their lunch to check on her and to say he didn't care for how it'd ended. She was the one who had to apologize, and Uncle Wade was so kind that she wanted to keep trying until she got it right.

There was enough daylight when she was close to the ranch to see the big cows she'd discovered the week before, and close to those were the cutest cows she'd ever come across. They reminded her of her favorite cookies, and she wanted to have a conversation with Uncle Wade about all the new breeds he was introducing to the ranch. The house had a few cars in the drive, and she remembered that Friday meant Frida was cooking for not only the family but the ranch hands as well. It was possible Asher was in there since technically she still worked at the ranch even if she was a rodeo star.

Rickie opened the front door and came out to help her with the cake, and her presence meant Asher was indeed inside. "Hey, I didn't get to talk to you much the other day. How are you?"

"I'm good. Working and going to school keep me busy, but I'm enjoying my freedom. Are you enjoying being back?" Rickie walked in as she held the door for her. The front room was full of guys in clean jeans and ironed plaid shirts. None of them were Asher.

"I've been so busy settling in there hasn't been too much time for fun." She followed Rickie into the kitchen, and she thought of all the memories that centered around Frida cooking at the big stove. This had been her refuge when she needed a break from everyone and everything. "Hey, Frida. I hope that cake is big enough."

"Once they eat a steak the size of their head, they go easy on the dessert. Sit and have a glass of wine. Dinner's almost ready and we're eating outside at the big table."

Her father had built a large patio outside to fit the table he and Asher had made from an old fallen cypress tree on the property. It was massive and sat thirty people easily, and they'd been so proud of the finished product she could remember their smiles. The pits on the edge of the space were big enough to accommodate feeding steaks to that many people. If she'd grown up to be a vegetarian, her father would've written her out of his will.

"Hey," Wade said, hugging her like it only meant something special if her feet came off the ground. "I'm happy you're here, and I hope you're hungry."

"Thanks for calling," she said, kissing his cheek. "And we both know it should've been me who apologized."

"Let's sit and eat, and afterward we'll go for a walk. I'll explain later why you should stop apologizing."

The dinner was so like all the others she'd sat through in the years she'd lived on the ranch. The people who worked for Uncle Wade and her father never changed. They were hardworking, easygoing, and fiercely loyal—the old phrase *what you see is what you get* was coined for ranch hands, and it was refreshing.

Of course people sometimes did put up walls to protect the secrets they had. It was those secrets that prevented anyone from truly knowing who they were. A great example of that was Steph and her need to keep her options open.

She helped Rickie, Frida, and a couple of the guys bring all the dishes in, but Uncle Wade waved her out before she could start putting them in the dishwasher. "Come on," he said. He headed through the barn and to the pastures beyond it. There were cows sitting in clusters while some of the calves still ran around despite the hour. The little ones had always been her favorites on the ranch, and she remembered Asher teasing her about it.

"I know what you said," she said and held her hand up when he started to say something. "Me leaving the way I did wasn't fair to you, and the way I acted isn't something I'm proud of. For all of that I'm sorry."

"It might come as a shock to you, sweetheart, but not even you get every situation right. That's a lesson your dad and I learned real quick, and the fact that you never completely learned that one should be the thing you remember about this conversation." He walked along the fence line and jingled the change in his pocket. "We're your family, we're always going to be family, and nothing you do or don't do is going to change that."

"I meant what I said." She took his hand and loved the rough calluses she could feel. "I'm taking on a new assignment, and if I'm lucky, it'll give me more time to spend out here."

"Good." Wade stopped and fanned himself with his hat. "I mentioned before about the decisions we have to make."

"Are you okay?" If he was sick, she didn't think she could handle it.

"No, nothing like that." He put an arm around her shoulders and kissed her temple. "I want to start taking some time off, so how would you feel about selling off some of the land? I'm not saying selling off the whole thing, but enough that we can run a smaller operation."

"You and Daddy worked so hard to accumulate all this land, and now you want to sell it?" She would've been less shocked if he'd said that he wanted to take up drag. "I'm not sure how I feel about that."

"If you don't want to sell, we won't, but last year I started to downsize the herd. For now I'm keeping all the full-timers on staff but not bringing on the seasonal guys." He stared out into the darkness like he could see for miles. "The cattle I bought recently were to maintain the reduced numbers."

"I'm not saying to change your plans, Uncle Wade. That you even started thinking retirement shocks me." She squeezed his hand and stopped him from taking another step. "Are you sure you're okay?"

"I'm old, Reagan, not sick." He laughed, just like her father's laugh. It was both comforting and saddening.

"Good, and I can see your point. This place is nothing but hard work, and I'm sure after years of it, you're ready for some downtime."

Wade shook his head and put his arm around her again. "I love the work, the land, and what we do. Frida, though, isn't going to wait around forever to see some of the places she's got on her bucket list." His smile made him appear younger and happier.

"You and Frida? Really?" She glanced up at him and laughed. Her dad had given up that part of himself when her mother left, always saying he didn't have time. Maybe if he'd had someone at home aside from her waiting for him, he'd have quit sooner.

"Sometimes you think too much," Wade said, tapping the side of her head as if he could see every thought in there. "Thinking is overrated when doing is so much better."

"I'm happy for you. I love Frida and I love you, so I'm happy you two figured it out." They started walking again, and she enjoyed the heat that lingered after the sun had set. Summertime on the ranch wasn't for the faint of heart, but she loved the quietness that surrounded them, like they were in their own little world where nothing bad could touch them.

"It takes us Wilsons ages to see what's right in front of us sometimes, but we get it eventually. I noticed Frida a long time ago, but she keeps telling me she's not the marrying kind. That first guy put her through the seven levels of hell, so I'm happy she loves me." He shrugged, and she could see the kind of life he wanted from the tone of his voice.

Frida might not have been the marrying kind, but Wade was. It might be too late for a family, but there was no reason they couldn't make each other happy until the day one of them died. Hell, it was the same thing she wanted, only she had yet to find it.

"Frida's a smart woman, so she'll come around eventually. As a card-carrying member of the Wilson family, I know for sure we're hard to resist."

"Next time, then, bring your friend. I know you have one, and it'll be nice to show her where you come from."

It made her laugh to think of Steph on the farm in her nice suits and Italian leather shoes. Getting manure on those would send her into a tizzy. "Let's start by getting me used to being back here first, and we'll work up to that. I did have a good time tonight, so thanks for that."

"We're going to prove to you that coming home is a good thing."

"I think I figured that one out all by myself." She went up on tiptoe and kissed his cheek. "I love you, Uncle Wade. Never forget that."

Chapter Eight

Saturday came before Asher was ready for it, and she stood in the shower trying to enjoy the hot water beating down her back. The event Red had put together supposedly at the last minute was actually something he'd been working on for over a year, and she'd somehow missed it. The Superdome was an ambitious place to start what Red said would be an annual event.

Wade had been happy to tell her the event was sold out, and not only that—all the tickets sold in two hours. According to him there were plenty of locals ready to see their homegrown star shine. The only upside to the whole thing was that a win with enough points could potentially move her into first place, especially since her main rival— Tyler Wheeler—would be competing.

Tyler was never outright ugly to her, but she knew his thoughts on her success. Life according to the great Mr. Wheeler was that women belonged in the kitchen so dinner would be on the table when he got home. If he had his way, her only role going forward would be one of spectator and not competitor.

"Hopefully tonight I can serve you up a big crap pie when I take this." She dried off and put on her lucky jeans, rodeo boots, and a dark blue shirt with plenty of sponsor logos on it.

She was driving herself since Wade, Frida, and the rest of the guys were all going together. Wade would make his way down to her once he had them all settled, and in a way, she was happy this was so close to home. She was psyched to do well. It wasn't often Frida and the others were able to come and see her since the ranches couldn't be left unattended. The doorbell rang as she put her wallet in her front pocket and grabbed the keys from the bowl in the kitchen.

"Hey," was all she was able to say before Jaqueline stepped into her arms and kissed her.

"You look good enough to eat, and I'm in the restaurant business so I should know." Jacqueline kissed her again and palmed her ass.

"Don't get me all worked up right before this thing."

"Come on, let me give you a ride, and if you win, I'll let you give me a ride," Jacqueline said and winked.

They drove into the city after she'd put all her equipment in the trunk. Jacqueline drove like someone whose sister was about to marry a detective who could fix any ticket she could ever get, and Asher figured riding the bulls was somewhat less exciting.

"Good luck, and I'll be in the stands with Wade and the group. Make us proud." Jacqueline kissed her one last time before she let her off at the back of the Dome close to dozens of horse trailers.

"Thanks, and if I haven't mentioned it, I'm glad you're here."

Tyler was watching her from the large roll door, shaking his head when she came closer. He was truly the quintessential chauvinist. "Do you drug these women to go out with you?"

"I believe that's your dating strategy, so no." She shook her head trying to dispel the urge to punch him in the face for saying something like that in a joking manner. "Jacqueline is a friend, and extra incentive to beat your ass."

"Come on, Evans, I was joking. I know I'm an ass, but I'm not disrespectful to women."

"Last time I checked, I'm a woman," she said, narrowing her eyes at him.

"You're Asher Evans," he said, shrugging. "That's different, so I don't really see you like that beautiful woman who dropped you off. You're more of a rider with the big boys, so live with it."

They laughed together and shook hands. Despite all his faults, she and Tyler had formed a tentative friendship that would only blossom if he changed his attitude. But first, one of them would need to retire so the competition between them could die down. Their conversation tonight made her think he might have a learning curve after all.

"Come on, they're drawing lots. With any luck we'll be close together so the judges can see this is a man's sport."

"Or that you ride like a girl, you mean?" So much for learning curve. The other men around them laughed and it stopped Tyler from saying another word.

They stood around, waiting for the draw, and Asher could already hear the crowd. There'd be a few competitions before bull riding, so she sat in one of the comfortable chairs the sponsors had set up and closed her eyes. Meditation, she'd found, relaxed her and allowed her to mentally go through the steps she'd have to complete to win. Someone put their hand on her shoulder what seemed like a minute later, and it was Wade.

"You ready, Buck? It's time to give the folks a show and impress that nice girl you invited." Wade handed her the rope she'd need and her gloves. She glanced at the scoreboard, and Tyler was leading with a ninety-two. "You should bring her to dinner."

"Let's not throw her into Frida's deep end just yet. Hell, we haven't even figured out what this is. Right now we're just having fun."

"Frida's already up there, giving her an earful. Nothing bad, so try to concentrate on the bulls and not your love life at the moment."

She put on her safety jacket and hat before following him to the chutes. The black bull inside was shaking his head and pawing the ground like he was trying to dig his way out. "Thanks, Uncle Wade. See you in a bit."

She climbed to the top as the rodeo workers wrapped her rope around the bull's chest. That seemed to perk him up like someone had poked him in the ass with an electric prod. She waited for the right time and climbed on. The worker held the rope up as she moved her hand up and down her customary ten times, tightening each time she slid her hand up.

It hit her then that there wouldn't be *that* many events before Vegas. It was going to be hard to let go of this part of her life—the adrenaline, the crowds, and the chess game between her and the bulls she drew to ride. It wasn't time to concentrate on that just yet, and she moved forward and clenched her legs to make sure she wasn't thrown off as the chute opened.

The crowd noise was amazing, but she shut it all out and threw her arm up. After whipping to the left followed quickly by a buck to the right, the damn bull came completely off the ground. Their landing jarred her entire body, and she was glad she was wearing a mouth guard—if her teeth had had the chance to smash together, she'd have chipped a tooth.

Her right bicep was burning from the strain of hanging on until the buzzer that came what felt like an hour later. She waited for the best window to dismount and had to jump clear of the damn bull before he gored her. He did end up bumping her on the shoulder before she was able to get away from him.

She tipped her hat to the crowd and went through the gate as the clowns had a hard time getting the bull out and into the holding pen. He'd be ready to go again in a bit, and hopefully he'd be someone else's problem. Wade was waiting, but her score was announced before he could say anything.

"Asher Evans, ladies and gentlemen." The crowd started clapping when the number came up. "Highest score so far. Evans for ninety-six, everyone."

"Your shoulder okay?" Wade asked as soon as she was close enough to hear him.

"My bicep was about to snap trying to hold on, but I'm okay. Two more rounds to go and I can hit the hot tub." She followed him back to the chairs and accepted Tyler's handshake before she sat.

"Good ride, Evans. I'll take you in the next round." He slapped her on the back and went back to his manager.

"There's something about that guy that chaps my ass," Wade said, his eyes on Tyler's back. "Your form is good, but be careful on the dismount. Red screwed everyone by throwing in one more chance for you all to get hurt before the championships."

"This purse, though, will go a long way toward paying for the hay barns I had planned for the property." The ooh the crowd let out probably meant someone did something that was cringeworthy. When the medical team ran by with a stretcher, they all got up and went to the gates. It was hard to see the guy lying there, not moving, with blood on his face. "Where in the hell did Red find these bulls? It's like they injected them with something that made them killers."

"He does love to put on a show," Wade said, "and part of that is carrying someone out on a stretcher. Red is successful, but he's a bastard." Wade put his arm on her shoulder. "Just take care out there, Buck. I got a bad feeling about this one."

The crowd gave the injured man a standing ovation, and there was a slight intermission while they reset the arena and took the bull out of the rotation. Her second ride after Tyler resulted in a score of ninety-four, a point higher than his. She was in the lead, but it was slim. There was another forty-minute break before she had her last ride, and another rider was taken out by the medics, only this time the man was conscious.

"Make this one count," Wade said, and she nodded.

Her bad luck was drawing the same bull from the first round, and it seemed like he remembered what the hell was about to happen and was a wild thing in the chute. The workers had a hard time getting the rope around his chest, but she waited patiently at the top of the chute trying to concentrate. Getting her legs jammed up against the sides would be an invitation to join her two friends in the emergency room.

"Remember, hang on and think ninety-two," Wade yelled, and she only nodded.

The bull let out what sounded like a scream before he bucked back and slammed the back of the chute with enough force to bend the metal sheet that made up the wall. That was the distraction the workers needed to get ready for Asher to climb on. When the animal bucked back again, she climbed on as his feet hit the ground. She squeezed her legs and pressed the heels of her boots to his side to get the rope taut, this time going through her ritual a little faster than normal.

"Ready, Asher?" the rodeo worker asked.

She bit down on her mouth guard and nodded. The sweat running and pooling at the small of her back made her crave a shower, but that would have to wait until this was over. As always, the beginning of any ride made her hyperaware of every sensation in her body. Her scalp itched from the flood of adrenaline, her fingers were tight in the rope, and her other hand was sweating in the leather glove that once belonged to Silas. Silas always said all of it was a sign that she was alive, ready, and aware of what she had to accomplish.

The bull surprised her by twisting savagely, making her momentarily lose her center of balance, but she hung on and tightened her legs. She went with him as he bucked, and bent slightly at the waist to get a groove going. The judges were looking for how well she handled and controlled the ride, and the bull was doing the rest by giving her one of the most energetic rides of her life. He was making that screaming noise again followed by grunts, and despite that, she could swear that she could hear the creak of the rope as it bit into her hand and the rasp of her jeans against his skin.

Eight seconds only lasted a lifetime when you were riding a bull, and it was no different for her this time. The buzzer was the trigger that released the floodgates of the crowd and the yells of the clowns who were ready to jump into action. She got ready to jump clear, and the bull did what she expected and bucked again with enough power to give her whiplash, but it gave her enough momentum to land four feet from him. The crowd seemed to appreciate her ride, and she tipped her hat again.

"Buck, look out," Wade yelled as he waved his arms frantically.

For the first time in the arena, time seemed to slow so she could appreciate and remember every second. It was like watching a movie a frame at a time as it ticked by at a rate that accentuated every bit of action. The clowns hadn't been able to lure the bull toward the barrels they used to protect the riders. She'd let her guard down for a moment, and despite that she'd started moving, it was too late to get away clean.

The first blow landed on her ankle, and the sudden pain brought about not only acute pain, but a bout of nausea that she hoped would subside before she embarrassed herself in front of all these people. There had to be broken bones, but she concentrated on making it to the gate. The damn bull had other plans, and his horn caught the back of her thigh and sliced through her pants.

She collapsed right outside the gate, but Wade prevented her from hitting the ground. As she was loaded on the stretcher, she heard, "Ninety-seven!" At least the night wasn't a total loss. This win with Tyler in the competition moved her into first place, and this might be as far as she'd get this year, depending on what was wrong with her leg.

"You'd better be okay." She didn't recognize the voice right off, so she opened her eyes to Tyler. "I want to kick your ass in Vegas and in all the events leading up to that. I don't want people telling me I won because some bull squashed you like a bug."

"You should go into motivational speaking, asshole." They laughed together, and she smiled when he took her hand. "Thanks, and don't worry, unless they cut the damn thing off, I'll be there." She hoped that was more than wishful thinking. She was in pain, and the one thing running through her head was what Reagan would have to say about this.

An *I told you so* right now would not sit well and it made her almost grateful Reagan wasn't a part of her life any longer. She took some deep breaths and did her best to will away the pain, but if her boot got any tighter on her foot, she'd have to beg Wade to cut it off.

"Think good thoughts, Buck," Wade said as he walked along with the stretcher and got in the ambulance with her. He was on the phone, probably talking to Frida.

They started moving, and someone banging on the side stopped them. She lifted her head to Jacqueline at the door. "Head to Baptist on Napoleon Avenue. Dr. Harry Basantes is waiting on her in the emergency room," Jacqueline said, and the EMT nodded. "I'm right behind you, babe, don't worry."

"Thanks." She let her head drop and closed her eyes with Wade's hand in hers. If this was her last competition, she'd have to accept it, but she wasn't quite ready. It had nothing to do with the money she'd leave on the circuit, or the buckles that would go to someone else. She wanted to be remembered as the best at what she did not because she won, but because she competed.

That simple fact made her understand Silas more than even his daughter did.

❖

Reagan had watched the coverage of the rodeo event at the Dome and cringed when she saw Asher go down. Rationally she knew it was only a severely broken ankle, but she was still…Well, she wasn't quite sure how to put what she was feeling into thoughts she could understand. Seeing Asher's face when the bull charged her brought back all the times she'd watched it happen to her father, and it soured her mood. It was two weeks later, and she was still angry.

"Do you want to talk about what bug crawled up your ass today?" Kendra asked as they were going over the schedule. "Because it's good and wedged in there now."

She shook her head and couldn't find the energy to form a smile.

"It's nothing with work, and I'm not going to blow up at any of the patients. I'm more professional than that."

"Then you admit that there's something wedged up in there," Kendra said and winked. "You don't have to tell me, but I'm here and willing to listen."

"I'm not ready to talk about it, but it's all about the past and how history is repeating itself. It's not really my problem, and yet it still pisses me off." She took a moment to calm down. "Forget about it for now—let's concentrate on the schedule."

"To get you in a better mood, you have your first private client, so smile and act like you're having a great day." Kendra handed over a card with an address on it. "I set up an appointment for this afternoon for you to go over the prelims and set the schedule."

"Is it a secret, or are you going to tell me who it is?" She schooled her features to not show surprise when she saw the address. It was on the same road as Uncle Wade's, so she had some idea of who her patient was. If Asher was living in the shack on the property, it sure as hell didn't have an address. Frida had said it burned down, but she had a feeling Asher rebuilt it since she wasn't living in the big house.

"We were hired by a service, and Dr. Harry Basantes asked for discretion. Try to remember she's one of the owners here." Kendra held her hand out. "If you want to pass because of whatever is on your mind, then tell me and I'll take the client. I'll be happy to, so let me know, and if that's what you want, all you'll have to do is manage the clinic until I get back."

"No, I'm not saying I don't want to do it, but you might still have to go." She might be mad at Asher for everything that had happened, but she wasn't arrogant enough to think Asher would welcome her like an old lover she'd been pining for since she'd left.

"Okay, that will need an explanation, and before you say no, think again. I need the entire story with a slide presentation so I can follow along." Kendra pointed at her like she was daring her to refuse her. "Start talking."

"I can't be a hundred percent sure, but I think our new client is Asher Evans. She got her foot crushed a couple of weeks ago at the rodeo, and we grew up together." She gave Kendra enough to satisfy her curiosity but kept most of the story to herself. "She might turn me down."

"Only one way to find out. The appointment is for two. Don't be late."

She spent the rest of the morning going through the motions of her job and not really enjoying herself. That was one more thing to blame Asher for. If there was one place she'd found escape from everything, it was her job.

Her drive east seemed to take an eternity, and she turned at the road her GPS prompted her to. The address wasn't at all familiar and she started to doubt it was Asher she was there to see, after all. She stopped at the gate where an arch bore the name *Pemberley*. The beautifully crafted wrought iron gates were firmly closed, so she pulled up to the intercom.

"I'm here from Riverbend Sports Clinic for the two o'clock appointment," she said when a man said hello.

"Just follow the black fence to the house. Someone will meet you and tell you where to park."

The black fences went on for as far as she could see, and the horses on the other side weren't the breeds she'd seen all her life. Farther away in the distance she thought she could spot the large cows she'd noticed on her way to dinner. Whatever this was, she was confused. And where the hell was the house?

She drove slowly, kicking up a little dust, until the house came into view and she stopped, wanting to appreciate what she was looking at. The house was beautiful and nothing like where she grew up. It resembled an old Acadian-style home, but it had to be new with its wraparound porch and large swing at one corner. If she had a dream home, this would be it. If it was named after Mr. Darcy's home in Jane Austen's *Pride and Prejudice*, it completely fit.

"Right over there, miss," a ranch hand said, pointing to a parking pad in front of the large garage to the left of the house. It was a separate structure that had a covered walkway leading to the back of the house.

She grabbed her purse and headed down that path until she reached the back door, which opened before she could knock, and came face-to-face with Rickie. That was the confirmation she needed of exactly who she was there to see. What she didn't expect was the slight frown on Rickie's face when she stood there, barring her from going in.

"Oh, they sent you," Rickie said as if that was the worst thing that could happen.

"Where is she?" Not that she disliked Rickie, but she didn't have time for this. "I'm only here as a physical therapist, so if she wants someone else, she can tell me that. It's not up to you."

"It's not my business who she wants—I'm just surprised you'd want to come." Rickie stepped aside and closed the door behind her. "Right this way."

Reagan walked slowly, noticing the inside of the house didn't really fit with who she imaged Asher had become. The old Asher who loved riding and learning things from Reagan's father and believed in putting in a hard day's work wasn't really reflected in the beautiful art and decorating that could easily be found in any magazine. An irrational streak of jealousy ran through her when she thought this might be Jacqueline Blanchard's influence.

The room Rickie led her to was a combination of a study and library with at least twenty-foot ceilings, the big oak desk that was a replica of the one her father owned, and book-lined shelves that took up two of the walls. It was a large room with equally large windows behind the desk that had a great view of the fields outside. Asher was lying on the leather sofa with a book on her chest and her foot, encased in an Aircast, elevated on some pillows. She was asleep with her mouth slightly open, and her hair was a mess across her forehead.

She wanted to back out and leave Asher alone, not wanting to disturb her. But Rickie shook her awake, and Reagan felt bad when Asher startled even though Rickie had been gentle.

"Your appointment is here," Rickie said, stepping aside and letting Asher see her.

"Ah," Asher said, and she couldn't decipher what that meant. "I'm sure this wasn't your idea, was it?"

"I'm sorry you got hurt, and if you'd like someone else, my boss said she'd be happy to fill in. If you've used the clinic before, the therapist who usually makes house calls is on maternity leave." She sat without being asked and took out a notebook. "Can you give me the details, or do you want me to contact the doctor?"

"The packet you'll need is on the desk." Asher placed what appeared to be a strip of leather in her book and placed it beside her. Reagan almost asked her what she was reading, but the more professional they kept this, the better.

She stood and walked to the other side of the large room and stared at the top of the desk. It wasn't a replica as she'd originally thought—it was her father's old desk. Granted it had been refurbished, but Asher hadn't sanded out the cigar burns on the corner. Her dad had chuckled every time she lectured him on leaving a burning smoke on the edge, telling him he'd burn the house down. There was an ashtray on the surface with a Cohiba snubbed out. Obviously, Asher had picked up a lot more from her father than just bull riding.

"Is this Daddy's desk?" She closed her eyes at Asher's sigh.

"He left it to me, and when the house was done, Uncle Wade had it delivered. If you're upset about it, I'll have it brought to your new place." Asher sounded so resigned but also somewhat angry. "There are a few things he gave me, but I'm not willing to part with all of them."

"I don't want it, Asher. It was a simple question." No sense in admitting that it wasn't simple at all. This was a minefield of problems all tied to the past, and their feelings now would prevent them from even thinking of the good times. Too much had happened to both of them to even consider there'd ever be a reconciliation they'd both be happy with. "I'm glad it found a good home. It looks good in here."

She glanced to the right, and the wall was covered in belt buckles, little plaques with the date and place they were won. All of them preceded Asher's time riding, so they were her dad's. His accomplishments were something celebrated here no matter her feelings on the subject.

It took effort to move her head and concentrate on why she was there. She was new to town, but she was familiar with Dr. Basantes and her work. The file contained pictures of what Dr. Basantes had done, along with instructions for postoperative care. She'd performed an ankle fracture open reduction and internal fixation, which simply meant she'd used a plate and five screws to repair the broken fibula. This would stabilize the ankle, and once Asher healed, she'd be fine.

"You can't put any weight on it for four weeks. Sitting around for that long is going to be a pain, I know, but let's keep you from needing more reconstructive surgery." She made some notes in the file and spoke with her back to Asher. "Can you tell me what happened?"

"I was trying to get out of the way of a big animal, and he stepped on my foot. Nothing more than that." Asher sounded almost detached, and Reagan wanted to blame the pain meds she must still be on. "I have an appointment tomorrow to have my stitches taken out of my foot and thigh and to change the cast again. If you want, you can wait until I can start to weight-bear to come back."

"That's not how it works," she said, turning around. "What time is your appointment? And what works best for you, mornings or afternoons? We can always adjust, but we'll be together for a minimum of eight to twelve weeks, so let's try to make the best of it."

"My appointment is at eleven, and I can work around your schedule. The only pressing things I have is reading a few books, so I can do that anytime." Asher moved and grimaced. The throbbing wouldn't quit, day or night. "And my offer is still good if you want to skip this altogether. You can tell your boss it's me who made the decision."

"Will it make you uncomfortable to work with me?" That was maybe the question she should've led off with.

"Not to be blunt, but I was never the one with the problem. I take that back—you were the one who thought I was brain dead for choosing this life, so I'm positive being around my Neanderthal ass isn't on your list of good times. It wasn't then, and I doubt you've had a change of heart about that." Asher was perhaps too blunt because her teeth clicked together so harshly that it sounded like it should've hurt. "Sorry, I'm in pain but that's no excuse to be rude. You're here to do a job."

"Don't worry about it. We'll get through this and get you better." She finished her notes in the chair close to Asher. "Do you have any questions for me?"

"How have you been?" Asher asked, and she seemed interested in her answer.

"Busy, but good. I went riding with Uncle Wade last week." The new cows and horses suddenly had an explanation. "May I ask you something?"

"Sure," Asher said, sounding anything but.

"The big cows, and the other ones with the white stripe down the middles, that's your doing?" Asher's face never really changed, so it was hard to decipher if she was happy, sad, or mad. It was the same blank expression she'd witnessed in television interviews she'd seen in the years they'd been apart. Asher was a private person who only showed her true self to very few people.

She'd never had that expression aimed at her, not until now, and it was irrational that it hurt as much as it did, but it did. She wasn't used to Asher hiding her feelings from her because she never had. Even in the letters she'd written her in college when she could only hear Asher's voice in her head, she could sense the emotion and feeling in them. Asher had been the most honest and open person she'd ever met much less been with, and all that was lost to her now.

"The new breeds were brought in after extensive research as to the best beef cattle on the market. Those are the big cows you mentioned, but the other ones are some of the best dairy cows on the planet. I'm diversifying because I'm interested in putting the best products on the market." Asher tapped her fingers together, but her expression never changed. "I formed a partnership with an organic dairy company to cover the costs of the new barn, and we should break ground soon."

"Uncle Wade was okay with all that?" The conversation she'd had with Wade made no sense now. If he wanted to slow down and thin the operation, everything Asher had said was the complete opposite of that.

"Why wouldn't he be?" Finally, Asher showed something other than disinterest. Confusion wasn't what she was going for, but that's what she'd gotten.

"He was talking about slowing down when I talked to him."

Asher nodded as if understanding what she meant. "Moon Touch belongs to you and Wade, but Pemberley is mine. Your dad and Uncle Wade took care of my interest until I was of age, at least the age my father thought was good for me to take over here. I moved here when I turned twenty and have been building my operations ever since. Wade's a good sounding board, but he has no say here."

"You're not helping him?" One of these days she was going to have to learn to curb her accusatory personality until she had all the facts.

"The ranch hands he has on staff take care of his livestock, and me and my people take care of everything else. I'm not in the habit of deserting the people I care about, Reagan, so learn to ask before you start firing shots." Asher's confusion had given way to anger, and Reagan couldn't be upset about something she'd totally caused.

Asher's message was clear. She'd stayed and taken care of Uncle Wade, Frida, and everyone else. It had been Reagan who'd run and ignored her responsibilities to family and the ranch. She hadn't been needed because Asher had taken care of everything.

"I'm sorry."

"Maybe this isn't a good idea. If Kendra's available, then have her call me, or I'll call her when I get back from my appointment." Asher's mask slid back into place, and there was nothing short of telling her to fuck off that was going to get her to open up again.

"If that's what you want," she said, not being able to help the little bit of snark, even if she wasn't entitled to it.

Asher laughed. "When in the world have you ever been concerned with what I want?"

She stood and left, not wanting to be subjected to Asher's contempt another second. Granted, she deserved that and so much more, but the pain in her chest was real, and it was making the battle to keep her tears at bay a losing proposition. Her face was streaked with them when she made it back to the kitchen, and of course Rickie was in there working on dinner.

"Take this with you," Rickie said, handing her a bottle of water and some tissues.

"Thank you."

"It's none of my business, but the easy out here is to give her what she wants." Rickie stared at her as if daring her to look away. "If you do that, then don't come back. You do that and you leave her alone. It took Uncle Wade and my mother a lot of time to put her back together, so don't come here with your wrong assumptions and half-assed guesses. She's suffered enough, don't you think?"

"You heard her," she said, upset she couldn't keep her voice from cracking. "She doesn't want me here, and it's not an unreasonable request."

"My mom was wrong about you, then. I didn't pay attention to why you left when you did, but I've been working for Asher for two years now. She's not that hard to understand." Rickie pointed to one of the stools on the other side of the large island. The move reminded Reagan of Frida. "If you're moving back here, and going out to Moon Touch, then it might be a good time to start figuring out who the hell Asher is. Not who she was when she was wild about you. That Asher doesn't exist any longer—no offense to you, but what you did kind of sucked."

"That it did," she said and laughed. Therapy might have been easier if she'd gone to someone like Rickie.

"Thing is, she's spent years building this place up and riding the circuit. We won't talk about that part since I hear you're sensitive about the subject. Pemberley is a world class operation, and it's all because of Asher and her hard work. That's all she's done from the time you left, and it seems almost comical that you've come back just when she's shown interest in someone."

"I'm not here to mess things up for her if that's what you're worried about."

"Asher will boot you out of here before I can worry about anything, so that's not why we're having this conversation, a conversation I will deny until I'm dead, so keep that in mind." Rickie went back to chopping meat into small pieces. "Asher needs to forgive you, not so much for you, but for her. She'll never move forward free of her past until she does."

"Ah, so you're not talking to me for me." The humor in all this did get her to stop crying. "You're very insightful for someone who's barely twenty."

"I'm older than that, and you're kind of an idiot." Rickie didn't put any heat behind her insult. It was just a statement of fact. "I'm talking to you and dispensing all this wisdom because my mother called and told me to. She said if you pick the easy way out, it'll prove you're only book smart, and that'll be a real shame. Life is too long to be such a fool every single minute of the day. All those minutes and days add up, so it's time to wise up."

"Good old Frida." She understood Rickie better now. She'd graduated from Frida's school of blunt. "Thanks for the water and the talk. I appreciate you taking the time, and make sure she keeps her foot elevated. I know the doctor recommends doing that for a week, but I think it reminds patients, especially patients like Asher, to take it easy until she can put weight on it."

"She's in good hands, don't worry."

She nodded and moved around to hug Rickie even if she seemed the prickly kind. "I know she is."

Chapter Nine

"Two more weeks, Asher." Another stitch was removed, and Asher kept her eye on Dr. Harry Basantes's hands as she steadily cut through the row of black sutures running up from her ankle. "That means fourteen days, not ten," Harry said as she put her instruments down.

"I got it." Asher tried not to sound whiny, but she figured Harry was on to her. "You could cut me some slack and say nine days."

"Don't give me shit. I know you." Harry laughed as she checked over her leg. "This looks good, so we'll put on the permanent cast." The supplies were laid out, and Harry started to get them ready.

"I know you're busy, Harry, so have the nurse do it if you want." She stared at the bruise on her foot, and a vivid picture of that damn bull came into her head. "I promise I'll be good."

"I like to stay in practice, so sit back and relax. Now if you want to finish the season, you'll listen to me. That means sit there and take some deep breaths while I put a bright pink cast on you." Harry winked as she held up the black roll. "Did you meet with the therapist Kendra set up for you?"

"Yes." It was all she could say on the subject. Having Reagan around every day for weeks wasn't something that was going to be easy. It was like being asked to shower with an aggressive rattlesnake every morning. Could it be done? Probably, but why would you want to?

"That's an interesting answer. Is there a problem? I know Reagan's new, but her résumé is terrific. We were lucky to recruit her. From what I understand, the Seahawks were close to offering her a permanent position." Harry started by placing a protective layer of padding on her foot before rolling the fiberglass cast material to right below her knee. "I'm sensing a problem, though, so tell Dr. Harry all about it."

"Don't give me that shit. You've probably talked to Frida and Wade, so you know exactly who Kendra sent to my house. And you did it anyway." She was about to rev up her argument when the door opened. Seeing Reagan in black scrubs made her think her placement was something either Frida or Wade cooked up. They were meddling busybodies, and no one could convince her otherwise.

"Good morning," Reagan said. Her tone was bright as if she wasn't the woman who'd imploded her psyche and walked away like it didn't matter at all. "Dr. Basantes invited me so I could ask questions about the regime we're going to follow."

"Thanks." Asher cursed that she couldn't put any weight on her foot. If she had one pet peeve it was being manipulated. And this shit was some major manipulation. She'd bet the ranch on it, but protesting would only make *her* out to be the asshole.

"Hey, Reagan," Harry said, "would you mind waiting outside for a few minutes? I was talking to Asher about something, so it won't take long."

"Sure." Reagan walked out like yesterday, and not once ever looked back.

"Tell me you didn't know she's Silas's daughter and Wade's niece and I'll drop it," Asher said. "Only I know there's no way you did not know, so cut the shit." Deep breathing wasn't helping the pain, so she closed her eyes and concentrated on the back of her eyelids. "I'm sure they all want a happy reunion, and that is not happening in this or any other lifetime."

"Wait." Harry put her hands on her shoulders when they were alone again. "Before you tee off on me, I really didn't know anything about the history here. I respect you more than that as a friend, and as a patient."

"Then how did I end up with Reagan?" She wasn't going to cause a scene in Harry's office, but it took effort not to raise her voice and demand to be taken home. Owen was in the waiting room, and one call would get her out of here.

"When my partners and I started Riverbend, our first priority was the level of care. That starts with our staff, so it doesn't matter if you're new to our clinic team or if you've been here from the beginning, you're going to have experience. Kendra put Reagan with you because she's the most qualified for the type of injury you sustained. She's dealt with this injury before—only on the football field." Harry sat again and moved her hands along Asher's leg, molding the cast until she was satisfied. "I can't force you, but think about it. The whole purpose of rehab is to get you back to where you need to be to compete. If you're fighting your therapist the entire time, that's the last thing that'll happen."

"If I say no, then I'm the bad guy?" She laughed and made a fist with the hand in her lap.

"No, if you pass, it makes you the patient. Patients in my practice get to decide what and who they want, and if Reagan isn't going to make you comfortable, then we'll get Kendra involved." Harry seemed pleased with the cast and finally glanced up at her. "I know your timeline, Asher, so PT is going to be important to getting you back not only on your feet, but on a bull. There's no way in hell I'm worried about you putting in the work because that's a given. If anything, I worry about you overdoing, but to put you in the right frame of mind, I'm going to need you comfortable with your care."

"It's okay, Harry. It's PT, not a date. If you think she's that good, then bring Reagan up to speed. All I need is for her to know why the timeline is important." She relaxed her hand and tried to will herself into silence. "She's not a fan of what I do, and she's not been exactly shy about her opinions on the subject."

"Physical therapists don't approve of a lot of the things their clients do. I have professional football players who need rehab for whatever happens to them on the field, and we do it. We do it with the full knowledge that when they're able, they'll be back on the field every Sunday where the chances of it happening again are high. That's not our call to make, though."

"Let's get the show on the road, then," Asher said. "I've got two more weeks of forced relaxation, so I'll take that time to wrap my head around all this." She sat back on her hands and waited for Harry to send Reagan in. With any luck, it'd be Reagan who called it quits, and she could get Frida and every other busybody in her life off her ass.

"Okay," Harry said, slapping her hands together. "Beginning tomorrow, Reagan will start coming by to start your rehab."

"I thought I couldn't put any weight on this, and you just put this spiffy cast on me." This was a new one. The last time Harry put her through the paces of PT, it was for her shoulder after a rogue cow slammed into her. PT didn't start, though, until she'd at least been out of the brace.

"I also know you, so I know sitting on the sofa eating bonbons isn't going to happen. Reagan's going to be there to make sure your continuing upper-body work doesn't interfere with your ankle recovery." Harry pointed at her as if she could read her mind. "Two hours a day should do it to start. And if you put any weight on that foot before then, I'm admitting you and strapping you down."

"All right already, I get it."

"What time would you like to start?" Reagan asked as if she'd made up her mind to do this. "I can do mornings or afternoons, but I need to reschedule my clinic patients, so if you can let me know, I'd appreciate it."

"Whichever is the least amount of work for you. I'm not set on either, so make it easy on yourself." She let go of some of her anger when Reagan stared at her as if trying to surmise if she was working an angle. This close she was reminded of how beautiful Reagan was. She had only gotten more so since she'd last seen her.

"Thank you, Asher," Reagan said. "I'll see you at nine in the morning unless you want to start later."

"Nine it is." She was ready to go and meditate away all the phantom itches going up and down her leg that couldn't be scratched now. "Anything else, Harry?"

"I'll go over everything with Reagan, so call me if you need anything or have any questions. Remember, above all else, be good," Harry said, shaking her hand then handing her a lollipop. "See you in two weeks."

She slid off the table and stood on her good foot until the nurse locked the wheelchair. The pain was manageable, and she tried to concentrate on her breathing to keep it that way. Now pain of another kind was going to blossom, and all she had to do to get rid of it was to get better. Once that happened, Reagan would go back to her life, and she could go back to hers. The two wouldn't intersect after that.

"You ready, boss?" Owen asked.

"You have no idea."

❖

It was four thirty a.m., and Reagan knew there'd be no more sleep. "This completely sucks," she said to the ceiling. The night before she'd sat outside with a glass of wine and a peanut butter sandwich. She'd found the small patio outside was the spot she felt the most comfortable talking to her father. So far it'd been a one-sided conversation.

"You've been awful quiet, Daddy." It wasn't that she was a firm believer in ghosts coming back to give you advice, but an afternoon with her father would've been fantastic. Even if all she got to do was sit and look at him, she'd have been happy. "I could really use your advice before today really gets started. We can start by discussing what a bitch I've been." She covered her face with her pillow and screamed into it. "Don't say anything if you agree." The quiet of the room made her scream into her pillow again.

She didn't need the ghost of her father to appear to know he'd agree with the assessment of her behavior. Not that he ever ignored her, because he didn't, but his relationship with Asher had been special. It was something she remembered with fondness and love. They'd been so cute together especially as Asher got older and some of the idol worship had worn off. Then Asher had worked hard to earn her father's respect, so he'd see her as a worthy partner for his only daughter.

What Reagan had done wouldn't have sat well with him. She hadn't been raised to run away from her problems, and especially not to treat people with such cruelty. It hadn't been her intent, but if she was honest, that's exactly what she'd done.

"Your silence means you're probably giving me that face you'd hit me with when you were disappointed in me." The knot in the beadboard on the ceiling she stared at didn't come to life to disagree with her, so she went with that.

She got up and took a long shower to clear her head. It was either shower therapy or start drinking, and it was way too early for that. There was still time to kill after she doubled her water bill, so she decided on a quick visit to the ranch to fortify her resolve. But her first stop was for coffee at the shop on the corner by her place, not to procrastinate, but to fool herself into thinking she wasn't procrastinating.

The drive to the east wasn't bad, considering all the traffic was bottlenecked in the opposite direction despite the early hour. All the suburbanites coming into the city for work from their big homes on the other side of Lake Pontchartrain were choking four lanes, and she'd seen at least three accidents. Her appointment with Asher wasn't for another couple of hours, which gave her time to live up to her promise to spend more time with Uncle Wade.

The mist caused by the river being so close clung to the ground, giving the cows the appearance of floating on clouds in the fields. Morning had always been her favorite time on the ranch, especially when she'd ridden out with Asher to check fences or put out hay. They'd been young, but Asher was a great conversationist who loved talking about the books she'd read, and the dreams they shared. At eighteen, she could've listened to Asher for the rest of her life.

One of the ranch hands pointed to the big barn closest to the house when she asked about her uncle, and she walked up to see Booker being led out of it. A large horse trailer that appeared nicer than her first apartment in college was standing open with a beautiful woman on the ramp.

"Good morning." Everyone turned around at her greeting, and she took a deep breath to keep from being instantly accusatory. "What's going on with my horse?" So much for that. Maybe after work today she'd look into a charm school if those still existed.

"Hey, sweetheart," Uncle Wade said, kissing her on the forehead when they hugged. "Booker's got a date with a handsome fella to see if they get along. If they do, Booker's going to make you a grandma."

"Hi"—she held her hand out to the woman—"I'm Reagan Wilson."

"Sorry, I'm forgetting my manners," Wade said. "Reagan, this is Helki Jaci. She's the horse trainer over at Pemberley. Helki, Reagan's my niece."

"It's good to meet you," Helki said, offering her hand. "I promise to take good care of her, and your foal will be beautiful. Booker will be right next door, so feel free to visit whenever you like." Helki shook her hand again before overseeing Booker getting in the trailer. "We also have the best vet in the city on call, so if we can get her with foal, she'll get the best of care."

"You okay?" Uncle Wade asked.

"I'm fine, just wanted to stop and have coffee with you if you're free." She put her hand in the bend of his elbow and pulled him toward the house. "I have an appointment with Asher in a few hours."

"Do you now?" Uncle Wade gave her the small laugh that meant he was highly amused. "You remember that she's a championship bull rider, right? You're not going to try to hypnotize her into taking up knitting instead, are you?"

"Yes, I remember, and she got off lucky when that damn bull only got a hold of her ankle and thigh. And if I knew how to knit, I might give it a try, but it's only PT. Believe me, I didn't volunteer for this assignment, but her agreeing might mean she'll work overtime to get rid of me as soon as possible." There were ranch hands around saddling up for the day, and they all tipped their hats as they walked by.

"Buck would do that no matter who Basantes sends out here. If she's actually letting you in the house, maybe you should start asking questions." Wade put his arm around her shoulders and waved Helki off with the other hand. "Asher isn't who you left behind, and she's someone worth knowing."

"The evidence points to her being the same person I knew way back when." She reached up for his hand. "But I promise I'll be good."

Frida was in the kitchen whisking eggs and frying bacon when they entered. Some things never changed, starting with Asher and that Frida would be cooking bacon. "Sit—I hear you have plenty of time to eat."

"Your spy network is still working, I see." She went to her regular seat at the table and stuck her tongue out at Frida.

"Tread carefully, Buckaroo. She's got plenty of knives back there, and I'd hate to have to run you to the emergency room before my second cup of coffee," Uncle Wade said. "And remember one thing."

"What's that?" She thanked Frida when she put her plate down.

"You're a Wilson, and Wilsons don't go running scared." He started eating after that, and they engaged in small talk until she had to go.

Not wanting to drive through the pastures, she rode back to the road and headed to Asher's main gate. The black fence line was impressive, and she couldn't really believe how much land Asher had been able to procure. Her spread was beautiful, and the animals looked amazing. It had been their fathers' and her uncle's philosophy all their lives—cows and horses were their business, so they had to be treated with respect. That strong belief had certainly carried into the next generation.

Another ranch hand pointed to the carport, and she gazed out at the big backyard, surprised to see Asher standing on one leg at the fence with her crutches leaning against it. The black horse lipping at her hair was gorgeous, and he seemed totally infatuated with Asher. It was almost as if he was kissing the top of her head. She smiled at the sight and the knowledge that Asher's love affair with animals was something that hadn't changed.

"Are you supposed to be out here?" she asked when she went out to meet her. She kept her voice calm, not wanting to spook either Asher or the horse. "And that's one beautiful animal."

"This is Albert," Asher said, patting the big neck with affection.

"Albert? That doesn't sound very horselike." Albert stuck his tongue out at her as if he'd understood the slight.

"Albert Einstein Evans, since he's pretty smart." Asher held on to his neck when he lowered his head and placed it against her chest softly as if he understood she was hurt and he needed to be careful. "I was just giving him a pep talk since he's got a date later. A couple, actually, so I want to make sure he understands he has to be a gentleman no matter what a stud he is."

"Is Booker one of those dates?" She bent and grabbed an apple from the bucket at Asher's feet. Even with the treat in her hand, Albert eyed her suspiciously. She would've sworn in court that Asher had trained him to do that.

"Booker and another gray mare we picked up last week. Albert's pretty young, but Helki thinks he's ready to enter the land of parenthood. We'll see how he does, but you have my word I haven't forgotten what Booker means to you." Asher kissed the tip of his nose and pushed him back into the field. "Take a run and leave some of the buttercups for the ladies. They like that kind of stuff."

Albert shook his head and danced a bit on his front legs but did as Asher asked. In motion he had be one of the most handsome animals Reagan had ever seen. She watched Asher studying his stride and could still make out the passion for the things she loved. That kind of devotion was hard to mask.

"Do you want anything before we begin?" Reagan asked, staying away from Asher and the crutches.

She walked next to Asher at her pace as they made their way back to the house, bypassing the kitchen for another door farther down the porch at the back. The workout room was impressive and as well-equipped as the clinic, so it would be easy to work from here. Asher sat at the weight bench and pointed to the chair ten feet from her.

"I'm good. What's your plan?" Asher asked.

"Dr. Basantes wants you to continue with your upper-body work as long as you don't put any weight on your foot as you make the circuit." She did a quick inventory of the machines and figured it'd be easy to keep Asher engaged for the two hours Harry had in mind. "Once you're done, I'll set up a massage table and work on your legs. Increasing the blood flow to your lower extremities will promote healing."

"Massage?" Asher stared at her as if she had no clue what she was talking about. "That's not something that's been part of my rehab routine before."

"How many times have you had to have rehab?" If Asher was anything like her father, it had been a constant throughout her career. With that kind of experience as a patient, she wasn't really necessary.

"Just twice for stuff that happened here," Asher said as if Reagan's thoughts were floating above her head in bright pink neon and dancing flamingos. "Cow got overexcited when we were moving them into the barn and butted my shoulder. The other was a stupid accident—my horse spooked when a snake snuck up on us. You know how it is here in the spring and summer."

"This is your first accident in the arena?" It was hard to believe, but she'd never heard of Asher getting hurt before now. She'd never admit it, but she'd followed Asher's career like Steph had for very different reasons.

"You probably don't believe me, but no. I'm not careless or unaware of what could happen. The bull that did this"—Asher pointed to her foot—"was a momentary distraction that cost me."

"You don't owe me any explanations, Asher." Eventually she'd have to find a way to apologize and make Asher believe in her sincerity. That wouldn't be today. Asher's walls were too high and thick.

"You're right I don't, but if we come at this from different points of view it's not going to work. Right now, I'm in first place in the standings, and I plan to be back on the circuit as soon as I possibly can." Asher held her hand up when she opened her mouth. "If you can't accept that, then thank you for your time. You can go."

"I'm a professional, Asher, and I'm not here to judge you."

"No, you've already done that." Asher had a way of talking with no emotion that Reagan didn't like. The flat delivery was a clear message that she didn't matter any longer. She'd hurt Asher, Asher had healed, and the scar that remained was thick and impenetrable.

"Let's get started, and you'll see that it's all about the job."

That was the biggest lie she'd ever told Asher. It came right after telling her that she didn't love her, and she wanted nothing to do with her. She was back, though, and if it took doing something she didn't necessarily believe in, then she'd do it. Now that she was this close to Asher again, all she wanted was to put things right. It was the only way to move forward, to forgive herself and free herself of her mistakes. Once that was possible, she could find some semblance of happiness.

What form that happiness would take was a mystery to her. It had to be better than what her life was now, so she'd deal with the aftermath when it finally came.

CHAPTER TEN

A sher spent the next week working out with Reagan in the mornings and riding out to the barn site in the afternoons. The cement floor was poured and curing, and the pasture was starting to green with the new grass her hands had planted. Her plans were starting to come together, and she was disappointed she wasn't more involved in the work. That was going to have to wait since there was another week to go of crutches and no weight-bearing.

Every morning, she tolerated Reagan's hands on her. Their conversations had been short and centered on therapy, but for those minutes when Reagan touched her, she closed her eyes and tried her best to think of something else. It wasn't that hard. She had experience listing all the reasons this woman wasn't someone worth her time. Remaining apathetic was the best course of action.

When Reagan left for the weekend with a quiet good-bye, Asher needed to get out of what was familiar. There was a restlessness in her that would only build into wanting to peel her skin off if she didn't get out, so she showered and got dressed. New scenery would reset her mindset and stop the loop of aggravation she was stuck in. Forced convalescence wasn't something she'd ever taken well, and this time it came with an obstacle course of problems.

She'd had to argue the point, but she sent Rickie home early and told her to forget about dinner. Two of the hands drove her into the French Quarter, having taken her up on her offer to have dinner at the sports bar they liked. They dropped her off at the Royal Sonesta Hotel on Bourbon Street.

Restaurant R'evolution was one of her favorite places to sit and read as the kitchen staff performed a synchronized dance easily visible from the dining room. The chef's table wasn't as grand as the one in Keegan Blanchard's kitchen, but the chaos and noise of this place was an easy way to get lost in a crowd. Anonymity wasn't such a dirty word sometimes.

"Hey, Asher," the waiter said, holding his hand out. "What can I get you?"

"Cinclaire small batch neat." She didn't drink alone often, but Silas had taught her a good bourbon every now and then could cheer up the dead. She propped her foot on an empty chair and took out the breeding book she'd started the day before. Helki had made the entries and was waiting on her approval before moving forward. Having a horse breeding program hadn't been in her plans, but having Helki run it with the guarantee they'd make money made it an easy sell. It was also more challenging than cows, so it could be fun if they grew it.

And then a voice made her glance up to see one of the sous-chefs place something in the brick oven. That's all she was willing to concentrate on, because turning around wasn't going to happen. "Fuck." The word exploded in her head, but she took a deep breath and kept her eyes on the brick oven.

There were bad days, and then there were days you wanted to press fast forward and put them in your *done* category. Reagan's voice had a distinct quality to it, and she'd recognize it even in hell. If she was half a poet, she'd say it was imprinted on her soul, but now it was like a bad rash that irritated the inside of her skull. The waiter put her glass down and took her order.

She was tempted to leave, but she wouldn't be run off from the places she enjoyed because Reagan had decided to crash her town. She also wasn't going to turn around and make herself known as the pathetic loner who read books about horses while nursing a drink. It turned out she didn't have to turn to see Reagan and her date from the first night they'd run into each other. They were four tables over in the corner. The only lucky thing was that Reagan's back was to her, but she could see from the back of Reagan's outfit that she wasn't in the scrubs she wore every day when she came to the house. Nope, this was more date-wear.

The woman with Reagan wore another great suit and was talking with her hands like whatever was coming out of her mouth was the most fascinating thing ever told. "I thought that was you." Gia startled her when she hugged her from behind and whispered into her ear.

"Are you supposed to be out drinking and reading about horse sex in public?" Gia moved around her so she could squeeze her face and kiss her on the lips.

"Albert has a much better sex life than I do, considering it has to be recorded for posterity. And it's only one drink and dinner." She put the ledger to the side and smiled.

"Cry me a bayou, sweet pea. You know there are plenty of women, including me"—Gia pointed to her chest—"that'll date you. That can start tonight if you want to join me." Gia held her hand as she sat to her right.

"Are you wining and dining, or wooing?" Gia had been fun and was still a good friend, but their dating history was done.

"I got a call from some clients who read the article about your house and want to hire me, so thank you for that. Now tell me, who are you spying on?" Gia picked up her glass and took a sip. Boundaries had never been Gia's thing. "You're being super covert, so you're either watching someone or I have a bug on the top of my head and you're afraid to tell me."

"I'm not spying on anyone. I came out tonight for a bowl of Death by Gumbo and some veal with a sinful amount of crabmeat on it." She spoke softly, not wanting to draw attention to them. "It was one of those nights when I had to get out of the house or start howling at the moon."

"So those two women in the corner aren't of interest to you?" Gia discreetly pointed in their direction. "I don't know the blonde in the killer dress, but the other one is Steph Delmonico. Graduated from Tulane Law and moved to Seattle after graduation but is back as the star of a firm in the city that specializes in corporate shit."

"Is corporate shit a thing?" She had to laugh at Gia's vivid descriptions of things. She did have the tea on most topics, though. That was a new bit of slang Rickie had introduced her to, then had to explain it meant having gossip and not in fact tea in a glass with lemon.

"People like Ms. Delmonico help the rich stay rich and keep the little guy under their heel. Tell me she's not a friend of yours." The waiter came back and delivered another drink when Gia lifted her hand. "She's a real bitch who takes pleasure in the kill."

Asher drained her glass and shook her head. When Reagan had said they were no longer compatible, she had no idea her new type would be this. "I really am an idiot."

"That's the last thing you are, and that"—Gia pointed to Reagan's back—"is not who she brought as her date to the young leadership group I belong to. The woman with her then was a media consultant, I think, and Delmonico introduced her as her girlfriend." Gia tapped her chin with her index finger. "That she's here with someone else means she's not just an asshole in court."

"There's a couple waving at you from the door," Asher said, tipping her head in that direction. "Go wow your clients and offer them a tour of the house if that'll seal the deal for you."

"Are you sure you don't want to come sit with us?" Gia squeezed her fingers.

"I'll be okay. Enjoy dinner and I'll see you soon."

"You're the best, good-looking." Gia kissed her again and followed the older couple to a table.

She accepted another drink and knew it would be her last. She didn't need to get tipsy and fall, breaking her other leg. Her horse book had lost its appeal, so she reached into her coat pocket to get the small book her old English professor had given her. *The Divine Comedy* wasn't exactly light reading, but sometimes you had to go through other people's hell to make your own seem not as catastrophic.

She'd fallen in love with the poem in college after reading the line from *Purgatorio* that she tried to live by in life: *If the present world go astray, the cause is in you, in you it is to be sought.*

Her life and everything in it existed because of the choices she made. That's what she'd taken from that line. She couldn't blame anyone else if the landscape wasn't all rainbows and sunshine.

As she thought about those lines, she realized that was the only reason she'd stuffed the book in her pocket. It was a reminder of what was important to her. The truth of who she was didn't revolve around her mistakes, her triumphs, or the woman who'd broken her. That truth lay in how she lived up to the ideal set by the three most important men in her life. Character couldn't be bought or polished back to perfect, her father had told her often. It was something you had until you didn't, so you had to take care of it. She'd lived that as best she could, making sure to be true to the foundation of what made her, well, her.

"Asher," Reagan said softly as if not to startle her, "I'm sorry I didn't see you. Are you okay?"

"Do I look not okay?" She made a mental note to calm her fingers before the tapping on her glass could be interpreted as nervousness. That would only project weakness, and she wasn't about to give Reagan the satisfaction.

"No, not at all. I'm just surprised to see you here. Are you alone?" Reagan glanced in Gia's direction, and her face was unreadable. The woman Gia had identified as Steph Delmonico was staring at them like the cure to cancer and dancing girls would be the prize for figuring out what the hell was going on.

"I am, and I don't want to keep you." Her fingers, the traitorous bastards, were tapping on the glass hard enough for her to hear it. "I'll see you in a couple days, so feel free to have a late night or a great weekend. We've been through the routine often enough that I don't mind going it alone if you want some time off."

"You're not keeping me from anything, and there's no reason for you to be sitting alone. Why don't you join us?" Reagan sat on the edge of her seat as if waiting for some rude dismissal.

"That's okay. Being alone doesn't bother me. This is more about getting out for a bit and giving Rickie a break from all my problems. She's getting ready for finals, so I thought I'd give her time to study. I didn't mean to interrupt your date." She didn't want to be completely rude, and with effort she made the corners of her mouth lift in a smile. It felt like there were weights tied to her lips, but she did it.

"Steph is a friend, not my date." Reagan placed her hands on her lap and sighed. It was like she was trying to not show any emotion herself.

The wall between them and the emotion that was thick enough to be visible like smog were more tiring than ranch work, so she sighed herself. "If you want, invite your friend to move over here. I'm not sure if you've ordered, but the chef loves to feed you if you're trusting."

"Are you sure?" Reagan stared at her as if trying to see if she was being set up.

She had to laugh at that because she was anything but sure. "Believe it or not, I'm not your enemy, I don't hate you, and I can be mature when called for. If a meal proves that, then let's have dinner, the three of us."

Reagan finally smiled as if she meant it. "I don't think I've heard you laugh since I got home." It surprised Asher when Reagan's eyes got glassy. Those tears had made her do plenty when they appeared—all except change one fundamental thing about herself. They'd been so sure when they were each other's whole world, but she couldn't change everything about herself to make someone happy. That was true, even if the person she was disappointing was Reagan Wilson.

"There hasn't been much to laugh about lately, but then I remember that life is that much longer if you learn to not take things so seriously." She pushed aside her empty glass and reached for the ice water. "Tonight, I remembered that we're both free to be happy about different things. That's normal, and there's no harm in it."

"Daddy used to say that all the time, and I think I forgot that myself." A few of Reagan's tears fell, and it was hard not to reach out and wipe them away. "You're never going to forgive me, are you?"

"What exactly do you want me to forgive you for?" It was puzzling that Reagan would be interested in that now. They'd been together alone for days, and she'd barely said anything, so of course a busy restaurant would be the perfect spot for this conversation.

Reagan opened her mouth a few times before shaking her head. "I hurt you, and I am sorry even if you don't believe me. What I did… the way I acted—"

"Please stop." She reached over and placed her hand on Reagan's forearm. "It's not necessary. You might not believe me, but you don't have to apologize for doing what you thought was best for you. There's no law that says you have to end up with the first person you kissed."

That made Reagan snort. "If Silas Wilson was alive, I doubt he'd agree with you."

"Uncle Wade tells me all the time that shit has a way of working itself out. It doesn't need a lot of input from us, so forget about it." She pointed to the woman still watching them from the corner. "Call your friend over, and let me prove there's no hard feelings."

"You've gotten better about telling white lies. You never could before without giving yourself away," Reagan said when she stood. "Thank you, though, for not shutting me completely out."

"I'm not that complicated, and tonight is just about dinner." Her appetizer arrived as Reagan walked off.

The ramifications of having to spend the night entertaining Reagan and her girlfriend made her lose her appetite. Perhaps Dante was right, and the path to paradise began in hell. Tonight could be defined as hell, but if she could truly learn to see Reagan and who she'd become, it could lead her down the path of letting go. Paradise, hers at least, could be defined as leaving Reagan where she belonged—in her past.

Chapter Eleven

A re you serious?" Steph asked when Reagan got back to their table. Reagan had been upset with herself for accepting Steph's invitation from the moment she'd said yes. It was time to cut ties and get on with the rest of her life, but the silence had a way of making her weak. Weak enough to say yes when she really just wanted to wish Steph away like a bad dream. They were never getting back together no matter how many dinners they had.

"We can stay here." She stood next to their table and wished for guidance. Nothing seemed like a good choice given the ones she had. "But she invited us."

Steph was up and handing her purse over as if not giving her a chance to change her mind. "Let's go, then."

"Unbelievable." There was Steph the successful attorney, and then there was the fangirl who couldn't resist the opportunity to sit with one of her idols. "Asher, this is Steph Delmonico. Steph, Asher Evans."

"It's great to meet you," Steph said, shaking Asher's hand so hard it shook the table. "I'm a big fan."

"Thank you," Asher said, sounding as if it took effort to form simple words. "I'm not sure you've ordered, but I can sign you up for the chef table experience."

"Thanks," Reagan said. She'd owe Asher big for this. Her old friend wasn't the type to suffer someone like Steph without major heartburn. "That sounds lovely."

Steph seemed about to start bouncing in her seat, and Asher was nice enough to engage her. "What is it you do, Steph? It seems only fair to ask since Reagan tells me you're a rodeo fan."

"I'm a corporate attorney," Steph said, and Asher glanced across the room toward the woman Reagan had seen at Asher's table. From their greeting earlier it seemed they were old friends and maybe more. "I moved back to New Orleans to concentrate on oil and gas litigation."

"How'd you two meet?" Asher put her foot and her book down when more dishes were placed on the table. *The Divine Comedy* as Asher's dinner read of choice would not have been Reagan's final answer on Final Jeopardy. This was like a parallel universe where everything was upside down.

"I bought her a drink one night," Steph said and laughed. "We hit it off, started dating, and ended up moving here together."

"Where'd you move from?" Asher would've made a good detective. "If you don't mind me asking."

"Not at all. I doubt our lives are very exciting, but Reagan and I met in Seattle. It was fate that we were moving at the same time to the same place. I was glad to have her while I started over here."

If there was a way to stuff a piece of bread in Steph's mouth and not kill her, Reagan would've done it to get her to stop talking. The way Asher scratched the tablecloth with her index finger made her think it'd rip. That was her response to Steph too, but what she didn't understand was why *Asher* was upset.

"She found the cutest place here," Steph said, finishing her report on all things Reagan. "It's a great location for work, and Reagan did a great job decorating."

"Sounds like it was fate, and a place you can make your own. Both of you, I mean." Asher shoved a bite of food in her mouth as if to keep from saying anything else.

"Steph doesn't live with me," Reagan said, needing to clarify that. Like she did in court, Steph had a way of weaving a story that wasn't necessarily true.

"Do you mind me asking about the rodeo?" Steph for once guided the conversation in the right direction. "Reagan tells me I was the only fan in the state of Washington, but I fell in love with it, growing up in Louisiana. I never got to see her dad, but you I've followed from the beginning of your career."

"Sure and thanks." Asher's face went from no emotion to a bit of a smirk. "What would you like to know?"

"What's it like?" Steph appeared almost childlike when she asked. "That's the one thing that's always fascinated me, and no one's ever given a good answer."

"Growing up, I watched my uncle Silas ride, and I wondered the same thing," Asher said, and Reagan suddenly couldn't wait for this answer.

"Can you share it with us?" Steph asked. "I mean, your experience or if he told you his."

Steph was right—no one ever gave a satisfactory answer as to the why of it. Not even her father could articulate that. She doubted she'd suddenly fall in love with the sport or accept it from one answer, but it was something to consider. "I can only speak for myself and my first time."

"Only the first time?" Steph was persistent.

"The first time defined all the rides that followed." Asher kept her gaze on Reagan even though she was answering Steph. "When the chute opened, it was so many things at once. It was violent, jarring, and terrifying." That was so true and why Reagan hated that people she loved would even think about doing it. "But it was mesmerizing."

Reagan sat quietly, thinking that she'd never heard Asher sound so open and poetic. This was what she hadn't given her a chance to say when they parted—the *why* of why Asher wanted to follow her father into something she so vehemently detested.

"It is that," Steph said "That's why I've never been able to look away, from the first time my dad took me to my first rodeo in Baton Rouge."

"I don't do it to prove anything to anyone," Asher said, still staring right at her. "Uncle Silas was the only person I saw that made it look like an effortless thing. It's why his championship score has never been replicated."

"But what's it like?" Steph tried again.

"You've never heard a good answer to that because there isn't one. It's personal to every rider. That one thing that makes it yours."

It was no answer, and she knew Asher did have the right words, but she wasn't going to share them with her and Steph. They didn't deserve to know, and they'd have to be happy with the little she did share. She put her hand on Steph's thigh, hoping she was smart enough to not ask anything else. The rest of dinner was like trying to find something to say, and Steph for once saved them all by telling them about her ongoing case.

It was enough to suck up the next hour and the four courses the waiters delivered. "Thanks for everything," Reagan said as Asher signed the bill. That Asher asked intelligent questions as Steph went on about her favorite subject was surprising since she doubted Asher cared one way or another. Asher had done it to be kind, and she was grateful her old friend was so generous when she'd been anything but.

"You're welcome—it was nice to have company." Yes, Asher had gotten better at the white lies. "It was nice meeting you, Steph."

"Trust me, the honor was mine. I don't usually go all fangirl, but I really have followed your career from the very beginning. I'm really sorry this happened to you now. This was your year."

"Thanks." Asher stood and seated her crutches. She'd texted someone and Reagan figured it was her ride. "Have a great rest of your night."

There were a few people who stood and talked to Asher as she left. It proved one important thing to Reagan, something that had never occurred to her. She'd left a tall skinny kid years before who wanted nothing more than to be like her father and her own. It had been Asher's goal to be honorable, hardworking, and loyal above all else. Asher was that, but the years had polished her like a stone tumbled by a violent river until she'd become this person who was interesting and social in a way that made people successful in business.

"I have to say, I never expected her to be that put together," Steph said, and Reagan resented her for polluting her thoughts with words.

"What's that supposed to mean?"

"She's not exactly the mindless cowpoke, is she?" Steph handed over her valet ticket and slipped her hands into her pockets. "You can get mad at me now, but I dug a little into her. That question I asked at first—she's the only person I ever wanted the answer from. You grew up with the rodeo and all the ranch stuff, but I've always wanted to know what groomed her into becoming someone who makes magic on the back of a bull. It doesn't sound right to call it magic, but that's what it is."

"What exactly did you look up?" At any other time she would've been pissed, but the answers were more important because she'd never get the answers from Asher.

"Your ex is, at the moment, despite the injury, the number one bull rider in the world." Steph opened the door for her and gave the valet a tip. "She also owns a ton of real estate, not buildings but empty raw land that she's amassed an acre at a time, and she's almost finished what will make it worth a fortune. Asher Evans is a different animal, and I found her totally charming."

"Cows and land are all ranchers know. How much it costs and how they get it almost doesn't matter. It's not a business," she said barely above a whisper staring out the window. The buildings of the Quarter were, as always, perfect in their imperfections. Their age and wear were what made them special, different than anything else in the country. They were unique and one of the reasons she loved this place, but tonight they were a blur. "It's a passion, and the money doesn't matter. Only the animals and the way of life matter."

"I understand that. We're friends, and I didn't grow up in the same kind of place you did, but I think I understand better than you." Steph stopped at the light on Canal Street and finally turned her head to look at her. "There's more, but you're going to have to find it on your own. All I mean is, when I read about her, I thought I'd like her, and I was right."

Steph stopped in front of her place but made no move to get out of the car. "Thanks for the invite." Reagan placed her hand on the door handle and glanced back. "Would you like a drink?"

"I think it's best if I go. Thanks for coming at the last minute." Steph didn't appear tempted even if it was Reagan offering this time. "I realize I'm an asshole, but I don't like eating alone."

"Not the night either of us planned, but I guess we both learned something." She didn't repeat the offer, and Steph waited until she was inside before driving away. Once she closed the door, she fell back and cocked her head back against it. In a city that very seldom slept, she'd never felt more alone. "Could I get any more depressing."

She hung her dress over a chair and debated putting on her pajamas. It didn't take much to convince her to put on jeans and grab her keys. The drive was different at night, but the traffic pattern was the same. People who were headed back across the lake were home by now, and only the people headed for some fun in the city were stuck in the opposite lanes.

The road toward her uncle's house veered to the spot she wanted, and the cows she could see were grouped together under a tree. With the window down she could smell the rain in the air. People might've thought that was a myth, but she—and the cows—could tell. In the distance she could see the levee and the four-wheeler parked at the top. So much for not putting any weight on her foot for another week. Asher might be way different now, but in many ways, she was still the same.

"Are you breaking the rules?" She sat on the slope at the edge of the blanket Asher had put out.

"I didn't run here, so I'm not sure what you mean." Asher had changed into jeans as well, and the white T-shirt was tight at her biceps. "Is this some new round-the-clock service you're providing?"

"I couldn't sleep." She lay back and closed her eyes. Now she could sleep and couldn't help the yawn. "But maybe I should've given it a few minutes."

"The mosquitos will carry you away if you try that here." Asher seemed almost welcoming, but she did have a talent for convincing herself of things that weren't always true.

"Will you tell me about them?" She pointed over her shoulder.

"The cows?" Asher turned her head, and that dark hair made Reagan's breath catch. God, how she'd loved running her fingers through that hair. "They're a gamble that paid off."

"You don't like answering questions, do you?" She smiled at the bemused expression on Asher's face.

Asher shrugged and didn't lose her smile. "I don't want to bore you, and you've never struck me as being interested in cows."

"How about for the next hour we call a truce and pretend I'm interested in all things bovine." She put her hands at her sides and sighed.

"The big cows you mentioned are beef cows, and the Oreo cows are dairy. I know we never raised dairy cows when we were growing up, but I want to be more than just beef." The stalk of grass in Asher's mouth was a habit she'd had since they were children. "I started small and add to the herd every year to diversify the stock for breeding. Once the barn is finished, we'll be producing organic milk with a high fat content." Asher rattled off the information, and Reagan could almost make out her contained excitement.

"Is all the black fenced land yours?"

"Yes, I needed the acreage to keep growing, and this is something I believe in, so I didn't mind the work I had to put in to make it a reality. People thought I was nuts, including Uncle Wade, but I wanted to try new things. At least new things in the realm of what I know." Asher had the kind of voice that weaved into your head and lulled you into agreement. It was like the sound held some superpower to make you want to please her.

Reagan sat up and rested her weight on her elbows. The river was moving as always, but the summer water levels were always lower than the rest of the year. She had memories of walking out quite a ways when she was younger, holding Asher's hand the entire time. Those were the days she had every belief that Asher not only loved her but would keep her safe from anything that could harm her. She didn't realize she was crying until Asher ran her fingers along her cheek.

There was coming home, and then there was this. "Sorry," she said, not backing away.

"I didn't think you felt so strongly about cows," Asher said and smiled.

"You're such an asshole sometimes." She swatted at Asher's shoulder and laughed as she kept crying. "I was thinking of when we used to walk out there."

"We've got a few more weeks before you can try it. The rains this year have kept the levels up." Asher's voice seemed to fade. "You should know, you've been back awhile."

"I have." It was all she could admit to.

"Can I ask why you didn't let Uncle Wade know?" Asher shook her head and glanced away from her. "I know you were forced into being here with me because of this damn injury, Reagan, but he loves you. He never mentions you a lot when he's with me, but I can tell it bothers him that you just left."

"There's no real explanation," Reagan admitted, "except that I've been angry for a long time. I left to stop hurting, but that only lasted so long, and the pain came back." She cried harder, and it made her head hurt. It was the first time in years she'd let go like this, so of course when she finally decided to have a meltdown, it would be in front of Asher.

"Hey..." Asher raised her hand, and it was the only invitation she needed. That she gave in so quickly proved in spades she was losing her mind faster than she could keep up, but falling against Asher, even if it was for a moment, was worth taking the chance. She expected to be dumped into the water, but Asher proved her wrong.

The crying turned to sobs when Asher hugged her closer. "I'm so sorry," she got out in a shuddering snot-filled voice.

"Don't apologize, and I'm sorry I asked. All I wanted was for you to spend some time with him and Frida. They're really cute together, and they're happy, but I'm thinking they'll be happier with you in the picture."

"I'm not good at making anyone happy. Not for a long time." She took a deep breath and leaned harder into Asher. Not a great time for her brain to throw a pheromone party, but damn if Asher didn't still smell the same. She wore a crisp sort of citrusy cologne that triggered a certain response she couldn't allow herself to feel. "I should've stayed away instead of making you all miserable."

"If that's what you think, you're dead wrong." Why the fuck did Asher always have to sound so reasonable and believable?

"You didn't see Frida's face when I first went out to the ranch, or Rickie's for that matter when I showed up at your house." In a way she deserved to be unhappy. She'd certainly spread it like seeds in other people. "They hate me."

"Hate you?" Asher pulled back to look at her but didn't let go. "You think Wade, Frida, or Rickie is capable of that?"

"Not when you ask like that." She buried her face in Asher's shoulder.

Asher rubbed her back and proved what a great job her father and uncle had done in finishing raising Asher. Uncle Dustin had set a solid foundation, and hell if it didn't stick even if he died before the job was done. With effort Asher had built plenty she could be proud of, but none of that superseded her kindness. All Reagan had done was use what her father and uncle had built to run away. She was good at her job, but that's all she had to show for her life so far.

"You okay?"

"I'm not okay, and I'll be embarrassed every time you look at me from now on, but it'll be okay." She tried to pull back, but Asher hung on to her. "Come on, Buck, I promise you don't have to piece me back together."

"Think of it as me being generous." Asher let up on the pressure, so if she wanted to break the hold she could. "And you can talk to me. You might not believe me, but I don't hate you any more than Frida or Rickie."

She slapped the side of Asher's neck but Asher didn't flinch. "Sorry, mosquito."

"You sure it wasn't our old history?" Asher laughed. "Help me up, and we'll go somewhere less buggy."

"Why are you being so nice to me?" Asher laughed louder and let her go. "It's a reasonable question. When I saw you that first night, you didn't appear thrilled to see me."

"Wasn't my best behavior, was it?" Asher took her hand when she stood and offered it. She then folded the blanket and followed close behind as Asher made it up the slope on crutches.

"I'm not saying you were wrong, but this is a definite about-face."

"Life's too short, Buckaroo, and we were friends once."

"Do you think we can be again?"

Asher looked at her and sat on the four-wheeler. "You and I are family, and there's no changing that."

CHAPTER TWELVE

It had to be the drinks. Asher couldn't blame anything else, and if she threw Reagan off the back of the four-wheeler, she'd be the asshole. Nope, she'd committed to a destination and issued the invitation, so she was stuck.

Then again, it could've been the tears.

The fucking tears. She'd never fully understood their power and, as a woman herself, never learned to use them effectively. She wasn't a monster, so of course she cried, but only when it was called for. Funerals...She started a mental list, then her mind went blank. That was her short list, she guessed—death. Other women, though, they had a much longer list, and it got her on a quad bike in the middle of the night, going places she didn't want to go to make them stop.

"Did you say something?" Reagan said right into her ear. The woman was plastered to her back, so why wouldn't she do that? Asher shook her head, but it was to clear Reagan out of her mind. That worked as well as trying to teach a cow ballet. "You're muttering. If you want, we can turn around, and you can leave me at my car."

The cabin was another mile, and she stopped, not turning off the engine. "Do you want me to leave you at your car?" This was why she needed to keep her distance. While she'd been mentally debating how she'd gotten here, Reagan had come to her senses. The experiment was over, and she was ready to move on.

"No, I want to see what's over there," Reagan said, pointing toward the lights of the cabin.

Okay, so she was wrong. So she throttled the engine and got them moving again. That old cabin they'd spent so much time in had been hit by lightning and gone up like dry kindling. It seemed apropos at the time, considering that's what her soul had felt like—a charred heap of trash—so she'd rebuilt. She didn't need another home, but it was nice to come out here and sit. The small cabin was as different from the house as she could make it, and to her, it was an escape because it felt less empty.

"You didn't put it back where it was," Reagan said. She climbed off the back and got Asher's crutches for her.

"We use this place during calving season and to check on the shyer cattle in the herd." She navigated the stairs and headed for the swing. It made her think of Jacqueline and how she hadn't heard from her in a few days. "The old spot was lower ground and not as protected." The trees a few hundred feet away did make a natural windbreak during bad storms.

"This is beautiful." Reagan sat next to her, moving as if the swing would fall if she wasn't careful. "Can I talk to you?"

"I thought that's what we were doing." This was a good thing. Getting this out of the way would satisfy everyone in her life who had ideas of what her happily ever after should look like. "Let me start by saying that you don't need to apologize for anything. It took some time, but I understand taking care of yourself. Your dad was someone I loved, and his death was a shock I'm still not over. He was your father, though, and only someone who's lost what you did that day could understand."

"But I did everything wrong." Reagan's eyes filled with tears again that didn't spill over.

"Everyone processes differently, and that's all we can do."

"How'd you get so smart?" Reagan reached over and placed her hand on her forearm.

"Time is good when it comes to lots of things like clearing away dark clouds, Reagan. To be honest, I didn't like you very much for a very long time. You, leaving the way you did, made me realize that loving someone isn't always enough." Dammit all to hell when the words choked in her throat and her vision blurred. "That pain, though, was good for me. It forced me to face my future and drove me home. The house my dad built was where I belonged, and I broke the two ranches apart like they were when our dads first started this place."

"Uncle Dustin didn't name it Pemberley, though." Reagan leaned back and didn't move her hand.

"No, the name came after a few years of riding the circuit. Bull riding was…*is* something you hate, and I understand that. It made all this possible, though, and in a strange way, helped me grieve your dad." She wiped her face, sensing that every tear that fell somehow stripped away her strength and dignity. "All those afternoons of him teaching me always repeat in my head when that chute opens."

"I didn't leave because I didn't love you, Asher. It was the fear for you that drove me away." Reagan was crying again, and Asher didn't push her away when she moved closer and rested her head on her shoulder. "Daddy died, and the thought of a world without either of you in it terrified me."

"I know what you wanted from me, and I'm sorry I couldn't give it to you. If we're honest, we can admit you outgrew me even before you left." That was the hardest thing to admit to herself, much less to Reagan or anyone else.

"You're wrong."

Asher laughed. "Am I?" She glanced down, daring Reagan to look away. "Steph Delmonico is, or maybe was, more than a friend. That was plain by the way she held you that first night when she thought you were hurting."

"She lived with me for a few months, and then she cheated on me. We're only friends, and barely that," Reagan said softly. If words could be painted with regret, Reagan had done an excellent job. "She's nothing like you."

"I'm sure that's true, but that's what you wanted. Someone who was your equal in every way. This life wasn't something you wanted, and I don't think you realized that, not until freedom from it was possible." The anger was back, and she took a breath to tamp it down. It wasn't called for now. "It's been a few years, but I don't think you'd let anyone in your life unless it was someone you wanted. I know it's not her, but it's going to be someone like her, and you deserve to be happy."

"It wasn't like that even if you don't believe me." Reagan tightened her hold on her arm. "I was lonely, and Steph was uncomplicated."

"You don't owe me any explanations." She held the leg in the cast up as she pushed off with her good foot, setting them in motion.

"Don't I?" Reagan shot back.

"No, not anymore. We were kids, and now we're adults with vastly different lives. There's no sin in it." Being honest and admitting to the things she'd rather forget was painful. All she could remind herself was she wasn't that pathetic kid Reagan left behind. She'd shed that kid years before, and she wasn't coming back.

"No forgiveness for the stupid, then?" Reagan stood up and moved to the end of the porch. She stared out into the darkness as if she wanted to disappear into it.

"Come back here," she said with more force than was necessary. It took a moment for Reagan to do anything, appearing at war with herself. "I know this is the last thing you want to hear, but I made a promise to Silas Wilson, and I intend to keep it until I'm dead."

"What, to take care of me even if you have to do it with me kicking and screaming?" Reagan finally laughed.

"Your dad was a smart guy," she said, shifting on the swing to get more comfortable. "I was the slow learner in the barn."

"I doubt that, and he'd agree with me. I miss him every single day, but I dread what he'd think of me if he was still here." The tears started again, and Asher placed her arm across the swing in invitation. "He would not be proud of me."

"He knew," Asher said in a low voice. Silas had made her promise not to have this talk until Reagan came to her.

"He knew what?"

"He knew you weren't happy with him, and he tried to prepare me—for when you left, I mean. I just didn't think I needed to be prepared for anything." She remembered the day they'd had this talk, her and Silas. It was the last time they went riding together, and he'd aimed them in the direction of her current house. He'd pointed to all the stuff that needed to be fixed. "There were things neither of us understood about him." She wondered often if he knew, knew that death was so close and his time was up.

"He died, so there's no making up that last meeting. God I was angry, so angry, and then he died." Reagan's weeping was reaching a new level, and Asher pressed Reagan to her chest. "I can't make that up to him."

"He wanted me to wait until you were ready to hear this." She rested her cheek on Reagan's head. "We went riding the week before he died. He made me promise to make you understand how much he loved you. When you got accepted to school, he was so proud of you, and he knew your life wouldn't be the life he and I chose." She rubbed her hand up and down Reagan's back, trying to calm her. "Listen, that was okay with him. The one thing he was proudest of was that he raised a kid who could stand on her own. You're strong because of him and despite him."

"All I want is one more day," Reagan said, twisting Asher's T-shirt in her fist. "I want him to know how much I love him."

"He knew that, darlin'. What you've accomplished and made of yourself honors the man he was and proves he was right. A whole life isn't boiled down to one day, and you're going to have to let that go. The truth of it is simple. Silas loved you, and I'll always be here for you."

"That's a promise you don't have to keep. I know I hurt you, so I'll never hold you to it."

"Sorry," she said putting her other arm around Reagan. "It doesn't work that way."

"Thanks, Asher. I'm glad he had you to talk to." Reagan relaxed as if the emotion had drained out of her and she was left empty. "Can I ask you something?"

"Sure," she said, hoping this openness only had to last the night.

"Why'd you name this place Pemberley?"

"*Pride and Prejudice* was my favorite book in school, and I liked the idea of finding that one person I could be happy with, who I could make happy in return." *Pride and Prejudice* was one of the few things Reagan had shared with her in the short letters she'd sent her when she was in college. She'd written so passionately about it that Asher had kept the letter. When it was her turn to read it, she could see why Reagan had loved it so much, since growing up she'd been a romantic at her core.

"We didn't read that in high school," Reagan said, gazing up at her.

"No, I read it at Tulane along with a lot of other books, not all of which I cared for."

"Wait," Reagan seemed to perk up at that. "You took classes at Tulane?"

"It took me a bit with all the work around here, but I graduated and went on to get my MBA. The ranch is hard work, but it's also a business." She shrugged, not used to talking so much about herself. "It made sense to learn the business side of things."

"You were so dead set against it." Reagan had a talent for crucifying her with a question. "College, I mean."

"I was dead set against going to school in Washington. That was the right decision for you, but I needed to stay close to run this place and help Wade."

Reagan didn't say anything for a while, but the quiet didn't bother Asher. She'd grown used to the quiet long before now and didn't see the need to disturb it. They sat like they used to, and in a way, it made it easier for Asher to think of them in the done column.

This is what they could've been, but Silas had warned her that day that Reagan might want different things. It didn't make her wrong or bad, just courageous enough to pick what would make her happy. He and Reagan had argued for days about his decision to try for one more championship, and he could hear in his daughter's words what she thought of this life even if she wasn't direct. It was the life Asher also wanted. Silas had been smart enough to know he wasn't the only one Reagan would punish for the dream of bull riding.

She'd made him the promise to talk to Reagan if something happened to him, that was true. He'd also made her promise not to give up on the family he knew she wanted. When it came to love, he'd said, he'd lucked out in the children God blessed him with. The one he'd helped bring into the world, and the one who was of his heart. It made the woman, Reagan's mother, who'd broken his heart and the loss of his best friend worth it. She'd pointed out he'd never looked for love again, and she wouldn't need to either.

She'd been sure there was no way Reagan would leave her, leave home, and leave behind the plans they'd made together. She was naive enough to think no one did that to someone they loved. He'd been right, though, and she never imagined being wrong could hurt so much for so long.

In the end, Silas had left first. The pain of that was a hot poker through the eye, and then Reagan left, and she was numb. It was only then that she understood why Silas had never tried again. That someone who loved you, or supposedly did, could do that killed that part of you that carried hope. What had hurt the most was that Reagan hadn't seemed that affected by their parting. Reagan had Wade drive her to the airport and hadn't waited for her to get back from her morning chores. Their end had come swift and final as if Reagan had taken a scalpel to their relationship.

"Thank you for telling me, Asher. Daddy loved you, and I'm sorry I missed so much." Reagan seemed almost reluctant to break the peace between them, so her words were hesitant.

"Maybe he knew," she said, voicing something she'd thought for so long. "Maybe he knew and hoped to die doing something he loved instead of in a hospital like he did." She squeezed Reagan to her and took a deep breath. "All I know for sure is he loved you. Christine gave birth to you, but it was Silas who dedicated his life to loving you. Remember that when you question that last day."

"I don't deserve you being this nice, but thank you. When I decided to come home, I was scared to see you again." Reagan flattened her hand on Asher's abdomen, and the feel of her was more familiar than riding.

"No need to be afraid." Her cell rang, prompting Reagan to move away. One of the ranch hands had found Reagan's car on the road and was worried it was someone messing with the herd. "Ride to the cabin and pick up the keys. You can park it by the house."

"I apologize for keeping you out so late. If you give me a ride back I'll get out of here, and we can start later than usual tomorrow." Reagan leaned forward and rested her elbows on her knees and combed her hair back with both hands.

"You get a break tomorrow, remember? I have a doctor's appointment, so with any luck this thing will come off, and Harry puts me in a boot, so I can reach all those phantom itches." She glanced at her watch, and it was after two. "And your choices are staying with me or in your old room at the house. It's late, and I don't want anything happening to you."

"Asher," Reagan said as if that's all she could think to come up with.

"Do you want to drive home this late?" Reagan shook her head. "Then take one of the spare bedrooms at the house and drive home in the morning."

"Can I see the inside of this place before we go?"

Asher fished the keys out of her pocket and handed them over. The place wasn't very big, but it was comfortable. The bathroom was the only other room off the open space and the fireplace was way too big, but she liked the solidness of it. Reagan stood in front of the hearth and touched the stones. It was surreal, in a way, seeing her standing here.

"It's not much, but it comes in handy when I want to save myself the hour's ride to get out this far."

The arrival of the ranch hand for Reagan's keys meant the end of their night, and she was glad. She was exhausted and yawned as the hand told her four of the cows were in labor, and they'd call if there were any problems.

"You must be tired," Reagan said when she went back in. "Why not save us the bumpy ride back? I'll take the couch."

"Sounds good." She pointed to the bathroom after pulling out a sleep shirt for Reagan to borrow. The last thing she remembered was sitting on the sofa to wait for Reagan to finish. It had been an exhausting day, but it did seem like she'd put down a heavy load, and she had no plans to pick it back up.

❖

The fog outside was thick as the sky started to lighten from the dawn. It was another too-early morning for Reagan, but this was so different than the previous day. She was in Asher's bed watching her sleep on the sofa, her feet hanging off the end and her arm thrown over her eyes. It was surprising Asher was still asleep considering a lifetime of waking early to do hard physical work. Cows waited for no one, and they expected to be fed, milked, and pampered no matter the weather.

So she sat with her knees bent, alternating staring out the window to staring at Asher. Once she woke up, she had a gut feeling they'd go back to their corners and the night before would be forgotten. What she knew for sure was not having Asher hold her again would hurt as much as it did the first time she lost the privilege. She'd always prided herself on her intelligence, but it turned out she was an idiot for ever thinking she'd be completely happy away from here.

"What are you thinking so hard about over there?" Asher's voice was cigarette-and-too-much-whiskey rough, and the sound of it made her nipples hard.

"It's so beautiful out here." The rest she'd keep to herself. "You picked the perfect spot."

Asher lifted her head and squinted as she looked outside. "It's been a while since you woke up with cows in your yard, I bet."

She laughed and got up to turn on a lamp. The small kitchen had a coffee maker, and she pulled two double shots—she couldn't imagine Asher not liking coffee. Asher sat up and made room for her on the couch. "Does Uncle Wade know you drink high-end Italian coffee?"

"I'm not stuck in my ways when it comes to all things," Asher said and smiled. "Thanks for making it. Moving around with hot liquid on those damn crutches is a pain."

"Do you have time for breakfast?" She was pushing her luck, but stretching out her time with Asher was worth a few chances. "I see you have eggs."

"That'd be nice if you don't mind." Asher held her cup with both hands and stretched out, putting her feet on the coffee table. "Did you sleep okay?"

"I did, and I'm glad you talked me into staying. At the risk of forcing you to throw me out, can we talk some more?" It was encouraging when Asher's reaction wasn't to tense up.

"Sure. We haven't spoken in years." Asher turned her head, and the intensity in those hazel eyes cut right through her. That face visited her in her dreams more often than she liked, and she wondered if she'd ever be free of it. "What would you like to talk about?"

"You," she said, and it got her a belly laugh. That's one of the things she loved about Asher—her laugh was as genuine as her. She stood and moved to the stove.

"You're off-limits, then?" Asher patted the seat next to her as if encouraging her to come back. If they were going to talk, they weren't going to do it across the room from each other.

She sat, but on the edge of the cushion. "I'm an open book with a lot of blank pages."

"Ah," Asher said with a smile that reached her eyes. She'd known her long enough to know the difference. "You know what?"

"What?" God, she wanted to be held again. She didn't want to compare Asher to everyone else she'd been with, but last night had made that impossible. There was no comparison, and not realizing that at eighteen damned her to this life she didn't like. Not one damn bit.

"I want to be mad at you, and stay mad," Asher said. "All those steps they talk about when it comes to grief are true. Anger came up the list fast and stayed."

"I'd argue with you, but it'll be hard to explain a cast up my ass at the emergency room." She tried humor wanting to keep Asher talking.

Asher obliged her by laughing. "What I figured out, though, is it takes a lot of effort to stay mad at you, and I'd rather concentrate on something else." Asher lifted her finger when she opened her mouth to thank her. "Before you thank me, just remember that I'm trying to rush PT so I can compete again. That means real bulls and not those mechanical rides outside the grocery store. You haven't liked me for a long time because of the choices I made."

"I've always liked you even when my brain went on vacation. You're a part of me, Asher. I can take it that you're mad at me, but I can't stand that you don't want me as a friend."

"That's what I'm trying to tell you. I'm tired of being mad at you." Asher seemed so sincere. "But if you can't accept what happens when this cast comes off, you need to tell me."

"It was always about the fear. Not the best excuse, but I was eighteen and terrified of losing you." She reached over and placed her hand on Asher's thigh. "Bulls scare me, and you on a bull scares the shit out of me."

"I started because of Silas, but I'm finishing for myself." Asher took a couple of deep breaths and placed her hand over hers. "It's kind of strange you'd come back now."

"Why?" She had to calm down and be patient not to scare Asher into silence.

"This is my last year. It'll either happen or it won't, but my life is here. Don't tell anyone since I haven't made that public yet, but this should prove to you that I don't hate you. In retrospect I think you were the person who deserved to know first."

"Don't quit because of me. That'll make you hate me forever." The words were coming out of her mouth, but it was like she had no control over them. She shouldn't mean them, but she did. "And you don't have to say it to get me to help you."

"I'm sorry, but did you forget everything about me?" Asher squinted again as if trying her best to see her clearly. "There are plenty of physical therapists in the city, Reagan. I'm telling you because it was what I decided before you moved back."

"You won't hate me?"

"According to you, I already do." Asher smiled in that lopsided way she'd had since she was a kid, and Reagan wanted back in to her heart more than she'd ever wanted anything in her life. Man, had she been wrong about so many things, but especially this. She'd known love, and no one could tell her she'd been too young for it to be real.

"But you don't. Not really," Reagan said as a ball of emotion formed in her throat. "Please tell me that's true."

"It's true, but I need an answer. I want to finish this season, so don't try to talk me into an earlier retirement. If it makes it easier, we can take up this friendship once I finish." Asher reached for her crutches and stood with ease. "Think about it. Let me hop to the bathroom, and I'll take you back."

"Not until you have breakfast." Reagan watched her walk away before moving back to the kitchen. "Maybe you *were* listening, Daddy."

She whisked eggs and heated butter in a perfectly seasoned black iron skillet. The eggs went in as Asher came out of the bathroom. Once upon a time this was all she knew how to cook and she'd fantasized about taking care of Asher and a family every morning. She was ashamed for ever making fun of that particular fantasy.

"Hey, you didn't have to go to all that trouble." Asher sat back on the sofa and rubbed her face, then combed her hair back, only to have it stick out in a hundred different directions.

"It's a thank-you for last night." She plated the plain omelet and carried it over to Asher. "And I don't need to think about what you said. I'm going to be your therapist, but I would like you to answer the question Steph asked you last night." She handed over a fork and napkin when she sat with another plate.

"What question?" Asher instantly cooled, and Reagan panicked, not wanting to lose ground.

"What's it like? I never gave you the opportunity to tell me." She tapped her fork against her plate and sighed. "I yelled at you, then ran off like a shit. Back then I didn't really want to know why."

"But now you do?" Asher stopped and took a bite of her eggs and chewed as if navigating this conversation was like tangoing through a minefield while having a rattlesnake wrapped around her head. "Why do you want to know? The circuit was and, I suspect, still is something you hate."

"I *need* to know because it's a big part of you. It won't matter if you retire this year, or a decade from now. You've rewritten history when it comes to the sport. You love it, and you're good at it. Not many people can say they're the best in the world at something." It appeared the right thing to say since the tension left Asher's shoulders.

"The United States is a bit conceited when it comes to declaring things like that. There might be some kid in, say, Norway who's way better than me, he just doesn't compete." Asher was funny. She'd always had a talent for making Reagan laugh, but she seemed to have a sharper wit now. "I was being honest last night. There's no easy answer."

"I don't want the anyone else's answer to why they climb on one of those beasts—I want yours."

"Are you going to use my answer against me?" Asher's question didn't seem to have any kind of malice behind it, and again she couldn't blame her for the suspicion. She'd made her skittish with her past behavior, and it was time to change that pattern.

"I want to understand because I doubt you did this only to please my father." She tapped her fork against Asher's plate and smiled. "Now, eat and answer my question."

"Your dad got me started, but he couldn't prepare me for the moment that chute opened. At first I thought you were right and I'd lost you over something that was totally foolish, not to mention stupid, but then I remembered my training." Asher sounded so animated. "It's strange."

"What is?" She took another bite of her eggs, hoping Asher would keep going.

"The crowd is always so loud right before I bust out, but once the ride starts my head goes quiet, and I only hear the creak of the leather, the bull's snorts, and the sound of my breathing. It's like nothing else I've ever tried, and I've gone as far as I can in the sport. That means I can walk away and not regret that choice." Asher finished her breakfast, and Reagan took her plate. "I took advantage of the opportunity Silas gave me, and it's helped me build all this."

"You're not quitting because of me, are you?" Reagan heard how that sounded. It was self-centered and conceited. "Listen to me," she said and laughed. "This is about you, not me."

"I'm quitting because I want to enjoy the rest of my life without facing a lot of this," Asher said, pointing to her foot. "Your dad stayed at the party a little too long, and I can understand that. This isn't some noble pursuit, but the chase is addictive. Wanting to win is hardwired."

"Like you said, he died doing what he loved. I might not have liked it, but he would've been miserable if I'd kept him under lock and key." Letting go of the anger and the regret wouldn't be that easy, but she had to try. Talking about it would help. "All I want is for you to believe me when I tell you I acted the way I did because I was scared."

"I do believe you. The only thing I don't understand is why you were gone so long." Asher still sounded like she wasn't upset, but there was a chance that would change.

"Think of me as a runaway cart going down a steep hill. Once I started making mistakes, they got easier and easier to pile on." She wiped her face, not believing she was crying again. "I didn't want to face the mistakes, and they only compounded."

"We grew up in the same house, Buckaroo. You should've learned that your family is always going to forgive you, and they missed you." Asher smiled at her, but in a way, the smile made Asher look sad.

"How about you? Did you miss me?" She was pushing her luck.

"Feel free to lie in a big way."

"I'd be lying if I said I didn't think of you often, but let's not talk about what I thought about." Asher laughed, and it was another one of those great laughs that made her nostalgic.

"I'll just bet." She took the dishes to the sink and practiced some more deep breathing.

"Come back here," Asher said to be heard over the running water. "You're dating an attorney, so you don't get to act like the wounded party here."

"Would it be better if she worked in the restaurant business?" If acting like the wounded party was out, then acting like the jealous girlfriend was not one of the multiple-choice answers.

"Jacqueline is a good friend and a customer." Asher's smile made her want to wipe it off. "Come here," Asher said again.

She dried her hands and sat on a cushion across from Asher.

"There's no way I can handle you piling on, Asher, even if I have it coming."

"Leave the dishes," Asher said, taking her hand. "The guys will come by and take care of things, and we have places to be. Maybe it's time you remembered what you've been missing."

"What are you talking about?"

Asher pulled on her finger and her smile widened. "Go put your pants on, and I'll tell you."

Chapter Thirteen

The ground was still wet from the heavy dew, making the four-wheeler skid a bit as they drove through the pasture, heading to the farthest eastern side of the property. Asher had received a text at four that morning that the cow was in labor so they should make it in time.

She stopped far enough away to not spook the cow that was braying as if she had plenty to complain about. "You want to go help out? I'd join you, but the crutches will make me useless." Asher turned and offered Reagan the opportunity.

"That's a big cow," Reagan said.

"It's going to be a big baby, so get in there."

Reagan was a mess by the time the calf was standing next to her mother and nursing for the first time. With any luck they'd repeat the same process another twenty or so times before the day was out. Their birthing season had been successful so far, and if Reagan and Wade were willing to let it go, she wanted the rest of the land to fit a bigger herd, but she'd be happy with what she had if they didn't. If experiences counted for anything, today would get Reagan more involved next door.

"You're going to have to lend me a towel," Reagan said, holding her arms away from her body.

"Tell me that didn't bring back memories." Asher smiled when Reagan plucked at her shirt. When a cow needed a little help calving, it always turned into a messy situation. There was nothing like it, though. Even if she was supposed to be a rancher and tough bull rider, the birth of a calf was something special, and she was lucky enough to experience it all the time.

"You're still a softie when it comes to these guys. It's good to know not all things change," Reagan said. "The only thing is, you didn't think this through, did you?"

"What's that supposed to mean?"

"You have to give me a ride back to the house, and I'm not taking my clothes off to climb on behind you." Reagan was a smart woman, so she knew exactly what she was doing when she said that.

Asher cursed the heat in her ears that confirmed she couldn't control her blush. "There'll be a shower waiting for both of us, so don't worry about it. Let's get moving," she said gruffly, but Reagan only smiled. "I have that appointment with Harry, and I'm sure you're ready to get the hell away from me."

"If that's what you think, you're wrong," Reagan said. "Thank you for last night and this morning." Reagan's voice was like velvet, and it wove into her ear like a warm breeze. She got back on the four-wheeler and leaned in to her.

Just like the blush, Asher couldn't control her response, and like Pavlov's dogs, her body reacted like it had hundreds of times before when Reagan was this close to her. All she could think to do was nod and start the engine. She needed to put some space between them and concentrate on a life where Reagan was only her friend. There would be nothing more.

"Do you want me to drive you to your appointment?" Reagan asked when they stepped into the house.

"I don't want to monopolize your time. One of the guys can take me." She led the way to the main bedroom and took out a pair of shorts and a shirt for Reagan. "You're welcome to use my bathroom, or the guest room next door is fully stocked."

"Asher, please relax." Reagan kicked her shoes off and accepted the clothes. "And please don't be upset that we might be on our way to being friends again."

"Why would that upset me?"

Reagan placed her hand on her shoulder and squeezed. "You're tight as a drawn bow, and you're frowning. Sit, and I promise I'll be quick, and once we're both clean, I'll drive you to the doctor's office."

It didn't take long for both of them to get dressed, and Reagan only stared at her when she started the Land Rover and the classical music came on. Silence had never bothered Asher, and from the beginning of their relationship there hadn't been a need to fill their time with small talk. This morning was no different. She waited in the car while Reagan ran up to her place and came down wearing khaki shorts and a black shirt with the clinic's name on the front.

Harry didn't say anything when Reagan led her into the exam room after her X-rays and watched as the cast came off. "The boot will be next, and if you try walking without it, the cast goes right back on."

"We'll start slow on the range of motion exercises," Reagan said.

"I'll talk to Kendra," Harry said, "so she knows you're going to be tied up with Asher for more time than you have been. It's okay to extend the two hours you've been doing and kick it up a notch. We both know who we're dealing with, so do your best to tire her out. It's the only way to make her behave." Harry typed notes into the computer in the room and ignored Asher's glare.

"I'm sitting right here. You remember that, right?" Asher wiggled her toes, glad it was less painful than before. "Stop talking about me like I'm out in the waiting room."

"I do know that, and you can tell me I'm wrong, but we both know I'm not. Be prepared to spend most of your days with Reagan, and when she's done with you, I promise you'll be grateful." Harry fitted the boot on her foot and pumped air into it for a snug fit. "I'll see you in two weeks, so we can assess from there."

"Thanks, Harry." She stood, and Reagan handed her crutches. She was cleared to put weight on the foot, but Harry warned about overdoing it.

Reagan led her through the circuit in her home gym, adding to the routine until Asher's eyes burned from the sweat falling into them. She was tired, and her body was tight from all the lifting Reagan had her do, but nothing scared her more than when Reagan called it a day and pointed to the massage table. This had never been part of her PT experience before, but Reagan was a licensed massage therapist, and she'd spouted off all the studies that showed it promoted healing, so Asher didn't argue.

"Can you take your shirt off?" Reagan's question made the top of her head tingle. "If you don't relax the muscles in your shoulders and back, you're going to regret it tomorrow." Asher watched as Reagan removed her boot.

It was a dare, had to be. If she refused, Reagan would know she'd wormed in more than Asher had planned to allow, so she had no choice. She walked to the table and sat. Reagan didn't look away when she dropped her sweaty T-shirt to the ground and waited for further instructions. She smirked when Reagan unfurled a sheet and held it up for her. If someone was going to walk away affected, it wasn't going to be her.

"It's pretty private back here, so I don't think we're going to need that," she said.

"Are you sure?" Reagan asked. "The shorts and sports bra have to go too."

"I'll leave it up to you." She stripped and lay down, closing her eyes when the cool surface of the table raised goose bumps when the front of her body hit it.

The sheet stayed off when Reagan worked her way down her body with sure, firm hands. She'd put on the same music she'd played in the car, and it helped Asher forget she was naked and being touched by Reagan. When she rolled over, Reagan covered her body, only moving the sheet to uncover the area she massaged. Asher never remembered falling asleep, but Reagan was watching her when her eyes opened.

"I'm not a creeper, I promise, but I couldn't take the chance you'd roll off and hurt yourself."

"Thanks," she said, sitting up. She nodded her thanks when Reagan handed her shirt over and put her boot back on. "How long was I out?"

"An hour but you must have needed it, so no worries. Do you want me to go?" Reagan sounded unsure of herself again.

"Do you mind driving again?" She put her shorts on before standing up and grabbing her crutches.

"No, did you need to go somewhere?"

"It's meatloaf day, and Frida and Uncle Wade are expecting us. I just have to shower and throw on less stinky clothes." She wasn't surprised Reagan followed her to her bedroom and sat there to wait for her.

She stood with the weight off her foot as the hot water made her sigh from how good it felt. There were interesting days, and then there were the last couple of days. Asher couldn't define them. If she wanted to romanticize it, the truth was her heart needed Reagan in her life. Having her close was like being given back an important part of herself that had been missing for way too long. Her brain, though, knew better. To keep herself grounded and safe, she had to proceed with caution.

"Ready?" she asked Reagan.

"Yes, I am," Reagan said, and it sounded as if she meant more than just meatloaf.

❖

A week of working Asher through her new therapy and exercise routine followed by a massage was systematically dismantling Reagan's willpower. Years of spending time in the gym had changed Asher's body in big ways that were hard to see if you weren't really allowed to look. As Asher's therapist, Reagan wasn't supposed to be *looking,* much less fantasizing about doing the massage naked.

"Are you busy tonight?" Asher asked when she hopped on the massage table and stripped. If Asher had been unsure about massage when they started, it seemed to have grown on her.

"No," Reagan said and had to clear her throat. She doubted Asher was teasing her, but she had to look out the window. Albert and Booker were chasing each other around the gated area where Asher kept them. She wondered if Booker was pregnant, which didn't matter since she doubted she could force Booker back to Moon Touch at gunpoint. It was like even her horse understood the allure of the Evans family.

"Would you like to have dinner? You've been stuck with me for a while, so I thought you deserved a treat." Asher lay down, and Reagan moved to cover her ass with the sheet. In a word it was perfect, and the sheet was the best reminder to behave.

"I don't think of it as being stuck with you." She dug her thumbs into Asher's shoulders and hesitated when Asher moaned. "Dinner sounds good, though."

"Good, how about we cut this short even if it's become my favorite part of the day," Asher said and laughed. "I'll deny that if you call me out on it."

"Your secret is safe with me, and I'll finish, thank you. Think of it as different pieces of a puzzle, so you can't skip any." She had a hard time losing her smile as she finished, taking longer than she usually did. "Are you okay?"

"I'm great," Asher said, standing without the boot to put her shorts back on. She'd never been shy and that hadn't changed. "How does seven sound?"

She glanced at her watch, seeing she had three hours to get home and dressed. "Sounds good. Do you want me to come back and get you?" Maybe in the time she had she could transform herself into someone Asher would have a hard time resisting.

"My foot feels good, so how about I pick you up?" Asher slipped her T-shirt on and put the boot on last. "I can drive without it, and I promise I'll put it on to walk anywhere."

"Do you remember where it is?" She followed Asher out of the gym into the kitchen. Being in the house for weeks and Asher's acceptance of her being there had softened Rickie's attitude toward her as well. Rickie smiled at her when she came in and handed her an iced tea.

"I haven't had that many blows to the head." Asher winked at her and waved before heading to her room. "See you soon."

Rickie took her drink back and poured it into a to-go cup. "You're moving up in the world, I see."

"Just a friendly dinner. See you tomorrow." She wasn't about to fall for Rickie's teasing.

All she could wonder on the way home was what the hell tonight was about. There was no way Asher would set her up after all this time. They'd moved squarely into the friend category, so dinner was just dinner. Right? Neither of them had mentioned their past relationships again—no new information about the gorgeous Jacqueline Blanchard.

"Shit," she yelled into the car. What if that's what this was. Asher had spent that evening entertaining Steph, so maybe this was payback. "I don't want to fucking do that." She didn't know for sure, but she'd put money on the fact that Asher and Jacqueline were more than friends. And if they were, there'd been plenty of benefits involved.

Her feet felt leaden as she walked up to her place, having convinced herself the night held nothing but heartburn. She could at least feel good about how she looked. She took out the white sundress she'd bought but hadn't found a reason to wear. She put her hair in a twist, put on makeup, and dusted off a pair of heels. All of it was date-wear as she called it, but she wasn't about to concede quietly.

She smiled at the knock on her door—six thirty. Asher, as she'd noticed so many times, was hardwired in many ways, and being early was a big one. When they'd been together, she'd taken pleasure in throwing Asher off those traits in numerous ways. She opened the door and whatever she was about to say was replaced by a deep breath. It was necessary when she found Asher in a suit holding a beautiful bouquet of flowers.

"Wow, you look great." Asher handed over the flowers and stepped in. The cowboy boot Asher chose balanced out the boot she'd promised to wear.

"You do too. I don't think you looked this good when we went to the prom." She took down the vase that had belonged to her grandmother and watched as Asher glanced around the room. "Do you want a tour?"

"Sure," Asher said, her hands sliding into her pockets. "It's nice."

It's nice probably meant Asher would die a slow death if forced to live here. Reagan put water in the vase and fixed the flowers, allowing Asher to finish her visual tour. "Thank you, and I know it's not your style, but it was the first place I liked and was available for a fast sale."

The doors to the balcony were open and that's where she led Asher first. "It doesn't matter if it's my style," Asher said. "All that matters is you like it. If it feels like home, that should be all that counts."

"It's missing, as you said, a few cows in the yard to truly make it home, but I like it." They walked around, and it hit her. The interior was nice, tasteful, and stylish. It was all that, but it also could've been in the Pottery Barn catalog, unlike Asher's place with the history of who she was along with the nice antiques that defined every space. "I bought it so I could sit out there even when it's hotter than hell and talk to Daddy. It's stupid, but I thought he'd hear me here. He never talked to me in Seattle."

"I talk to him all the time when I'm riding the fields, so it's not stupid." Asher placed her palm on Reagan's cheek and swiped away the few tears that fell. "That you found your way back, and into a job you like, should be proof he's listening. He led you here, and here's a hell of a lot closer than Seattle."

"No wonder he loved you. You inherited his outlook on life."

Asher smiled and offered her hand. "You ready?"

"I am, and I'm sure you're tired of all this emotion." She picked up her purse and put her hand in the bend of Asher's elbow to make sure she was okay on the stairs. They drove out of her neighborhood and headed into the Quarter again. "Are you going to give me a hint?"

"You mentioned Jacqueline, and we already had dinner with Steph, so I thought of a place that wouldn't remind us of either." Asher pulled into the Piquant, and the valet parked the car.

"Are we getting room service?" She raised an eyebrow and stared at Asher.

"We're getting a pedicab, but I'll keep that in mind if we're feeling more adventurous next time." Asher helped her up when a cab stopped by the car. "It's a bit of a walk from here, and this was the easiest way to get there. I didn't want you to fuss."

Being this close to Asher made it easy to smell her cologne and feel the nice material of her suit. It was going to be a long night. She glanced up at the small wooden sign where they stopped and took Asher's hand to get down. GW Fins was one of the new restaurants she'd heard about but hadn't been to yet. The only other people she knew well enough to have dinner with were Steph and Kendra, and she was glad it was Asher who'd invited her.

The next two hours proved to her that Asher was still a great conversationist. They talked about a wide variety of things, including subjects she thought didn't interest her. When she sat with Asher, the truest definition of a stunning butch with a great linen suit and perfect face, she was willing to listen to everything she wanted to tell her about cows.

"The dairy thing threw me. Why'd you decide on that?" Reagan was sorry they were headed home, and the night was almost over.

"When I moved home, one of the first things I did was to clean out my dad's old office. I found his journals and he'd laid it all out. He was planning to start small and build a dairy herd until he had enough to make a business out of it." Asher stopped in front of Reagan's building and got out to get her door.

"Would you like to come up?"

"Only since you have the day off tomorrow." Asher left her jacket in the car and followed her up.

She poured them both a drink and joined Asher on the couch after she'd taken her heels off. "So, are you going to be happy milking cows once you're finished competing?"

"It's what I've been working toward." Asher sounded committed to that future. She was passionate about what she did, like Reagan was. Steph had once complained that Reagan loved her job but didn't give anyone else the benefit of loving theirs. "You're welcome to come and check it out once we finish the barn and get going."

"Do you want me to visit even after we finish PT?" The love they'd had was always right under the surface, ready to break free. It's how she still felt but didn't know if Asher would ever get there again.

"I meant what I told you the night we spent out at the cabin," Asher said. "I'm tired of being upset with you, and if you're interested, I'd like you to come back as often as you want." Asher didn't pull away when Reagan reached for her hand. "When you asked about the name of the ranch, I didn't tell you the whole truth."

"Why?" she asked, staring at Asher's mouth.

"I did read *Pride and Prejudice* in college, but I remember it was the one thing you wrote to me about that gave me back a piece of you. When I got the chance to read it, I fell in love with the characters and the place they eventually called home."

Reagan put her glass down and moved closer. "I loved that book because it gave me hope for the future. All those misunderstandings, but they still found each other."

"You could write the SparkNotes from your own experiences," Asher said.

Asher didn't turn away from her when she pressed her lips to hers. She couldn't help it, having reached the limit of her control. Having Asher this close made her impossible to resist. Asher kissed her, but she was holding back. They'd kissed enough for Reagan to know that was true, and she didn't like it. She ended it and grabbed the hair at the sides of Asher's head and pulled gently.

"Either kiss me or go." She wanted Asher to stay, but the ultimatum was serious.

"This isn't too fast?" There was so much behind that question. *Why did you leave me? Why did you break my heart? How can I trust you?* All of those ran under the surface of Asher's hesitancy.

"Can I be totally honest with you?" When all else failed, the truth was the best course of action.

"I'd like that." Asher didn't move away from her so Reagan counted it as a win.

"When I made the decision to come home, I convinced myself it was for Uncle Wade. He needed me here, and I wanted to get close to him again." At that Asher did try to move away, but she held fast.

"Then I arrived with Steph in tow, and the last person I wanted to see was you."

"Damn, nothing like a little brutality with a story," Asher said and laughed. It sounded more humorous than pained, so she felt like she could continue.

"I didn't want to see you because I'm a failure compared to you. Jesus, you stayed, took care of my family, and you have that amazing spread. Add to that the beautiful woman I saw you with that night, and I was right." She didn't want to keep going, but she was all-in now. "I didn't want you to see what a bullet you dodged even if it was me who left."

"First, if the beautiful woman was a serious thing, I wouldn't be here," Asher said. She seemed comfortable enough to put her injured foot on Reagan's coffee table. "And I believe the Seattle Seahawks don't hire losers. Uncle Wade loves to brag a little when it comes to you. Besides, it shouldn't matter what I or anyone else thinks."

"The hardest thing sometimes is to forgive myself."

Asher put her arms around her and brought her closer. "This time worry about me forgiving you, and I do. Then concentrate on the fact that the past doesn't define you."

"You make it sound easy." She couldn't trust this, but thinking too much right this second might lead to waking up, and she didn't want to do that. That she'd been allowed to kiss Asher meant she was dreaming. Had to be.

"It's not hard unless you go out of your way to complicate it. I've known you to do that, but try to avoid it this time around." Asher kissed her cheek and didn't fight it when Reagan moved her head and kissed her on the lips again.

"Right now what I want is not complicated at all," she whispered in Asher's ear.

Asher shivered and chuckled. "Slow down a bit, Speed Racer. We fixed this recently, and I don't want to mess it up again."

"You don't want—"

"Don't think for me, Reagan, please. All I want is to not rush something that shouldn't be rushed." Asher was too mature for Reagan's taste at the moment. "It's hard to forget I'm not what you want."

"You can't believe that." Her actions would condemn her if Asher couldn't come to believe her now. She'd been so confused, and it wasn't until she was back in Asher's arms that she knew the truth of that. Coming home hadn't been only about Uncle Wade, but about getting back something she needed that was key to her happiness. "Will you be honest if I ask you something?"

"I'm not going to lie to you, honey. What purpose would it serve?" Asher wiped Reagan's tears and kept her hand at the side of her neck. "It's like you've worked yourself up into expecting everyone to act a certain way and getting upset when we don't follow that role."

"You're probably right, but that's not my question." She leaned into Asher's touch and remembered it all. "Why aren't you married with children?"

Asher laughed, and it was another one of those deep from the belly laughs. "Are you upset I'm not?"

"Asher, I hate that what I did to you might have something to do with the way your life is now." She felt Asher's hold on her tighten.

"If there's one thing I can tell you, it's that I'm happy with my life. Do I want a family? I do, but I'm not going to rush into it because it's the next logical step." Reagan closed her eyes when Asher kissed her temple. "All you should take away from today is that I don't hate you, and I'll be here if you need me."

"It's late," she said, not ready to let Asher go. It was strange after so many years of not seeing or talking to Asher that she'd be this pained by the thought of letting her walk out the door. "You can stay. I'll take the couch." She talked fast before Asher turned her down.

"I appreciate the offer, but I'll be okay."

She shook her head and held on to Asher. "Please, I'm going to be worried about you if you leave now."

"How about I go, and I'll call you when I get home?"

There was nothing she was going to say that'd convince Asher into staying. "If you go, then I'm coming with you." She stood and put her hands on her hips. "You're still hurt, and I don't want you driving alone."

"Okay, but I'm taking the couch, and I promise I'll be here in the morning." Asher started on the Velcro straps of the boot and freed her foot. The sock with sharks all over it was cute, and Reagan said so as she helped her off with the regular boot. "I'll be okay if you want to go to bed."

Reagan didn't say anything as Asher texted someone before

placing her phone and everything else in her pocket on the coffee table. What she wanted to do was unbuckle the alligator skin belt with the sterling buckle. Eventually she'd ask Asher when she'd developed such a sense of style.

"I'm not ready to let you go," Reagan said, sitting down and putting her hand on Asher's thigh. "And don't make fun of me by telling me I'm good at that."

"Only an asshole piles on, and I'd like to think I keep that side of myself down to a minimum." The softness of Asher's voice was familiar yet new in its pitch. She was familiar with a younger Asher, and that part of her was still there, only now wrapped in a more enticing package. "Go change and I'll tuck you in."

"You aren't going to run out the door, are you?" She made Asher laugh again.

"Maybe in a week I can pull that off. Tonight, you're stuck with me since you won't let me leave." Asher winked, and it made her stomach clench.

"I believe you. I'm the one who's good at running."

CHAPTER FOURTEEN

A sher stared at Reagan's back as she headed for her bedroom. She wondered if her broken ankle was somehow affecting her brain. The kissing had for sure shorted out her cognitive thinking ability to the point she didn't want to stop kissing Reagan, but protecting herself was her first priority in all situations. That she'd learned from the woman walking away from her. She also didn't have it in her to be as cruel as Reagan had been.

Thinking of it now, though, had Reagan really been cruel? She'd done what she'd needed to in order to survive. It had hurt to be left behind, but her dad had taught her that no two people processed pain the same. He'd been adamant that it wasn't their job to judge, but to try to love others even if it was hard. Loving Reagan even as a friend would be hard—she wasn't delusional enough to think otherwise. There was so much between them, too much, but the last week had opened her mind to the possibility—her heart would take more convincing.

She stood again and unbuckled her belt and took off her pants. The tight boxers she'd gone with would have to do for sleep. It was ridiculous to act as if it mattered, considering Reagan had her naked every afternoon for the massages she was fairly sure she didn't need to be completely naked for. Reagan had started covering her ass, which meant her ex was starting to sweat—which meant Asher wasn't alone.

The truth was that Reagan had gutted her, but it didn't make her less beautiful. It didn't make her less sexy, and for sure not any less desirable. Those massages had become something to sweat over, and now adding kissing to that equation meant resisting Reagan was going to be a route that not only led to hell but to failure. She knew enough about herself to know that. Everyone had a weakness, and hers wasn't exactly women, but this one particular woman.

"Do you really want to go home that bad?" Reagan asked, sitting next to her.

"I'm on *your* sofa in *my* underwear, so I'm not sure what you're talking about." She stared at Reagan and took in the navy-blue silk nightgown with the thin straps and perfect fit. One consistent thing about Reagan was she played to win. This was not what you wore to a friendly sleepover. "What are you talking about?"

"You were deep in thought and looking pained. I'll still go with you if you want to head home, but I don't want you to be miserable." Reagan scooted closer and took her hand. "Believe me, you've already given me so much. I'm grateful."

"You don't have to be grateful for something I want to do, and I took my pants off because I want to stay." She squeezed Reagan's fingers and let go. "Now go to bed, and I promise I'll be here in the morning demanding coffee."

"Are you sure you don't want to take the bed? My couch is shorter than the one in the cabin." Reagan came closer and laid her head on her shoulder. "Do you want a T-shirt? I doubt I have one that fits you, but it'll keep you from sleeping in that great shirt."

"You get me out of my clothes often enough, so don't worry about that either. Get some sleep, and we'll go to breakfast in the morning. The only good thing about my ankle is that early mornings of work are out until I can get on a horse."

"Speaking of, do you think Booker is pregnant yet?" Reagan seemed to be finding subjects to drag out their night.

"It's not for Albert's lack of trying. He's so taken with your horse he won't go near the other mare Helki talked me into buying." She leaned back and Reagan went with her. "Once I can start riding again, I doubt he'll be in the mood to leave the barn."

"Has Helki been with you long?" There was a tone to Reagan's question, and Asher had no idea what it was. "She seems nice."

"She is, and she's good with the animals. I'm glad she took me up on my offer to join us and expand the horse part of the equation. All the stuff I have going on will keep me busy once I retire. I wasn't planning on breeding horses, but they're making good use of the barn." She clenched her jaw to keep from yawning.

"You know how much I love horses, so I'm glad she's there."
Reagan moved closer and tapped the bottom of Asher's jaw. "Are you
tired?"

"I'm exhausted but glad to see you're following Harry's advice."

"What are you talking about?" Reagan placed her hand on her
chest and fanned her fingers over Asher's heart.

"You're wearing me out, but I'm starting to feel like myself
again." She couldn't fight the yawn this time, but she kissed the top of
Reagan's head when she finished. "I may not act like it, but I appreciate
it."

"You have plenty of credit with me."

That voice lulled her into closing her eyes, and she didn't resist
when Reagan eased her down the rest of the way. Reagan smelled
different, and she was too tired to figure out if it was her shampoo or a
new perfume. Whatever it was, it made her happy to be close enough to
smell it. That was the only thing on her mind when she closed her eyes
and fell asleep.

❖

She woke up at three in the morning and had to take a second
to remember where she was and who was lying half on her. A quick
inventory of the situation made her laugh at herself for her nonexistent
self-control. Her hand was on Reagan's ass, and that nightgown felt as
good under her fingertips as she'd thought it would when she first saw
it. The one thing she was sure of was Wade was going to give her shit
for this, and if she played with Reagan's emotions, he'd dish out a hell
of a lot more than that.

"Do you want to go to bed?" Reagan asked, her voice rough with
sleep. "It'll be more comfortable."

"Lead the way." Hell, it was no time to start pretending now. She
followed Reagan to the back of the condo and briefly wondered if Steph
had been at home here, sharing this space with Reagan. "Go back to
sleep, darlin'."

Reagan moved back into her arms and sighed before her breathing
evened out. She closed her eyes as well and relaxed her body, hoping to
go back to sleep. There were times when the restlessness caught up to
her and she roamed the house until Rickie arrived in the morning or she

saddled Albert and rode out to open the feed bins. In the early morning stillness now, though, she put her arms around Reagan and pretended she was eighteen again.

It felt like minutes later when she woke to Reagan running her fingers along her eyebrows. She hummed and closed her eyes again. Reagan must've taken it as an invitation and kissed her as she placed her hand against her neck. The kiss was soft, unhurried, and nice in a way that was like coming home after being away for way too long.

"Good morning," Reagan said as she moved to caress her jawline. "This is like a dream."

"Do you want to go out or stay in?" Right now, she'd be happy not getting out of this bed.

"I know you'd take me out again, but I'd love to make you breakfast, and then we can decide where we can go that you can wear an extremely wrinkled shirt," Reagan teased. "I think days like today are made to be a bit lazy."

"You think every morning is made to be lazy. Unless you've changed drastically, you've never loved early mornings." She didn't move much as Reagan lay completely on her. "If you're up for going out for a bit, I promise a day in. That might be the best for us."

"Where would you like to go?" Reagan framed her face before moving her finger to trace her lips. "I promise pancakes if you stay right here. I'll even feed them to you."

"I think you've taken the eight seconds I need to stay on a bull to heart. You're quick out of the chute after we haven't seen each other in forever." She was teasing, but Reagan was quick to move off her.

"I'm sorry, I thought…never mind. If you give me a couple of minutes, I'll be ready to go." Her sad expression twisted something in Asher that prompted her to reach for Reagan before she got too far away.

"I was kidding, honey. Nothing that's happened so far has been unwelcome," she said, pulling Reagan back to her. Reagan's face softened, and that lost appearance disappeared. "Just promise me one thing."

"What?" Reagan moaned when Asher started the next kiss, slipping her tongue between welcoming lips.

"If you only want casual, tell me now. It's not wrong, but I don't want another miscommunication between us to turn into another long stretch of years that leaves one or both of us hurting." Holding a sword over her own head was a risky move, but she needed to be sure before Reagan got so far in she wouldn't know how to cut her out of her heart a second time.

"I know you," Reagan said, "and because I do I know you won't trust easily. That means I'm not going to make big promises you might not believe, but I'm not going anywhere. My mistakes cost us both, and I'd like to think I'm smart enough to learn not to repeat them." Reagan kissed her while threading their fingers together. "I want you to give me a second chance."

"Are you sure? You said the last person you wanted to see when you got back was me."

"That's true, and if you want the real answer, I'll tell you why." Reagan put her head down but stayed on top.

"I thought you did. Are you saying that wasn't the truth?" Damn if this wasn't like being trampled by a bull that then backed up and kicked you in the head.

"What I told you was true, but I left out the most important part. You've become this success that makes people take notice of you, that part I knew from Uncle Wade. That and the interviews you've given, as well as the couple of magazine layouts." Reagan moved her hand to slip it into her shirt as far as it would go. "Seeing you, though—I knew from the second I packed my apartment and started driving here with Steph that if I saw you, I'd want this. I'd want it, and you'd refuse to give in because of what I'd done."

"No faith in me, huh?"

"It was more like I believed I deserved to be punished, but there was also the chance that I was too late. Living with that meant living without who I needed most."

"That's sappy, but I know what you mean. When Wade told me you were coming home, I expected married, or on the way to that." She laughed as she rubbed Reagan's back. "Old Uncle Wade for once wasn't full of advice, but I could tell he was itching to give me some. This time around I guess he thought we should figure it out for ourselves."

"Do you think we will?" Reagan asked with her lips pressed to Asher's neck.

"I'm in your bed in my underwear trying to forget what you're wearing, which I'm sure you picked on purpose," she said, slapping Reagan's ass. "We're well on our way."

"That's a good thing, right?"

"It is, so get dressed, pack a bag with dry clothes, and I'll get my pants back on. We need to make a few stops." She heard thunder outside and figured her plan was sound. It was better than thinking it was ill-advised. "Do you have patients today?"

"Harry assigned me to you until you're well enough to ride. Before I put you back on a bull, you're going to be strong enough to ride the worst hellion they think to put you on." Reagan sat up and straddled her waist. "And I promise that'll be way before you think."

"Good, go pack. I want to get moving before the deluge outside gets any worse."

A few minutes later, Reagan came out in shorts and a long-sleeved T-shirt with her hair in a ponytail. They didn't say much as they headed back to the ranch and an empty house. Rickie had school in the mornings, so Asher packed what she needed and called down to the barn for the hands to prepare the rest of what she wanted. Owen promised he'd get everything on her list and deliver it for her so she didn't have to worry about strapping it to the Gator. The four-wheeler was more fun, but the Gator had a roof, a windshield, and plastic doors that could be zipped up in bad weather.

"Put this on," she said, handing Reagan a slicker that went past her knees. The weather had turned nasty, and the hands were driving the stragglers who loved the open range to higher ground.

She handed Reagan a hat as she pulled hers low on her brow and pointed to the door. The rain was coming down in sheets, and the weather report said it would be with them for most of the day. Her hands had checked with Wade to make sure he and his crew were okay, which was one less thing for her to worry about.

Luckily she could find the cabin blindfolded, since the visibility was terrible. She went slow, not wanting to get stuck in a pothole, and zipped up the Gator before following Reagan inside. Owen had already been by and everything she'd asked for was on the counter, including the bag Reagan had packed.

"I should've thought this out better," she said, standing at the window. All she could make out was the porch. "We might be stuck for a few days."

"You say that like it's a bad thing," Reagan said as she went through the supplies and put some in the refrigerator. "I promise to keep you entertained—or is that what you're worried about?"

"Entertain away." She sat on the arm of the couch and unstrapped the boot before jamming her other foot into the bootjack. They'd left their slickers dripping by the door, so she took her socks off to put with those since they were soaked.

"Let me finish," Reagan said, already in her bare feet. If the nightgown the night before wasn't enough to make Asher nuts, the dark red toenail polish might tip her over the edge. "Want anything?" Reagan smiled when she caught her staring at her feet.

"I'm good for now. Do you want me to order you some books from the house? There's no TV, and the phone signal is for crap." She put her feet up and welcomed Reagan to her side with a short kiss.

"You're much more entertaining than that." Reagan sat on her knees so she could reach and kissed her again. This one was different in every way, and it caught Asher by surprise, so much so that her hands stayed at her sides.

"Are you trying to kill me?" Asher enjoyed the way Reagan held her face, the way she rubbed the tops of her cheeks and stared into her eyes. It made it impossible to hide anything from her, and she wasn't interested in that. The weather outside was nasty, but in here there was no place to hide.

"I'm trying to get you to see me," Reagan said as she moved to straddle her lap. "We'll go as fast or as slow as you want, but all I want is a chance."

"You're too deep inside me to ever forget." She put her hands on Reagan's hips and pulled her closer. "Is this what you really want?"

"Honey, please believe me." Reagan ran her fingers through her hair and pulled gently. "I've known you all my life, and more importantly, I know what you want out of life."

"Will it make me sound weak if I admit I'm scared?" Asher asked. It actually terrified her. "You ran from this life, and I can't leave it. I've built something here that I'm proud of, and it kills me that you didn't want it—won't want it still."

Reagan's tears started again at Asher's admission. "I'll keep saying it until you understand. I ran because I was afraid you'd die like Daddy, for something I didn't believe in. But the ranch, land, and the livestock are as much a part of me as they are you."

"Let's take it slow, then. Don't make promises you'll be unhappy keeping." She wiped Reagan's cheeks with her fingers, and her own eyes watered. "It's not wrong to want something that's not this."

"I rode with Uncle Wade a few weeks ago, and I was reminded of where I belong. He doesn't force anything on me, but I know he wants me to take some responsibility for Moon Touch." Reagan sighed and closed her eyes for a moment as if trying to gather herself. "I can't do that if you hate me. I can't be this close and know you picked someone else."

"I haven't, and I don't hate you. It's going to take a conversation and a visit to explain some things to Jacqueline, but I'm not lying when I say it wasn't serious." Radio silence from Jacqueline most likely meant she wouldn't need much persuasion to change their arrangement, but she hadn't been raised to be an asshole.

"Do you promise?" Reagan asked.

Asher wasn't sure what the question meant. "Do I promise what?"

"You'll be happy trying?" Reagan cried a little harder when she nodded. "Then I promise you won't be sorry."

Asher sat up and kissed Reagan like she hadn't in years, and it felt good…familiar. Reagan's legs tightened around her as much as they could in the position they were in. It was raging outside, but here on Asher's lap was the answer to questions she'd put to the back of her mind for too long. The kiss made Reagan slump against her, so Asher lay back and kept Reagan where she was.

"Close your eyes and listen to the rain," she said softly. She didn't want to go fast but resisting the urge to go any farther was harder than getting Albert to do algebra. "I'm glad you're here."

CHAPTER FIFTEEN

The loud thunderbolt startled Reagan awake, and she turned her head a little and watched Asher sleep. Their legs were tangled together, and she thought of all the other times she'd woken up with Asher. When she laughed, it woke Asher and she cleared her throat before making eye contact with her.

"What's funny? Am I drooling?"

"I was remembering a rainy day in the barn when you talked me up into the loft and got me out of my shirt." She laughed louder when Asher pinched her side.

"Your memory is faulty, Ms. Wilson." Reagan kept laughing as they wrestled on the couch, stopping when Asher flipped her over and threaded their fingers together over her head. "I remember being dragged up there and you willingly handing over your shirt. That your father caught us and threatened me with an ass full of pellets for messing with his little girl is a fact you always leave out of that story."

"It was the first bra I bought that I thought was sexy, and I wanted to share it with you. Who knew Daddy could be so light-footed." She lifted herself up and kissed Asher. "I miss that loft."

"Those plain white bras were plenty sexy," Asher said, lowering her head and kissing her again. "I didn't have a lot to compare them to at fifteen, but I knew enough to realize that."

"You were always a generous grader." She pulled her hand free and touched Asher's face, glad she had the freedom to do so. It was wonderful that Asher didn't seem to mind, and her silky dark hair was still as soft and thick as she remembered. "Do you want me to make lunch?"

"I'm not hungry right this minute." Asher began to move off, but

Reagan threaded her fingers behind her neck to keep her in place. "But if you are, I can eat."

"How about we reminisce?" She encouraged Asher back into a sitting position so she could straddle her again. It was nice to see how riveted Asher's gaze was when she began to take her shirt off. "I remember white being your favorite color."

That first set of matching panties and bra was still one of her favorite memories. No one had looked at her that way since. Asher had a way of making a woman feel like she was the center of her world, that she craved you. That kind of attention had spoiled her for the short list of lovers who followed. And when they were apart, thinking of Asher with someone else had driven her mad. She knew Asher was a memorable lover, and she'd seen that in Jacqueline Blanchard's face when she greeted Asher that first night.

She'd picked the bra she'd worn tonight a month ago with Asher in mind. Most people wouldn't pick white when it came to sexy lingerie, but it was hard to argue when those blown-out pupils were right in front of her. The massages had worn Asher down, but the silk and lace bra got her attention.

"Has that changed?" she asked as she put her finger on the center of Asher's forehead.

"What?" Asher blinked slowly and inhaled deeply.

"White," she said, starting another kiss. "Still your favorite color?"

"If it wasn't, you moved it up the list." Asher ran her hands up her back and smiled. "You can't claim you didn't plan this."

She laughed and shook her head. "Would I sound conniving if I did?"

"You say that like it's a bad thing." Asher repeated her words and laughed along with her.

"You're good at cows, honey, but sometimes you need a hint when it comes to other things." Asher laughed again. "I bought this for you." She lifted Asher's hand and placed it on her right breast. "Feel free to unwrap it."

"I thought we decided on slow," Asher said but her hands stopped at the clasp. It seemed like before she could think too long about what she was doing, Asher undid it and lowered the straps.

"It's been too long," Reagan said, dropping the bra behind her. "Make me feel...make me yours."

"Are you sure?" Asher asked as she stood, holding her up. Asher's foot briefly crossed Reagan's mind, but Asher was solid, strong, and determined.

"Please, honey." Asher put her down next to the bed. It didn't take long for her shorts to drop to her feet, and she could start on Asher's belt buckle.

She hadn't been a nun since they'd separated, but no one made her this ravenous. These belt buckles were earned, and Asher wore hers with apparent pride. Being allowed to touch it, undo it, and popping the buttons on Asher's jeans made her feel special, powerful, and like the woman Asher wanted to be with. All of that turned her on, and she yanked Asher's pants down, desperate to get naked.

She left on those tight boxers that went almost to Asher's knees, enjoying how long they made Asher's legs look. Asher watched as she shimmied her panties down and kicked them away before lying in the middle of the bed. She bent her knees and spread her legs. It made her feel feminine, and she'd feel even more so as soon as Asher pinned her down with her weight. That position wasn't something she'd allowed with anyone else, but it was different with Asher because she'd never try to dominate her.

"Please, baby," she said, holding her arms out. Asher gave her what she wanted and took her place between her legs. All that skin contact made her moan, just from that simple pleasure. She opened her mouth when Asher kissed her and pressed her tongue inside. The boxers rubbed against her, and she slipped her hands under the waistband and squeezed Asher's ass. It was a silent way of saying *I want you.*

"Tell me if you want to stop," Asher said respectfully.

"Not going to happen." She pressed Asher's head to her breast when she sucked in her nipple, making it harden against her tongue. Her hips pumped up into Asher as she tried to find some relief. "I know we said slow, but can we renegotiate?"

Asher moved her lips to the side of her neck and her hand between them. "Are you wet?"

"Yes," she said before moaning when Asher's fingers landed on her clit. "All for you."

Asher gave her what she wanted but at her own pace. She lifted her hips and glanced down at where her hand was, prompting Reagan to glance down as well. "Fuck," Asher said, squeezing her clit between her fingers. The way Asher said the word made her lift her hips. It sounded like Asher wanted her as much as she wanted Asher.

"Please, baby, go inside. I need you to fill me up." She lifted her hips and pulled the hair at the back of Asher's head.

The begging couldn't be resisted, and Asher kissed her again as she slid her fingers in. It sounded wet and so sexy. Asher moaned and didn't move.

"So long," Asher said, and the words felt pained. She pulled almost all the way out and went back in. "So fucking long."

"It's where you belong, honey. Now please give me what I want." She moved her hands to Asher's back and scraped her nails from her shoulders down to her ass. "Oh Jesus."

Asher kept her movements slow and steady, and it was driving her wild. Her desire was ratcheted up to the point she wanted to scream—it was so good but not enough. The combination of Asher's stroke, her breathing in her ear, and her thumb on her clit driving her close to the edge, but she needed more. Her entire body was on overload, and if she didn't come, something was going to explode.

"Baby, please…I need…need to come." Time hadn't changed how generous Asher was with her, especially in bed. Her strokes sped up, and they hit that one spot that drove her to an intense orgasm sooner than she wanted. "Yes, oh my fucking God, yes."

Her body tightened and arched off the bed as she soared over the cliff Asher had let her climb before she fell back like her bones had melted into the mattress. She held Asher in place, wanting her weight on her and her kisses against her neck. Now she felt even more foolish for having taken so long to come home because home wasn't at the ranch or in the city, but right here with Asher.

"You okay?" Asher rolled to her side but not too far away.

That question had so many answers through the years, but right now it had only one answer. "I wasn't for so long," she said, throwing her leg over Asher.

"How about now?" Asher maneuvered them under the covers and held her.

The muscle Asher carried now was different than a decade ago, but it was a good change as she ran her fingertips along her bicep. "Now I'm sorry." She had to hang on when Asher began to move away. "No, honey. I'm not sorry we made love—I'm sorry I left you alone to grieve Daddy. You loved him as much as I did, and you had to go through that without me. That, and that I hurt you. You letting me back in makes me very lucky."

"The sight of you surprised me," Asher said as the thunder started again, making Reagan shiver.

"In a good or bad way?" There was a lesson here about just saying she was okay. Honest Asher wasn't always what she wanted to hear, especially right this second when she wanted to enjoy the bliss she was in.

"It surprised me because I didn't much care for you being held by someone else. I lied to everyone, telling them I didn't care, but I could've punched Steph, no problem."

She slid more completely onto Asher and rested her chin on her chest. "Are you saying that to be nice?"

"Telling the truth is being nice?" Asher rolled her over and held her hands above her head. "Just take my word on it, and stop apologizing. Let's enjoy the rain and each other."

"Tell me it's not just for today," she said, opening her legs again. Asher could touch her as much as she wanted, but this couldn't be one-sided. "Tell me I can do this past today." She put her hand between Asher's legs and pressed up until she had her hard clit between her fingers. "Tell me I can put my mouth right here."

"Fuck me," Asher said, sounding winded. "I can't think when you do that."

"I don't want you to think, I want you to answer my question." She flipped Asher easier than she expected to, never moving her hand. "Answer me."

"Yes, anything you want." Asher sounded as if she was having trouble forming words. "This isn't a one-time thing."

She moved down Asher's body and knelt between her legs. Everything they'd done had turned Asher on, and she didn't want to make her wait another minute. The groan Asher let out when she lowered her mouth made her smile. She sucked wanting to wring every bit of want out of Asher, the end coming way too soon.

"Did your fuse get a lot shorter?" she teased as she kissed Asher's sex before moving back up.

That great laugh came again, and she sighed when Asher put her arms around her. "After all those massages, that nightgown, and those panties, you should be happy you made it in the cabin before I jumped you."

"I didn't think you were paying attention, and it was even more difficult to stay professional when you stripped every day for your massage." She moved to Asher's side and held her in place with her arm and leg. "This is a great place."

"I love the quiet, and it was the best design I could think of when our place burned down." Asher rolled to face her. "When lightning hit it, I thought it might be a sign to let you go. What I should've been doing was flying to Seattle to make sure that was the right move for you."

"I missed everything about you."

Asher tapped the tip of her nose and shook her head. "I'm sure not *everything* about me. Do you think you'll survive the events that lead up to the championship?"

"Honey, I might close my eyes when you're on those damn things, but I'm not going anywhere." She rose high enough to reach Asher's lips. "Just promise you'll wait until you're ready."

"I have a month, and then I need to start practicing. Do you think that's doable?"

If this was a test, she wasn't going to fail. "It's why I upped your regime, with Harry's okay. I wasn't kidding that I want you strong enough to withstand the strain of riding before you head into the arena."

"If you're serious, then I have one request," Asher said, sliding her hands to Reagan's ass.

She smiled down at Asher and raised an eyebrow. "Is it to come here as much as possible?"

"I was thinking more about those massages," Asher said, initiating the next kiss.

"Those won't stop even because of this," she said to put her at ease.

"I know that, but you should consider doing them naked," Asher said, and Reagan had to laugh this time.

One of the many things she'd missed about Asher was how much she made her laugh. She had a talent for instilling joy, and she'd been lacking that for a very long time. "You have a deal."

❖

Asher watched from the bed as Reagan cooked the steaks the hands had delivered, having to forgo the barbecue pit because of the rain. She'd been ordered to stay in bed and rest her foot, and she didn't mind, considering the view. Reagan was dressed in her T-shirt and nothing else, and she was concentrating on getting the sear right on the two rib eyes she had in the cast iron skillet. After they'd gotten reacquainted way more than she had planned, they'd taken a nap. The rain on the metal roof she'd put on this place was better than any sleeping pill.

"Are you sure you don't need any help?" All this forced rest was starting to bend her mind. Her head kept trying to convince the rest of her that everything was fine and ready for action. If she tried that, though, she figured Reagan would take her out.

"You can get up when it's done. We're going to have a picnic in front of the fireplace and pretend it's winter," Reagan said, pointing a cooking fork at her. "I'm interested in more sweating before the day is out but not because we light a fire."

"Do I have to get dressed?" She stood and stretched, pointing to the stove when Reagan openly stared.

"As soon as I'm in no danger of catching splatter, I'm taking this off"—she indicated the T-shirt—"and feeding you steak and potatoes. It'll give you a chance to admire my breasts." Reagan winked at her and went back to the steaks.

Reagan plated everything on one large dish, cut the meat into bite-sized pieces, and did what she promised. They ate and laughed much more easily than they had, even at the beginning of the day. It was easy to fall back into what they both knew, at least it was for Asher. All the warning bells to be careful, to proceed with caution, and to not be so trusting flew from her head as Reagan straddled her and fed her until the platter was empty.

The rain finally slacked off in the late afternoon, but the sky stayed dark and overcast. They went out and sat on the porch wrapped in the bedsheet and watched the cows graze in the distance. There were no words to describe the peace of stillness, and of having Reagan pressed against her front. Asher had shared this with Jacqueline, but this was different. The history between her and Reagan was something she'd always wanted to build on, and she wanted to believe that was possible.

"You know, when we first started sleeping together"—Reagan spoke softly as she ran her fingers along the back of Asher's hand—"I thought you were the best thing I'd ever laid eyes on, and that's even more true now. It's too early to make big proclamations, but God, I've missed you." Reagan turned in her arms and kissed her neck. "I never dreamed I could be here again."

"How about we take it a day at a time and concentrate on getting to know each other again. Only this time we'll do it from a different frame of mind." She ran her fingers through Reagan's hair and loved the feel of it.

"What do you mean?"

She took Reagan's hand before answering and kissed the tips of her fingers. "We've been together for days and days, but we don't know anything about each other except the superficial. Let's find out who we are again and move on from there. Hell, you might not like me very much."

"Do you honestly think that could happen?" Reagan pushed up a little and stared into her eyes. "Do you think you might not like me very much?"

"Not what I said, but after I got over the urge to fire a few warning shots every time you drove up, I realized I like you a lot." She didn't glance away, wanting Reagan to know she wasn't trying to avoid the conversation. "I might be jumping the gun, so let me ask you one thing. Are you only interested in this"—she waved down their naked bodies—"or do you want something more?"

"Will I freak you out if I'm honest?" Reagan held her by the jaw as if wanting her full attention.

"All I'm asking is for you to be honest." She made a mental note not to appear freaked no matter what Reagan said. When she asked for honesty, she sometimes got it in spades, and it wasn't always what she wanted to hear.

"I didn't come back with any kind of plan. About six months ago I couldn't take it anymore, and I decided to come home. The emptiness in my life was painful, and it was like I was always alone." Reagan pressed her fingers to Asher's lips to keep her quiet. "You can call me out on whatever you want, but let me finish. I'm not here because I'm settling—that's the last thing I'm doing."

"Like I said, you don't need an excuse to be here," Asher said. "This is home, and you never lose that." She pulled Reagan closer and watched the rain falling in the distance. From the cloud cover, it looked like they were in for another night of bad weather. "We're not following a script here, so stop worrying I'm looking for an excuse to toss you out."

"You're amazing," Reagan said before she kissed her like she wanted it to last all afternoon. "Do you know that?"

"I'm glad you think so, and I want you to remember that when I'm getting on your nerves." That made Reagan laugh, which felt like an accomplishment. "How about a shower and we pack up? If we don't want to spend another night out here, we need to get going."

"Do you need to be somewhere?" Reagan stood and held her hand out. "Let's go inside and shower, and then we can plan what we're eating tonight. The earlier we do that, the earlier we can go to bed."

They got ready for bed after a light dinner Reagan made and made love again. They'd slowed down and found a bit of that old magic, and she liked how Reagan stayed close once they'd tired themselves out. Asher lay on her back so Reagan would be comfortable pressed against her and watched her sleep.

She'd had more orgasms in the last day than she'd had in months, and she smiled at how quickly life changed. It made her think of her father and how he always encouraged her to try since it was the only way to win. Right at this moment she couldn't talk herself into a downside to a relationship with Reagan.

"You're thinking," Reagan said, throwing her leg over hers. "Is that a good thing?"

"I was thinking about you." She was too comfortable to move, so she held Reagan in place. "This has been a good day."

"You're still scared, aren't you? Scared that I'm going to flake out on you again." Reagan held her and sighed.

"I'm not, really. There's no way to know what the future holds, but I'm not going to cut you out because I can't guarantee the outcome." She kissed Reagan as she pressed their foreheads together. "I'll be here, and I'm not changing my mind."

"You won't be sorry."

The next morning Reagan helped her stretch and guided her through some exercises to improve the range of motion in her foot. She was at a point where the movements didn't cause a tremendous amount of pain. Reagan was so careful, and she closed her eyes and waited for her to finish. All that was left was coffee, and then they had to head back to the house, which at the moment wasn't something she was looking forward to.

It was a long time since she'd had Reagan all to herself, and she wasn't ready to let the real world back in. The downpour had slowed down to a drizzle, and another day of this would be more than welcome. Reagan brought her daydreaming to an end when she tickled the bottom of her foot.

"Are you overthinking again?" Reagan moved from the foot of the bed to lie on her.

"I'm thinking I don't want to leave, but the damn cows don't deliver groceries. How about we go back to the house and spend some time in the gym—then I'll take you out to eat?"

"Is Rickie working all day?" Reagan asked as she moved her hand right under the top of her boxers. "If she wants the day and night off, my plan is to put you through your paces in the gym, followed by a naked massage so I can put you through your paces in the bedroom. After that I'll cook again."

"Let me take you out, babe. You've cooked plenty." The muted light in the room was enough for her to see the slope of Reagan's butt. This had always been one of her favorite views in the world. "If we go somewhere casual, I'll spend the night in town with you, and we can head back here in the morning. Or I can go into the clinic if you want."

"I like taking care of you, so I'm cooking. Now that I know you're not going to kill me, I'd like to walk around your place." Reagan didn't make a move to get out of bed. "If you bring me into town, I can pick up some clothes, and I'll stay so we can work longer."

Asher rolled her over so she could study every part of her. "Right this second I'll give you whatever you want." She put her hand between Reagan's legs and cursed in a soft voice. It didn't take much buildup for Reagan to scream and pull her down so all her weight was on Reagan.

"You've gotten much better, and that doesn't seem possible since you were excellent in high school." Reagan opened her legs wider and ran her hands up and down Asher's back.

"You're good for my ego," she said, pushing her hips down. "You're also driving me over the edge."

"I'd get used to that," Reagan said, putting her index and middle fingers between Asher's legs. "God, this is heaven."

"What?" Getting that word out while pumping her hips was harder than eight seconds on a bull. The sensation of Reagan under her and her lips against Asher's neck was driving her to orgasm faster, and her mind cleared. It was like coming out of the chute—everything flew from her mind. Now it was only Reagan she could sense. How she touched her, loved her, and brought her to the brink.

"I want to keep you this way, so you never come to your senses," Reagan said before they kissed passionately.

The declaration was all it took for her to jump off the precipice Reagan had led her to without fear. She wanted this…Reagan and everything she entailed. "Fuck," she cried out as she tensed, "fuck," this time much more softly as she slumped into Reagan. She tried to roll off, but Reagan crossed her feet at the small of her back and held her in place.

"I like this," Reagan said, pressing her lips to her temple. "It's not great to think about all the people we've been with since I left, but I never shared this with anyone else."

"What?" She drew herself up enough to see Reagan's face. The answer seemed important enough to need to see her expression. "You can tell me."

"With people like Steph and a few others, it was all about the release. To not feel so lonely, and not be so alone." Reagan combed Asher's hair back and traced around her ears with her finger. "It was always on my terms, though. I didn't want this, to be pinned down, touched, and devoured by anyone else."

"It's like coming home," Asher said, understanding what Reagan didn't say.

"Yes, exactly. You are imprinted in here," Reagan said, putting her hand over her heart. "We'll go as slow as it takes to convince you, but my heart knows you, Asher."

"We'll be okay, I promise." The dilemma now was whether to believe in salvation or total destruction. If Reagan got in as deep as she had before, then ran, the pain wouldn't be so easily conquered this time. It would be like being bashed against rocks by relentless waves that would leave her more battered than any bull ever could.

"We will, because I promise too," Reagan said as she framed her face with her hands. It was as if she could see the fear in Asher's eyes and wanted to reassure her.

Faith, Asher thought, was easier for some than others. A strong belief in something intangible and ethereal took courage. You had to believe no matter your doubts, and this was what Reagan was asking her to do—only this time, there was history to put cracks in that faith. Reagan was asking her to stand on the cliff that overlooked the waves and jagged rocks and trust her to keep her from falling, trust her to keep her and her heart safe. She was sitting at the table and gambling all she held dear.

"We'll have to have faith, then."

CHAPTER SIXTEEN

Two weeks of therapy and taking care of Asher in every way she could think of—from cooking dinner, to riding the ranch with her—was making a difference. The dairy barn was starting to take shape, and Asher was out of the boot for most of the day, so she was starting to take shape as well. Their appointment with Harry that morning would dictate their next step.

"Do you want your jogging shoes?" Reagan asked, holding them up as Asher was about to slide her feet into a pair of boots.

"Do you want me to wear my jogging shoes?" Asher laughed and put her boots aside.

"I don't want to put any strain on your foot until I absolutely have to." She sat next to Asher and took her hand. "Boots can wait for another week."

"I have a month to get in shape, darlin'. Putting strain on the foot needs to start somewhere. If it can't hold up, it can't hold up, but I want to at least try."

"Honey, you're going to do a lot more than try. I promised you at the beginning that I'd get you back on a bull, and I'm keeping that promise." She pulled Asher's head down and kissed her. "Right now I need you to put these on. If Harry approves your boot wearing, I'll polish them myself."

"Come on, smart-ass. If we leave early for the appointment, we might be out early enough to grab lunch." Asher stood and put her wallet, phone, and keys in her pockets.

"Are you getting tired of my cooking?" She smiled, jealous of Asher's shorts and linen shirt. Harry was her boss, so she had to look a bit more professional than that. "And Uncle Wade invited us to lunch at the ranch when we get back. I think he and Frida want to go on a fishing expedition since he hasn't seen either of us lately."

"If Frida's making fajitas, it's worth the interrogation." Asher held her hand out, but Reagan flattened hers on Asher's chest before they left the main bedroom.

"Is it going to bother you if he knows?" They'd been in a bubble where it'd been only the two of them, and at times Rickie.

"I'm not keeping you a secret, so I don't care who knows how close we've become." Asher had a way of sounding confident that everything and everyone would simply fall in line. "Unless you have a problem, I want to tell him and Frida if we go over there today. Do you think he's going to have a problem with it?"

"I don't, and he's going to be thrilled." Asher kissed her as if they had all the time in the world. "I'm sure he'll give me a talking-to, as he likes to put it, but I think that's a good thing. You need people who love you in your corner."

"Are you in my corner?" She'd been too afraid to ask if Asher had reached out to Jacqueline because it didn't seem like that was a closed story. "I keep waiting for the other shoe to drop and I can't help it."

Asher led her to the chairs next to the window that overlooked the back pastures. "Are you not sure anymore?"

"No," she said emphatically. "I'm sure, and I know what's coming. The real world hasn't touched us in days, and I'm scared what's going to happen once it comes crashing in."

"Tell me what you're afraid of. I can't help you unless you tell me." Asher held her hand and seemed open and earnest. "I've felt you wrestling with something every night, but I haven't pushed."

"Asher, I—" She didn't know how to finish in a way that didn't make her sound unhinged or bitchy.

"When you say you're worried about the real world," Asher said, "does that mean Steph and Jacqueline?" It was like she had a window on her forehead that allowed Asher to read her thoughts.

"Does that make me a fool for worrying?" There was no reason to deny it now.

"Think about where you are, and why. I want you here, and only you here." Asher stood and put her arms around her. "I haven't reached out to Jacqueline because I've been too wrapped up in, well, you. The way you should look at it is she hasn't reached out to me either."

"We're going to be late," she said, not ready to hear that Asher might still have feelings for someone else.

"You know me, baby. I'm not lying about what I want. If you want, when we get back, I'll give her a call. She should know I've found someone that means everything to me."

She inhaled, enjoying Asher's cologne. "You have a way with words, cowpoke, and you can take your time with your friend. All she needs to face is there will be no more benefits."

"Maybe we can all have dinner and introduce Steph to Jacqueline. I know you said you and Steph weren't together, but the way she looked at you made me think she'd missed that headline in the paper." Asher smiled when she moved her hands from her hips to her backside. "We should have dinner with Steph again no matter what."

"Why?" she asked as Asher picked her up and let her feet dangle off the ground.

"I wasn't in the best mood that last time, and I owe her some answers about the rodeo. She did sound like she was a true fan, but she needs to know you're off-limits." Asher kissed her again before putting her down and taking her hand. "Let's not be late."

Harry didn't keep them waiting and didn't show any surprise when Reagan followed her in and sat next to the exam table. She did, though, hike an eyebrow at Reagan—she guessed it was for holding Asher's hand when they stepped in. But dread started to set in with the knowledge their little routine was about to include bull riding. There was no way Reagan would have given Asher the go-ahead without Harry's consultation, but her lover was healed and ready.

"You should thank your brilliant doctor and therapist," Harry said as she manipulated Asher's foot in a variety of different ways. "Have you been weaning her off the boot?" Harry glanced Reagan's way, and she nodded.

"We're up to four miles without any pain. Only walking, though. I wanted to wait for clearance before she starts jogging." She couldn't help but let her eyes go to Asher. "No pain, and she's making it through the strength-building exercises well."

"You two can ask me, you know," Asher said and winked at her. "Reagan's been great. The Buffalo event is in five weeks."

The announcement was like a bomb exploding in Reagan's head, the shrapnel hitting her heart full force. She kept a smile on her face, but she could see that Asher wasn't buying it. "You're ready now," Reagan said, "and if you have any doubts, climb back on. The foot will hold. I did everything to make sure it does."

"Harry, could you give us a few minutes?" Asher asked.

"She's right, and you're done with me unless you have a problem during a practice round. Even a twinge and you call me, okay?" Harry shook hands with them both before closing the door behind her.

"Are you having second thoughts?" Asher asked, swinging her legs off the side of the table. "It's okay to say it, and it's okay to wait until I'm done. I realize it's a gamble to let you go for the next four months since I doubt I'd get you back, but I have to finish."

"No more letting go. Believe me, it was a hard mistake to walk back. But don't ask or expect me not to be worried." She stood between Asher's legs and put her hands on her shoulders and squeezed. "It's way too early, but I love you. I'm wildly in love with you, and imagining you hurt kills something in me. I can't stand it."

"How about we concentrate on the wildly in love part?" Asher held her as if she was the most precious thing she'd ever had in her arms. "That's mutual, by the way. I love you, Reagan Wilson. I have since I was twelve and didn't know shit about anything except that I was in love with you. We don't have to figure out the logistics of everything now, but I want a life with you and a bunch of cows and horses."

"Oh my God, really?" Her first thought was that her father was brainwashing Asher from the Great Beyond, as he always called it. Or maybe he really had heard all those wishes she'd thrown off her balcony and moved the heavens to make them a reality. Whatever it was, she was truly happy for the first time in years. She hadn't been totally miserable, but this kind of joy was hard to find once in any lifetime, much less twice.

"You weren't ever far from my thoughts, honey. Even when my head wanted to erase your existence, my heart wouldn't allow it."

The sound that escaped Reagan was a laugh combined with a sob, and Asher simply held her. She found a safe refuge from her emotions in Asher's arms with her face pressed against her shoulder. It was as if a door opened to the place she'd wanted to get back to after being locked away for years leaving her in a frozen tundra of her own making. It wasn't a shock that Asher was this forgiving—she'd always been considerate of her feelings—but this was a huge gift.

"Are you crying because you're happy, or because you're trying to figure out a way to lock me up for the next four months or so?" Asher asked softly, not letting her go. The joke made her laugh again, but her tears still flowed.

"You can't imagine how many times I thought of you saying that to me again," she said, holding on to Asher to keep herself tethered to the moment. "I didn't think it would ever happen because of my stupidity."

"Stop beating yourself up, and let's go home. I believe you said something about lunch with the family."

They drove to Moon Touch after she'd collected more clothes from her place, and she kept her eyes on Asher the whole way back. Asher's appearance had changed over their years apart—smile lines at the sides of her eyes, the muscle that made her appear solid and strong, and the smattering of white hair along her temples like her father Dustin's, who'd started to gray at an early age. She'd also retained so much of what Reagan remembered, which was mostly her smile. Asher smiled like she truly meant it.

"Do you remember the day in school when you told me—" She stopped, wanting the power to turn back time two minutes at a time. "Never mind."

"The first time I told you I loved you?" Asher reached across the console and took her hand. "I didn't have much romantic timing back then. English class wasn't the best place to tell you that when I had about a thousand places around here to let you know."

"We were reading George Bernard Shaw's *Pygmalion*, so I thought it was a perfect time." Her hand appeared so much smaller in Asher's, but they fit. "I'm sure the moral of the play wasn't that anyone could fall in love with someone who was their opposite, but I thought it was that there's a perfect match for everyone."

"I remember you saying that, and I thought about it after you left. Why do you ask now?" Asher was smart. There was no escape.

"It's a nice thing to remember. That's all, so forgive me if you thought it was something else."

They turned into Moon Touch, where the house was closer to the road than Asher's place. Before she could exhale and flee the SUV, Asher pulled over. The black fence was new across this section, a reminder that what was once one entity was now two, with one thriving and growing and the other slowly winding down.

"Was the fence your idea or Uncle Wade's?" she asked, her attention outside.

"When I decided to go home for good, I did it for me, that's true. I also did it for Uncle Wade. It was a break from having to sweat any visit you made." Asher rubbed her face as if it was tough getting the words out. "He didn't deserve for your time together to be awkward and distant because I was in the middle of that."

"He talked about you more than you know. Sometimes I don't think he knows he's doing it, but he wanted me to know what you're up to, and how you were." Wade had also tried to steer her back to Asher and find what she'd thrown away. "He and Daddy thought you coming to live with us was a story they'd tell our children because of how it'd turn out."

"We watched the game you worked the sidelines on when you were in Seattle. He couldn't stop talking about how proud of you he was, and how you'd built this wonderful life."

"It wasn't wonderful, honey. There were parts of it I enjoyed, like that game, but I didn't belong there." She was upset by the sad expression on Asher's face. "I'm sorry I brought it up."

"It's our new policy of talking, so don't sweat it." Asher put the truck in park so they weren't moving. "Do you remember the rest of what you said about Shaw's play?" Reagan nodded, not able to speak. "Once you find that perfect match, you figure out you have only one."

"Losing that person…isn't fatal, but you find that no one can be a total replacement," she said as her tears embarrassingly started again. "God, you must be tired of all this crying. I promise I'm not."

"No need to cry—you were right. If you'd been wrong, both of us wouldn't still be single." The gentle way Asher wiped her face righted something vital in her. Going through life a bit off-balance wasn't something she'd recommend to anyone.

"You're a nice person, and I missed that." Asher waited until she could get her emotions under control so as not to worry Uncle Wade. "Don't take any shit, honey," she said as they got out and noticed Wade and Frida on the porch.

"Did you get lost on the way over here?" Frida asked, her hand on Wade's knee.

Reagan wasn't sure how old Frida was, but she was still a beautiful woman who knew her place in the world. That came from strength, and the confidence she often said was taught to her by her Cherokee family. If there was one certainty in the world, it was you always knew where you stood with Frida. That was a trait she'd instilled in her daughter—Rickie wasn't one to hold her tongue.

"The doctor took longer than we thought," Asher said, making Frida smile right away. There were clearly favorites here, and Asher was at the top of the list.

"Everything okay?" Wade asked.

"Let's go talk about it," Asher said, glancing at her before walking away with him. They'd discuss later what a great idea it was to leave her alone with Frida and her bluntness.

"Why've you been crying?" Frida asked right out of the intrusive gate. "And don't lie and tell me you haven't been. I've got eyes." She went through the door Frida opened and took some deep breaths to fortify herself for the talk she couldn't avoid.

"Asher and I have been working through some things, and I got emotional." If this was what she was getting, then God knew what Uncle Wade was telling Asher. That's all she needed after becoming a weepy mess every time she talked to Asher.

"So is sex now called *working through things*?"

Of course Frida knew. When she was a kid she often thought Frida could read her mind. "You could've started anywhere but there," she said, shaking her head. "I don't want to jinx it."

"Jinx it? It's Asher, baby. That kid is wired to do the right thing." Frida poured her a lemonade and pointed to a chair at the table. "Don't take this the wrong way, but are you serious?"

"How can I not take that the wrong way? No matter what you and Uncle Wade think, Asher's not perfect." She was actually perfect for Reagan, but her family needed to show some support. "She rides bulls, for the love of insanity."

"She does, and if you start messing with her heart, it's going to mess with her head. Being in a small space with a big animal that is intent on killing her means you might not get another chance to work through anything." Frida sat next to her and took her hand. "You're right, though, Asher's not perfect. Never has been and the things that aren't have only become entrenched with time."

"You and I both know she's your favorite, so don't hold back on me now." She made Frida laugh and a load of bricks slid off her shoulders.

"For years your uncle has been after me to marry him. I've told him for that same amount of time that all we're missing is a paper from the state, but I've been taking care of him and this place for most of my life. I wouldn't have done that if I didn't feel married." Frida covered her hand with hers and took a deep breath. "Wade is someone easy to love. He cares for me and my child, even though Rickie should've been a Wilson, but I messed up. She's been a joy but a mistake I made twenty-four years ago."

"Uncle Wade loves Rickie, and he loves you." She often wondered about what had happened since she'd realized from the time she knew what love was that her uncle loved Frida. Why had Frida cheated? Or were they not together then?

"I can see your wheels turning like a hamster in a small cage. Wade and I became a couple when Rickie was eight. Her father ran and never looked back." The story wasn't easy to hear, but one glance at Frida's expression, and she realized it was even harder to tell.

"I hate to ask, but were you and Wade together back then?"

"I knew how he felt about me, but no. It took me a while to convince him I wasn't settling because I had a child when I finally said yes."

She nodded and fell back in her chair. "Thank you for trusting me enough to tell me. I'm not sure why you did, but it's nice to have the truth."

"I told you because we have a lot in common. You screwed up and left. Granted, you didn't come home with a kid, but it's going to take some time before Asher won't flinch every time you get in the car." Frida poured herself some water and it was like she was searching for something to do. "When I came back, it was for two reasons. The most important was for Wade, and also because this is my home."

"I came back for the same reasons, and I'm not going to mess with her, so don't think that." Reagan stood and stared out at the barn. "He's not in there shoving sharp sticks under her fingernails, is he?"

"Come back here and wait them out. I doubt Asher will let anyone change her mind." Frida seemed more relaxed after sharing her story and knocked on the table to get her moving.

"Let's hope not."

"Sweetheart, remember always that they're nothing like us. They think differently, see and live life differently, and they love differently." The declaration got Reagan back to the table.

"What do you mean?" She had to agree Asher and her family were a breed apart from everyone else.

"Where others would let betrayal rule their heads, I found Wade and your father more forgiving. It's like they understood that life is made up of choices that shouldn't define you until the grave." Frida choked up and stopped for a moment. "They know because they've made mistakes, and not having a forgiving nature damns you to an existence of wanting what you want but keeping it at arm's length."

"Do you think Asher can be that forgiving?" She needed to know because in the last few weeks *she* knew with absolute certainty that Asher was who she wanted.

Frida nodded. "Before I answer that, think of your father and ask yourself one question. Why do you think Silas Wilson poured so much into who Asher is? He taught her not only to be forgiving, but kind as well as driven. She was going to need all those traits to take care of what was the most precious to him."

"I hope you're right, and since you were right about me being a slow learner, I'll take it on faith."

Frida laughed and it filled the room. "Girl, if she wasn't forgiving, you'd be nowhere near her bed, and from the look of you, you've been there plenty."

"God." She felt her face heat up. "You do this on purpose." That was true, but she laughed along with Frida. The world was back on its axis.

CHAPTER SEVENTEEN

F rida bought tickets today for Italy," Wade said as they entered the barn.

The bucket of apples by the door was, as always, full, and Asher picked up a few for the horses that stuck their heads out of their stalls. "The ranchers in Tuscany raise some of the finest beef in the world. Make sure you order a steak when you're in Florence." She patted Wade's horse on the neck before moving to the next one. Whatever was on Wade's mind would eventually make it out of his mouth.

"I always order steak wherever I am, Buck. That's a given." He pointed to the haystacks at the back door and sat. "You want to tell me why Reagan was crying?"

"She was remembering something from high school, but it's nothing bad." She sat next to him and put a stalk in her mouth. "We've been trying to work things out."

"How's that going?" He sounded even-keeled, but she knew better. All that pent-up Wilson emotion was right under the surface like lava flowing underwater.

"You were right, old man. Shit has a way of working out." She enjoyed laughing with Wade because he laughed with his whole body. "I've been mad for way too long, and it took one kiss to prove that I've been wrong."

"Don't take this the wrong way, but don't mess with her. No one realizes more than me what Reagan's running did, and your reaction to it, but don't mess with her." He wasn't joking, and in the end, Reagan was his family. "I know what's going through your head, and you're my family too." She needed better control over her emotions. "Come on, Buck. I love you both, but Silas is gone, and she's my responsibility just like you are."

"If you know, you don't need to tell me not to be an asshole. Reagan is someone I never got over, but a happily ever after isn't possible until I get over all my trust issues." She leaned forward and rested her elbows on her knees. "I'm not leaving here, but she ran the first chance she got. Right now it's easy because we haven't made promises."

"Sometimes you have to walk a million miles before you realize where you started is where you belong." Wade put his hand on her shoulder and shook her gently. "It'll make combining the properties a lot easier if it works out."

"I convinced you, but she's not going to be that easy. No matter what happens, I still want to buy it." She turned and glanced out the door to a view she knew better than even her own land. "She just needs a little finessing."

"Fuck you," Reagan spat out behind her before turning and running out the door.

"Dammit." She stood and ran after Reagan. The bucket of apples, of all things, tripped her at the door, and she took a few steps trying to regain her balance. All she remembered after was the sudden shock of intense pain as her head collided with the door to the first stall. "Uh, what?" she said, shaking her head as she tried to get away from the awful smell under her nose.

"Jesus Christ, will you stop scaring the hell out of all of us," Frida said, waving the smelling salts under her nose again. "What in the world happened?"

She sat up and noticed Wade was gone. "I knocked some sense into myself before it was too late."

Frida held her down and grabbed her chin to make eye contact with her. "Your pupils are fine for now, but you need to come in the house and lie down."

"Sure," she said. The more agreeable she was, the quicker this would be over. When they stepped out and Frida turned for the house, Asher made it to her truck and got in as Frida shouted at her. She waved and drove herself home. "One of these days you're going to learn not to fall for the pretty words coming out of that pretty mouth. God, I'm a fucking idiot."

She fishtailed onto the road and wanted to ignore the phone but noticed Jacqueline's name on her screen. "Hey," she said as she turned in to her property.

"Hey, cowpoke, it's been way too long." Jacqueline's voice always sounded like it was infused with sarcasm. "How's the healing coming along?"

"Back on my feet and will get back to practicing in the next few days. I want to do a few more gym days before I trust the dismount." If Nero fiddled while Rome burned, then she was making small talk while her life dropped right back into a fiery hole dug by Reagan.

"Do you want to tell me what's wrong?" She heard a loud tapping as if Jacqueline was beating her finger on the receiver. "Think long before you say *nothing*. I'll ban you from all the restaurants for life."

"Remember I told you who my physical therapist was going to be?"

Jacqueline laughed before apologizing. "When's the wedding?"

It was her turn to laugh. "She just told me to fuck off at full volume, so that's not funny."

"Is it this girl who's not real bright, or is that you?" Jacqueline's question made no sense.

She pulled over under a tree and rolled down her window. "What's that supposed to mean?"

"Babe, women aren't that passionate unless they're that passionate. Reagan might've committed a laundry list of sins against you, but she still loves you. I saw it on her face the first night you saw her and acted like one of your cows plopped in your mouth." Jacqueline stopped a second, and it gave Asher the chance to laugh at the disgusting joke.

"I'm sorry I didn't call and tell you, and if you'd waited a day, there'd have been nothing to tell." Maybe she was meant to be alone. All she had to do was change her will and leave everything to Albert if something happened to her.

"No strings, remember? I've been busy here, but I've been on a few dates. Nothing serious but I've had fun, which is what I want you to do. Now, tell me you're not giving up."

"I'm not the one screaming obscenities." Another reason not to get too caught up in fantasy relationships was that they only worked out in books. "All I'm going to do is concentrate on what I need to do to get back into competition. If you're not banning me from the restaurants, I'll see you in Vegas."

Albert ran to the fence and neighed until she got out of the car. His girlfriend Booker was right there with him. At least one relationship was worthy of a romance novel. Why she did this to herself was something she had no ready answer to except that Reagan Wilson was her weakness.

"Asher, don't give up. Tell me what happened." Jacqueline said uh-huh as she explained, and it made her realize why Reagan was mad. If she wasn't angry before, she was angry now. "She thinks you played her to get what you want."

"I agree with you, and I promise I'll be okay, but I've got to go."

"Please, try to calm down, and talk to her. You're special to me, and you deserve to be in love and happy."

She said her good-byes and hung up. Being in love and happy with someone who thought so little of her wasn't going to happen. This had been their last chance, and Reagan had killed it yet again without giving her a chance to explain. There'd be no more chances.

❖

"Reagan Samantha Wilson, stop or I swear I'm grounding you," Wade yelled, and she did as he asked. "What in the hell is wrong with you?"

"What's wrong with me?" She gave as good as he did and screamed herself. "What in the hell is wrong with you? I didn't think my own family would conspire against me to sell off the land my father left me."

"Thank all that's holy you never became any kind of law enforcement officer. There'd be a ton of innocent people serving time." Wade took his hat off and didn't appear happy in any way. "Who do you think is conspiring against you? And I swear if you say the names *Asher* or *Wade*, I'm going to show you the door, niece or no."

"I heard you. Don't deny it. *She needs a little finessing.* Were you talking about Frida?" She knew he and Asher weren't since she'd heard most of the conversation. "I can't fucking believe I fell for her act that was only to get her hands on the deed to Moon Touch."

"Calm down the language and listen. Believe me or no, but Asher was interested in buying a large tract of land I'm not interested in using.

I doubt you are either, so it should go to someone who wants to use it and understands how special it is." He started back for the house, and she got the impression he didn't care if she followed him or not. "I told you we needed to talk about it, and you refused."

"I didn't think you wanted to sell. Have you thought about what Daddy would say about that?" Right now she couldn't give a crap about the land, but that Asher had so easily gotten her into bed and gotten past her defenses stung. "You both loved this place."

"I still love it, and I'm not going anywhere. All Asher and I discussed was grazing and pastureland. The house and a bunch of acres around it will remain with Moon Touch." He sat on a rocker and threw his hat on the table. "When you said you were coming back, Asher rescinded her offer to lease the land because she knew you'd never sell or give her use of it. I didn't believe you'd do that, but you just proved me wrong."

"Lease it?" Why wouldn't Asher have talked to her about this?

"She needs a way to get to the land she wants to purchase on the other side of us, but history is a bitch, ain't it. Asher figured you wouldn't want anything to do with her, so she told me she'd just have to put an outpost over there, like the cabin she has." Wade swept his sweaty but still thick hair back and glared at her. He didn't get mad often, but when he did it took a bit to calm him down. "I doubt she's going to want to have much to do with either of us now."

"Why didn't she tell me this herself? I ask because *finessing* isn't a word you use unless you're trying to get something over on someone." She saw Frida coming out of the barn with blood on her bright yellow shirt. "Now what?"

"What happened?" Wade stood and flew down the steps. "Are you all right?"

"I'm fine—the blood's not mine. Asher tripped and knocked herself out in the barn," Frida said.

"What?" Reagan stood and started for the barn. "And you left her in there alone? What's wrong with you?"

"I brought her to, and she insisted on leaving. Since she's an adult capable of making her own stupid decisions, I couldn't chain her to the wall until she came to her senses." Frida put her hands on her hips. "Girl, there's slow learners, and then there's you."

"This is not my fault." She wasn't making shit up, and Uncle Wade could bend the truth all he wanted but it wasn't going to change anything.

"Listen"—Wade pointed toward the porch—"the land belongs to both of us. I'm not going behind your back, and neither is Asher. If you don't want to sell or lease, then drop it. Accusing people who love you is not only rude, it's obnoxious. Before you keep doing that, if you have questions, we'll answer them."

"Why do you want to quit so bad?" No matter what he'd said, she couldn't shake the suspicion that he was sick.

"I was in the barn before, telling Asher not to mess with you. If she was serious about you, then I expected her to act accordingly. The other thing I told her is that Frida purchased tickets to Italy, and we're going after the finals." Wade held up a finger every time he made a point. "You're not interested in ranching, so I wanted Asher to lease so she'll keep our guys on. We'll keep the herds separate until we wind down, but they can start working for Pemberley and I won't feel guilty for wanting to retire and enjoy some downtime with Frida."

"I wish you'd said something," she said, close to tears.

"I'm not going to play that game with you, Buckaroo. You heard what you wanted to hear, and now it's time to apologize. It's also time to stop thinking the world is against you." Wade sounded tired, but his anger had subsided some. "How you ever thought Asher or I could've done something to hurt you is something I can't wrap my head around."

"I'm sorry, and you're right. I wasn't thinking, and I let my anger overrule my head and my heart. Those simple words won't cover it, but I am sorry." She stood and thought about how she was going to get back to Asher. She'd call an Uber, and the wait for them to get here would give her time to think of what to say. "You two go ahead and eat. I need to see Asher."

Uncle Wade threw her the keys to his truck and finally cracked a smile. "Don't take no for an answer and make it count."

She drove back to the road and headed to Pemberley, glad she had the code, doubting either Asher or Rickie would open the gate. Asher's SUV was parked, but there was no four-wheeler close to the house. God, she'd really fucked this day all to hell, and there was no taking it back. She sat in the truck and thought about what to do. The realization of where Asher was came to her as she stared at the barn.

This was one of the nicest barns she'd ever been in, and there was a staircase up to the loft. Both loft doors were open, and Asher was stretched out at the back with her ankles crossed and her eyes closed. There was a butterfly bandage over her left brow, and her shirt was streaked with blood. Reagan had done this, and she was ashamed of her behavior.

"I know you don't want me here, and as soon as I say what I need to, I'll go." She didn't move any closer, not wanting Asher to throw her out before she apologized. "I was wrong. I was wrong, and I'm sorry."

"Uh-huh," Asher said, not opening her eyes.

"This morning we were on our way to something wonderful, and I messed that up."

"You want to know the truth?" Asher said, turning her head and finally looking at her.

She took a chance and sat at Asher's feet. That Asher was talking was a minor miracle. "What?"

"I love you. You're killing me, but I thought about that when I was holding you this morning. I love you and today showed me that won't change even if we never see each other again." Asher put her hand up to keep her quiet, so she didn't say anything. "You think I don't know how important what your father left you is to you. Moon Touch will always exist as long as I'm alive."

"I was so wrong, and I can't imagine not ever seeing you again." She put her hand on Asher's ankle and moved it up to her knee. "Please forgive me."

Asher opened her arms, and she didn't give Asher a chance to change her mind. She dove into what was her salvation, and there was no doubt it always would be. The salt from her tears coated Asher's lips, but she'd never felt anything more exquisite than the kiss they were sharing.

"I don't deserve you, but I'm lucky you're willing to give me another chance." She pressed her face into Asher's neck and breathed in her scent. "And I love you too. I'm horrible at showing it, but I love you more than anything or anyone." She kissed the shell of Asher's ear and hummed to release some of her tension. "What changed your mind? About me, I mean."

"Jacqueline called me and told me to not give in to the anger, or something like that. She's right. I was plenty angry, but denying you would hurt us both." Asher sat up still holding her and pointed out toward the levee that was barely visible from here. It was at the top of the list of their favorite places, a place where they could look out at their tomorrows. "Are you sure about all this?"

"Will you keep Uncle Wade's hands on if you get the land?" She pressed against Asher, not wanting to be away from her.

"If they want to stay, but maybe you should take over for him. You could still work at the clinic after hiring a foreman. That way it'll stay in the family." Asher widened her fingers when Reagan took her hand. "That's not exactly what Silas wanted, but that might be a good reminder of what you love about this place."

"I know what I love about this place, honey. The cows, the land, the work don't add up to you. Being here with you, I've come to realize I belong here…with you." She turned, wanting to look at Asher and have her see how much she meant it. "The future I want is right here with you."

"Don't take this the wrong way, but this terrifies me more than the competitions I have coming up." Asher didn't turn away from her, and that, more than anything, gave her hope.

"It's about doing the things that scare us, isn't it?" She put her hand on Asher's cheek and leaned in to kiss her. "Sure bets don't come around too often, but I think you know this time, I'm sure."

Asher pulled her back in and kissed her with her hand on the back of her neck like she wanted to possess her. She moved but didn't break the kiss as she straddled Asher's lap. Once she had Asher's hands on her hips, she leaned back and pulled her shirt off and threw it behind her. Right now she needed Asher inside her, claiming what was hers.

"Please, love," she said, pulling Asher's hair. "I need you."

Asher twisted and laid her down in the hay, taking her own shirt off first so she could use it as a blanket to keep her from getting poked by the dry stalks. She wasn't sure how they were both naked so quickly, but it didn't matter. All she could think was that Asher's hand was between her legs and she was sucking on her nipple.

"Open it up for me," Asher said, lying next to her. She raised her knees and let them fall open. The want of Asher over her, putting her fingers in, and driving her to come was making her crazy.

"I need you to go inside…I'm so ready for you." She sounded

as if she was on the last mile of a marathon, but Asher was making her desperate and not above begging. "Like that," she said when Asher entered fast and hard. "You feel so good. Fuck me."

Reagan could hear the slap of Asher's hand as she kept up the stroke that she loved. It was slow, deep, and relentless. Her thighs closed around Asher's hand, and Asher opened her back up by lying over her. She scraped her nails up Asher's back as she lost control. "Like that, don't stop doing that." The orgasm made her tense and grab Asher's ass as she bucked up into her.

"Tell me what you want." Asher spoke with authority, and it turned Reagan on that much more. "Tell me or I'll stop."

"I want you...oh fuck...I want to belong to you," she said, looking up at Asher while she rode out the peak of her orgasm. "Tell me."

"I love you and you do belong to me." Asher circled her clit with her thumb and slammed in one more time. It was an act of possession and what Reagan had been waiting for. She had belonged to Asher for what seemed her whole life, and being away from her had damaged something vital.

"Yes, oh yes," she said before wrapping her arms and legs around Asher, not wanting her to move. "I do, you know."

"You do what?" Asher sounded tight and on edge.

"I belong to you." She released Asher and rolled on top as soon as she moved. "Let me show you how much."

She moved slowly down Asher's body, kissing all the nicks that'd scarred over from a lifetime of ranch work. They were markers of Asher's dedication to the things she loved. Reagan stopped and kissed over her heart knowing that's where the biggest scar lay, and days like this would be the only thing that finally healed it all the way through. She covered Asher's breasts with her hand and squeezed, getting that grunt she loved.

Asher not being overly vocal during sex was one thing that had remained consistent. Asher was as quiet in bed as she was most days. It's what had made those days in the cabin so special. Their talks had been the catalyst to this. She'd admitted her mistake, of tearing them apart just as much as Asher's kindness in making it right. While that hadn't been pleasant, there's no way they'd have gotten back to this level of comfort without it.

"God, baby, you taste so good," she said, sounding muffled since she hadn't raised her head from Asher's sex. She flattened her tongue, and Asher put her hand at the back of her head.

"Fuck," Asher said.

There was no way she was stopping, but she did open her eyes as she sucked Asher in and thought about how happy this view was going to make her for the rest of her life. She sucked harder and slid her fingers into Asher, wanting her to belong to her as much as she did to Asher. This was theirs, and no one would ever come between them.

Asher tensed and released faster than Reagan would've liked, but touching her had always turned Asher on, and it was nice that hadn't changed.

"Do you remember that first day we saw each other again?" She rested her head on Asher's chest and listened to her heart.

"At the restaurant, you mean?" Asher asked.

"Yes, I was so upset. It was the way you stared at me with that hard gaze that telegraphed you'd never forgive me." How close had she come to losing all this? If she had given Jacqueline the chance to spend lazy days in the loft, she'd be living with the truth that she had no one to blame for losing Asher but herself.

"I'm sorry about that. Frida told me you were coming back so I could start preparing mentally to see you again." Asher's voice was slow and thick like cane syrup in winter. It'd be easy to blame it on the lethargy from the sex they'd just had, but she knew Asher better than that. "When she said you were coming home with someone, I was glad I had a few months to perfect my poker face."

"I didn't say that to blame you for anything, honey. When you walked in and didn't notice me it was because the beautiful woman who greeted you with a boa constrictor kiss had your full attention. You have to admit, Jacqueline Blanchard is one beautiful woman." That same queasiness to her stomach and pain in her chest came again as she thought of Jacqueline kissing Asher. Everyone handled jealousy their own way, she guessed, like anger, and hers had always been like a virus that made her ill. "I wanted to pull her off you, but I didn't have the right."

"The hard gaze came from seeing you being held by Ms. Delmonico. I was irrationally angry that I'd been replaced." Asher ran her fingers through Reagan's hair and kissed her forehead. "Any need for a hug is my job from now on."

"How did I get this lucky?" She really was. Asher put a world of hurt aside because she loved her, and she wasn't ever going to take that for granted.

"You're Reagan Wilson. No luck needed." Asher gazed down at her and smiled. "You're imprinted on my heart, and only dying is going to change that."

"See, I never understood why you want to ride bulls when you're this poetic." She laughed when Asher did, and it was freeing. Asher always told her eggshells were meant to be broken, and there'd be no consequences if they were honest. The emotions of the day—no, really the whole time they'd been apart—crept up on her, and her laugh turned to tears. Through it all, Asher just held her and didn't say anything. She didn't have to because she knew her.

"I love you, and that's not changing. All I want is for you to be sure."

She was about to answer when she heard talking in the barn. A glance outside gave no clue as to who it was, but one of the voices was female. "I'm sure. I have no doubts, and I'm also sure we're about to get embarrassed."

Her shirt came flying up the stairwell and landed on Asher's head.

"It's Helki and her assistant," Asher said with a laugh. "They were due to come by today with the vet to check on Booker." Asher plucked the shirt off her head and threw it behind her.

"Please tell me she's not coming up here to get hay." She started laughing again when she gazed at Asher. Once upon a time it had been her father and uncle down in the barn, and Asher had been convinced Silas was going to chase her off with a shotgun. He'd at least given them time to get dressed, but they'd each had a slew of chores added to their slates because one of the legs of Asher's jeans had been hanging down into the barn like a big clue to what they'd been doing.

"No, and if we hurry, we can make it inside and into the shower before anyone else shows up."

She rolled off and grabbed her clothes as Asher put her underwear back on. That big smile on her lover's face meant that sex was going to be not only mind-blowing, but fun again. "Honey?"

"Hmm?" Asher said as she stood with her jeans on but unbuttoned. God, she was sexy. "I love you."

"I love you too." Asher moved closer and picked her up so their naked chests pressed together. "I love you and you're mine."

It might've sounded almost chauvinistic to some, but it's what she needed to hear. Belonging to Asher gave her a place, and a home, and her person back. "Are you mine?"

"Every bit of me, baby, and I'm going to prove it every single day." Asher kissed her, and that's all it took. She'd made it back, and she had to pace herself and practice patience because she wanted it all, and she wanted it right now.

"No need to prove anything. I see it every time you look at me." She touched the side of Asher's face and stared into those beautiful eyes.

"Good," Asher said, putting her down. "Let's get going then. We've got a life to get to."

"That we do, my love."

CHAPTER EIGHTEEN

The bulls were in the small pen and Asher stared at the herd as she took deep breaths. She had a few weeks to get back on the proverbial horse before competitions started back up again. Then a few more months before they ended up in Vegas, and she wanted to be at least in the top three. The top spot might not be something she could protect in the first competition, so right now all she needed was to be able to do well enough not to drop out of contention.

"Are you okay?" Reagan asked when she stepped next to her and put her arms around her waist. "You look a little nauseous."

"More nervous than nauseous. It's hard not to think about that damn bull and the pain in my foot." She'd promised to be honest, and that's what she was going to be.

"Baby, turn around." Reagan loosened her hold enough for Asher to face her. "I need your head in the game. The time we've spent together is special, and I'm glad I was able to help you get back on your feet, but I don't want to do it again." She stood on her toes and kissed her. "You're ready, and you're stronger than you were before the accident. Trust me, I made sure of that. If not, you'd be handcuffed to the bed right now."

"Okay," she said. The protective jacket she wore in practice was hanging on the fence, and Reagan helped her put it on. She then motioned for Owen to put the meanest bull in first. Might as well find out if she really was ready. She placed her hat over one of the fence posts and put on the helmet.

"Love you, honey, and I have one word of advice," Reagan said as she tugged on the front of the jacket.

"Forget this and let's head to the barn?" She smiled against Reagan's lips and moaned when she felt Reagan's tongue against her own.

"Thanks for putting that thought in my head, and I haven't been able to look Helki in the eye for the last two weeks." Reagan kissed her again, making Asher drop her hands to her ass. "And no. My advice is to remember to stay away from the bull when you jump off. You've got enough pins in that ankle to last two lifetimes."

"Yes, ma'am."

The rest of the bulls were on edge when the guys roped the one she wanted and put him in the chute, which made the bull she was going to ride a little out of control. She took another deep breath and got on, glad to have the mouth guard in when he kicked back and shook his whole body. The jarring shook the nervousness loose, and she smiled at the ranch hand holding up her rope. It all came rushing back—the adrenaline, the power of the animal, and her will to get on and try. She ran her hand up and down the rope her usual ten times and got into position.

"You good, boss?" the hand on the railing asked.

She nodded and tensed her legs. The bull twisted out of the chute in a way that almost dislocated her shoulder. For the first time in her career, she counted in her head. All she had to do was hang on, so she put her hand up and started. *Seven, eight*—she finally got to the magic number, and it was like the chains came off. Fear had to be respected, but she couldn't let it overpower her enjoyment of the sport.

The bull twisted again as if wanting her off, so she waited for him to straighten before she jumped clear of him, keeping her eye on him the whole time. Once she was on the other side of the fence, the relief at not losing this part of herself before she was ready to let go made her scalp tingle. She smiled when she felt Reagan put her arms around her from behind.

"I can't say that I'm not terrified, but I am glad that you're the best at this. Now finish up your practice so we can take a shower and cook dinner." Reagan came around and kissed right over her pulse point.

Once they'd admitted their feelings for each other, things had changed. Reagan was living at Pemberley, they put together most of their meals themselves, and Reagan slept next to her every night. It was everything they'd planned a long time before, and Asher was loving the experience. Being at home and taking care of the person you loved didn't sound exciting, but it's all she'd ever wanted.

"You want to head up to the house? Wade can help me finish here." She waved her hand to get another bull ready as she hugged Reagan to her.

"I'm not letting you out of my sight. Your foot seems to be holding up well, but I want to make sure it's not bothering you to the point you have a setback." Reagan stepped back and took her hand. "I'll be happy to sit with him and judge how you're doing for very different reasons. Though I give you a perfect score on how you look in these jeans." She laughed when Reagan slapped her ass.

She spent another hour riding before Wade called it a day, saying her form was almost back to perfect. The mechanics of bull riding never changed, only the strength you could maintain to stay on the bull. The worst of her ordeal was almost over. Now all she had left was to get ready for the first competition and try her best to win, to generate momentum for the rest.

When dinnertime rolled around, Reagan put a plate of grilled fish and vegetables in front of her, and she smiled. Their diet had changed to well-balanced and high-protein meals, but Reagan's talent in the kitchen seemed to help build muscle, so she never complained. The routine suited her, but there was that small voice in her head that warned Reagan would get bored and pull away. Their future seemed both real and intangible.

"What's going on in that cute head?" Reagan asked. She cleared the dishes and sent her back to her chair when she got up to help. "Relax and just tell me. You know I'll wheedle it out of you eventually."

"Nothing important." Not bringing it up would delay that dreaded conversation one more day, but she wasn't being fair. Reagan didn't act like she was ready to head back to her condo and away from her.

"Then let's talk next steps," Reagan said as if reading her mind. "We leave in two weeks, and I'm thinking once you start competing it's going to be a few months crammed with stuff to do before we arrive in Las Vegas."

"That sounds right. If you can't make every event, that's okay." It was like the fish had been seasoned with a healthy dose of depressants in it. She had to snap out of this before she ruined their night.

Reagan stared at her and wiped her hands on a dish towel.

"Listen to me because I'm only going to say this once. There's no missing anything on my part. I'm going to be there, and I've already decided to ask for leave from my job, which they should be okay with because Harry wants me at every competition." The dish towel landed somewhere behind Reagan, and she stepped between her legs and cupped her face. "Do you not believe me when I say I love you?"

"I do, and I'm being a fool." She had to make her actions match those words. "Want to take a walk with me?"

"Since you ate about three pounds of fish, I think that's a good idea," Reagan teased her. "You can tell me all about how you're going to make room for me in your closet."

"There's plenty of room in there now, so feel free to add more clothes than you have already." She held her hand out, and Reagan didn't hesitate to take it. "Do you need anything?"

"I have everything I need." Reagan smiled at her and squeezed her fingers. "I did want to talk to you about something."

"Sure." She opened the door and headed out the back. There was another car at Rickie's, and she imagined she was enjoying her time off after Reagan took over dinner prep. "What about?"

"It's about what Uncle Wade and you have planned for Moon Touch's land." Reagan moved closer and wrapped her hand around her bicep as if trying to keep her close.

She'd shelved plans for the expansion she'd thought incessantly about for two years. She knew Reagan believed Asher never planned to take something that important from her. The tracts of land Silas and her father had left them would stay separate. If Reagan thought Asher hadn't talked about her plans because she was afraid of where it would lead, she was wrong. There were more important things in life than bigger and better.

"Sweetheart, we'll figure something out so Moon Touch stays profitable even if Wade wants to downsize." That would work if both Wade and Reagan wanted to enjoy the livelihood the land afforded them. "Whatever you two decide is good with me, and I'll do whatever you both need."

"Honey"—Reagan stopped her from taking another step. She stood in front of her and put her arms around her neck—"if I hadn't been an asshole, you and my uncle would be on your way to the best deal for all of us. I read over all the plans you gave me, and I think it's the best way forward. What you built here deserves to be finished. There's only one thing I want."

"What?" She gazed down at Reagan, reminding herself how beautiful she was. Even from an early age, Reagan had lit up her brain when she smiled at her like this. Now it was even a bigger reaction, and she pulled Reagan closer. "Tell me, and I'll try to give it to you."

"I want you to listen to me. Stop living in your head so much, trying to figure out what I'm thinking." Reagan squeezed her face between her hands until Asher's lips puckered. When she laughed, Reagan joined her. "I'm telling you what I want, but it's like you don't want to hear it."

"You haven't specifically said what that is, so don't blame me," she said, sounding funny since Reagan hadn't let her face go.

"I want you to start merging the operations. Give Uncle Wade what he wants and in turn what I want. Our dads had a dream for this place, and I doubt it was to keep them separate." Reagan stood on her toes and kissed her softly. It was the kind of kiss meant to show how much someone loved you and only you. "Your dreams have to be mine and vice versa." That seemed to jog something in Reagan, given the way she dropped back on her heels. "Unless that's not what you want."

"It's time for both of us to stop guessing and just ask. I'm sorry for not talking to you, but I didn't want you to—"

Reagan put her fingers over her mouth. "I love you, Buck, but more than that, I trust you. It's been a while, but I'm guessing all those big cows you have need room to stretch their legs. Are they going to bully Uncle Wade's herd?" The sun completely set, leaving them in the purple glow of twilight, and she couldn't help herself and lowered her head again and kissed Reagan.

"Everyone is going to get along, I promise. And if we're going to do this, then we need to do what you said."

"What are you talking about?"

She combed Reagan's hair back and loved how soft it was. "We need to merge our operations."

"I can't accept that, honey. Uncle Wade has been downsizing Moon Touch, so it's not fair for you to offer me anything." Reagan took her hands and pulled her toward the rockers on the back porch. "All I want out of this deal is for you to keep the hands on. They love you, so I'm sure they'll be thrilled to join your place."

"Uncle Wade will be thrilled, and you need to think long-term. You can leave the day-to-day to me, but you need to be involved. It's the only way this is going to work. If you really want to be here, then help me with the big picture." She led Reagan to a rocker and knelt between her legs. "What I want is a partner in all things. If you're not interested in that, it's okay, but I need to know."

"Baby"—Reagan squeezed her shoulders—"I ran from this life."

Asher closed her eyes and gave herself a quick pep talk not to show emotion. "You did." The words didn't sound like they were being strangled out of her throat, at least to her. Giving in would make the pain that much worse this time around because she willingly inflicted it on herself.

"The thing is, though, I ran back to it even faster. That first morning we spent at the cabin, and I looked out at the mist, the cows, and you—it stilled my head. There was no thought, no regret, and I wanted to laugh at what a complete fool I am."

"For wanting this?" She wanted the answers to come faster if only to unravel the tension in her chest.

"For staying away so long. You, my love, are a hard person to forget, much less get over." Reagan smiled as she wiped the tears Asher only then realized were falling. "Why would I give that up after I'm lucky enough to have been gifted it?"

"Tell me—I need to hear it."

"I might be a fool, like I mentioned, but I want it all. Perhaps it's too early to say this, but I want you and everything that comes with having you." Reagan pulled her forward with one jerk and held her as if she'd disappear if she let go. "That'll mean you're mine. Only mine."

"That's a given." They'd kissed plenty since that first day, but this one was like what she imagined people sensed right after saying their vows. It wasn't just a kiss to entice, but something that proved you belonged somewhere and to someone. To Reagan.

"Thank you," Reagan said as she rested her forehead against hers.

"For what?" She glanced down when Reagan started sliding her T-shirt up. They had to get inside before any of her clothes came off.

"I thought this would take so much more time." Reagan smiled against her lips. "Spending more time naked so you'd warm up to the idea of letting me in."

She rocked on her heels and stood up to offer Reagan her hand. "I think we need to review that last part upstairs."

"You have the best ideas."

"Give me some time, and I'll show you how true that is."

CHAPTER NINETEEN

The clinic was full even though it was eight in the morning. Reagan hadn't come in since she'd started working with Asher, and seeing the patient load now made her feel a bit guilty. Not that she'd change what she'd done, since she'd gotten what she most wanted, but Kendra and the others had been good to her from her first day.

"Can I help you?" Kendra said, holding her hand out. "I'm Kendra, nice to meet you."

"Come on, you're the one who sent me out there." She pushed Kendra's hand aside and hugged her. "And I owe you an expensive dinner to thank you for that, by the way."

"The cowgirl got her head out of her ass, huh?" Kendra said softly before she stepped back.

"She wasn't the one with a bad learning curve, my friend, but she does have a good heart. It's been some wonderful weeks." They walked arm in arm back to Kendra's office, and she shook her head at the offer of coffee. "I wanted to talk to you about taking a leave of absence."

"Asher's pushing you to quit your job?" Kendra seemed surprised at that.

"No"—she shook her head—"Asher's actually pushing me to come back while she's finishing up the circuit that comes before the championship in Las Vegas. I can't prove it, but I think she's scared to have me watch. Like I'm going to change my mind if I'm there."

"When you first came back and finally told me about her and what happened, I would've thought Asher was right. You weren't a fan." Kendra sat next to her and placed her hand on her forearm.

"Still not a fan, but there's no way I'm letting her go alone. I love her, and I'm not going to be away from her that long." Thinking of being away from Asher now gave her more anxiety than the thought of seeing Asher did six months ago. "I'll quit if I have to, but I'm going with her."

"Don't get crazy on me. Take the time and keep Asher in one piece. When she's done, we'll talk about scheduling." Kendra laughed and squeezed her arm again. "Make sure to stay in touch, and if something happens, which I doubt it will, I'm a call away."

"Reagan said you were a good friend," Asher said from the doorway. "She was right."

It'd become one of her favorite things every day, to watch Asher exist in her skin—the broad shoulders she carried with confidence, the jeans that were just tight enough to make the ass worthy of staring at, and the legs that went on for a mile.

Today the jeans were faded with a small hole below the knee, and the golf shirt was tight at Asher's biceps, and it wasn't tucked all the way, just where the belt buckle she'd won at the Dome sat proudly, sort of a reminder of what could happen or how far Asher had come since the accident. She wasn't about to ask why she'd picked that particular one.

Asher was handsome but not in the way she'd describe a man. She was no man wannabe, but she was strong, solid, and hers. The way Kendra was staring at Asher reminded her she was going to have to get used to that too. Asher had that kind of effect on women. Even when they didn't fit, were from different worlds like Jacqueline, they appeared entranced.

"She is, and you weren't as long as I expected." She stood and wrapped her fingers under the buckle and tugged Asher toward her. "Did you get everything you needed?"

"I did, and Harry says hi. She told me to stop being such an ass and go with the fact that the girl loves me." Asher lowered her head and kissed her. "We have time for lunch before we head back."

"Good, let's go to my place. I wanted to talk to you about something." She put her arm around Asher's waist and turned to face Kendra. "Thanks for the time off, and I promise I'll be back when all this madness is over."

"Take care of yourself, Asher, and promise me you'll keep an eye on my friend. Call us if you need anything."

"Thanks, and thank you for cutting her loose. This will be hard enough with her there."

She patted Asher's butt when she said that, liking that she wasn't afraid to admit she needed her. "Don't worry, we'll stay in touch." Kendra hugged them both, and Asher held her hand back to the car.

The ride to her apartment was quiet, but they didn't have to fill the air with unnecessary words if they weren't needed. This place wasn't home any longer, and she probably should wait until they were back, but she needed to talk about it. "How about a sandwich?"

"How about you tell me what's on your mind, and we'll order something." Asher sat on one of the stools at her kitchen island and flattened her hands on the marble top.

"Honey, I don't mind making you a sandwich." She opened her refrigerator, hoping there was something in there so she could do just that. When she felt Asher's hands on her abdomen, she closed her eyes and leaned back. "What?"

Asher closed the refrigerator and turned her around and kissed her. The boots made Asher even taller, so she bent and picked Reagan up so she could wrap her legs around her waist. She didn't have to mention how much this turned her on as Asher started for the bedroom. This was the first time she'd be intimate with anyone in this condo since she'd moved in. Granted, she'd slept with Steph in this bed but had already suspected she'd been cheating, so having sex was out.

Asher put her down, and the comforter landed on the floor when she flicked it off the bed. Reagan still was surprised at times how quickly Asher made her wild, desperate, and wet. Some of it had to do with what she'd thought when Kendra had not so covertly checked Asher out. But it was the want in Asher's expression when she gave Reagan her full attention. Right now she could see just how much she was wanted, and it drove not only her love, but the lust that clouded her brain when Asher was this close.

Asher moved behind her and started on the buttons of the short-sleeved blouse she'd chosen that morning. The navy bra she'd put on felt nice against her skin when Asher covered her breasts with her hands and squeezed just short of painful. If she hadn't been soaking wet before, that would've done it. She moaned and counted on Asher to keep her upright.

"You make me wild," Asher said as her hands moved down to the button of Reagan's shorts. "I can't take my eyes off you."

Everything she was wearing had to go before she vibrated across the room from want. "Baby, please." She pulled her shorts down, needed them off.

"It's time to prove to you that you belong to me," Asher said, turning her around. Her shirt and bra came off, and she wanted to scream that she did belong to Asher in every way a person could. "And that I belong to you. Whatever ghosts haunt this place are about to be buried for good."

She grabbed Asher's shirt and yanked it up. The exercises she'd guided Asher through had really defined her muscles, and it made her want to rub against Asher all day long. They were so different in build, but Asher had always said they fit together perfectly. She put her hands on the belt buckle, needing Asher naked, above her, and in her. There wasn't time to think when Asher cupped her ass and picked her up.

The sheets were rough against her back when juxtaposed to having Asher's skin plastered to every inch of her. She inhaled that cologne that reminded her of the beach and citrus, and it fired the pleasure center of her brain. When they'd turned sixteen, Asher had touched her for the first time, and those hands had left their mark. It was like a tattoo that couldn't be washed off or forgotten.

"Please, honey," she said as Asher sucked on her neck. Reagan spread her legs and moaned when Asher dropped her hips to press against her. "I need you inside."

Asher lifted only enough to fit her hand between them and entered her hard and fast, only to still her hand once she had. "It's mine because I love you," Asher said before kissing her.

She clawed at Asher's back when she pulled out and started a relentless rhythm meant to make her orgasm hard and fast. It's what she wanted, but when Asher slowed and softened her movements, Reagan wanted to scream but it lengthened the pleasure.

All she could do was moan as the only sign she wanted whatever Asher was willing to give her. She bucked her hips when Asher sped her hand, as if not wanting to wait. Seeing her fall over the edge of the want Asher built in her had always turned Asher on. She'd do something about it, but right now she needed to come or pass out.

"Please don't stop. Don't stop." She put her hands on Asher's ass and squeezed to keep her in place. Slowing down or stopping would only be tolerated if the condo was engulfed in an inferno. "Oh my… fuck…oh fuck," she breathed into Asher's ear as she sucked on her neck. It was an overload of sensations—the lips at her neck, the press of Asher against her chest, and the way Asher's finger rubbed in just the right place.

"Yes, oh yes," she yelled as her knees fell open wider and she pulled at the back of Asher's head. She needed Asher's lips pressed to hers, and when they did, she came, her moan swallowed by Asher who never stopped. "No," she said when Asher started to roll off. Asher's fingers were inside her still-pulsing sex, and she'd never been more content or connected to the one person in the world who was perfect for her. "I need to feel you."

"I'm too heavy," Asher said. She tried again to roll off, but Reagan held firm.

"That's not true, and I like you up here," she said, running her fingers through Asher's hair. Asher smiled when she locked her feet at the small of her back. "I love you, and you make me happy."

"Happy enough to tell me what's on your mind?" Asher raised her head to look her in the eye. "I'll understand if you want to give the next few months a pass. Stay and work or whatever you want. You can stay at the house and ride, or move in with Frida and Uncle Wade. I promise, I'm coming back."

"No." She was adamant about that. "I want to go with you and take care of you because no matter how easy you make the impossible seem, it takes a lot to do. And I don't want to freak you out before we go." So of course those were the words that came out of her mouth, like she had no control over them. Was there ever a time when someone said *Don't freak out* that you didn't do exactly that?

"That sounds ominous." Asher didn't move but she'd become slightly more tense.

"Honey, I want to sell this place and move in with you," she said, holding the sides of Asher's face. "I thought it would freak you out since six months ago you hated my guts, but now I can't stand being away from you."

"Does that mean you want to move in and think I'll be dead set against it?" Asher appeared confused, but she couldn't blame her. "Or is it that you're upset that you're even thinking that?"

"I want you." She gently shook Asher's head. "That means I want to take care of you. That means we have to be in the same house for me to do that. The only thing that'll upset me is if you don't want that."

"Are you sure you want to sell this place?" Asher did roll off now but kept her arms around her. "You haven't talked about it much, but it seems to be your style."

"I bought this place because I figured it'd be the closest I'd ever get to Moon Touch and to you. Pemberley came as a complete surprise, but in a way not really. Do you understand?" She hoped Asher did since she couldn't make sense of it herself.

"I'm not saying no, sweetheart, but give it some time. Think about it, and if it's what you really want, I'll have the guys pack you up and get you home." Asher kissed her forehead and flattened her hand on her back. "Right now let's concentrate on what's coming."

"Do you mean it?" She squirmed against Asher, wishing she could move the clock faster.

"Mean what?"

"Home. Can you see me there?"

"Pemberley was built with you in mind. I didn't really know you well anymore since all my news of you came in snippets from Wade, so I couldn't be sure." Asher's voice was almost velvet smooth with a hint of smoke. It had a way of weaving around you until all you could do was wish it'd never stop. "When I finished the repairs, additions, and remodel, I seriously questioned my sanity. How in the hell was I going to exist in a place that was built for you?"

"That library got me that first day," she said, loving this talk. "I might not have consciously known it, but seeing you in that room made me warm."

"Sorry I was such an ass to you at the beginning."

"No need for apologies. We're both right where we need to be, though—this place is a one and done, I think, when it comes to you and me. The quicker the For Sale sign goes up, the quicker we'll get to cohabitation and fabulous sex where we belong." It hadn't gone as smoothly as she'd have liked, but Asher hadn't said no. Their future wasn't going to be miserable and apart like she'd been so afraid of since she'd lost Asher.

"I love you, and I want the same things, in case you were worried."

"I love you too, and I'm not worried, not anymore."

CHAPTER TWENTY

The plane ride to Pueblo, Colorado, was rough, but Asher still tried to sleep for at least an hour. They were flying into Denver before catching a small plane to Pueblo for the Pendleton Whisky Velocity Tour. She'd completed the first three rodeos that remained before the championship, and Pueblo would be her last chance to accumulate points before Vegas.

She smiled with her eyes closed as the scent of lemons mixed with honey invaded her senses, and she tightened her hold on Reagan. The first three events had rattled Reagan a bit, but she'd gone to every single one. With one win and two second-place finishes, she was in second but only a few points behind Tyler. They were almost in a dead heat, but he'd done well in Del Rio and had pulled ahead with his usual gloating.

"I can feel you thinking real hard about something," Reagan said, turning her head slightly and kissing her neck. "If it's that you want to stick your hand in my pants, you have to wait until we get to the hotel."

"Thanks for ruining my nap, and I was only partly thinking about that." She laughed when Reagan bit her neck gently. "Okay, I'm mostly thinking about that whenever there's not a bull in sight."

"Better, but now that you've told the truth, tell me what's on your mind." It was dark outside the plane, and the dim lights in the cabin had them speaking in a whisper. "Are you worried about us?"

"I'm thinking about the competition in a couple of days. Vegas will come pretty quick after that, and I wouldn't be here at all if it wasn't for you." She lifted her arm and put it around Reagan's shoulders. "So thank you for that and for being here. It's helped me to keep my head screwed on right, having you so close by."

"Honey"—Reagan moved closer and kissed her—"I love you, and

I'm going to love you even when you're doing crazy stuff. I hope you meant what you said and you're not going to resent me once you retire."

"I've been to the championships for quite a few years, and third is the closest I've come to winning. This year a win is possible, but if it doesn't work out, then I don't have anything else to prove. There's too much happening to keep this up, and I'd like to be able to throw you over my shoulder and carry you to bed and not drop both of us to the floor." The old man across the aisle laughed, having probably heard her.

"I'm all for that." Reagan leaned farther over and sucked on her bottom lip. "Once we're done, I'll have to talk to Kendra about my future with the clinic."

"If you're thinking of quitting, I want you to rethink it. You've worked hard to build your career." She closed her eyes as she leaned closer to the window with Reagan. "I don't want you getting bored."

"Get bored with the ranch, or with you?" Reagan had a way of cutting to the center of every steak in life. "You're an adorable fool, and you're mine no matter what's happening in life. That means we run the ranch, the house, and our business together. Boring doesn't begin to fit into that equation."

"Thank you, I think." These talks were getting easier to get through. "I never thought it'd make me hot to have someone call me a fool."

"Well, you are, so I hope this little talk put you out of your mental calisthenics." Reagan pinched her abdomen hard when she took a breath to say something. "Uh-uh, you had your time to talk. When it comes to my job, I'm not giving up anything, but I might not work full-time. You wanted a partner, and that's what I want to be."

"Cows were never your thing, baby."

"No, but you gave me an idea with Booker. I'm not as knowledgeable as Helki, but I'd like to help her with the breeding program." Reagan moved until her lips were next to her ear. "The one main thing I want is to be close to you, and you're just going to have to believe me."

"I want you to be happy, that's it." Letting Reagan find her way was the best gift she could give her. It was a gift to them both. "And Helki will be happy to share the load with you. Her thing is finding new stock to add to the program, so she'll be happy to have someone who wants to stay home and form some equine love connections."

"Then it's settled, and all we need is the two buckles you don't have to get started on all that."

The flight attendant announced they were starting their descent, and she noticed the lights of the city outside the window and kissed Reagan one more time before the mad scramble to get off. She carried their bags to their next departure gate while Reagan grabbed them a couple cups of decaf.

The last flight of the day wasn't crowded, and she hoped it stayed that way. The rodeo wasn't for another two days, so tomorrow she was planning to sleep late and enjoy some time alone with Reagan. She sat facing the windows overlooking the tarmac and waited for Reagan to get back. When her phone rang, she expected it was either Wade or one of the guys checking in. Seeing Jacqueline's name on her screen made her smile.

"Hey, pretty lady." She loved Jacqueline's laugh. It always sounded like she meant it and found a lot of things in life humorous. "Did you get my message?"

"I did, and I'm sorry it's taken me so long to get back to you. Sounds like it all worked out, though." Jacqueline sounded pensive. "Tell me one thing."

"What? I'm still your friend, and that's not changing." If anyone could've made her forget Reagan, it would've been Jacqueline. There wasn't a woman alive who could erase Reagan completely, but Jacqueline was in a category all by herself when it came to enjoying the hell out of life. That she chose her to come along for the ride for as long as she had made her fortunate.

"Remember that a girl loves to be romanced. You're good at that, and Miss Reagan should feel lucky you love her. I'm going to miss you, but I'm happy for you. I just wanted to call and check on you and wish you luck."

"I'll see you soon, and I'm the lucky one when it comes to not only love, but the friendships I've made in my life. If you ever need anything, I'm a phone call away." She loved Reagan, there was no doubt about it, but it didn't prevent her from mourning the loss of Jacqueline just a bit.

"I know that, cowpoke, and I can't wait to get to know your love. Don't forget to bring Frida and Wade along. Dinner will be my treat."

She hung up and tapped the phone against her chin, then noticed

Reagan in the reflection of the window, hesitating not that far way. Reagan only came forward when she held her hand out and helped her with the cups.

"Was she upset with the we-can-only-be-friends talk?" Reagan sounded like she wanted to be nonchalant, but a bit of jealousy seeped through.

"Jacqueline and I had that talk at the beginning of our friendship. What we had was fun, and we cared about each other, but she wasn't you." She put her arm around Reagan again and widened her fingers when Reagan took her hand as if to keep her in place. "The thing is, I would've eventually had to face what my life was going to be if you hadn't come back. I didn't want to be alone, but what woman was going to put up with the ghost of you haunting me until I got planted in that plot by the oak grove?"

"You *are* the love of my life. I figured that out when I was twelve, and I'm going to keep showing you that until I'm in my nineties." Reagan turned in her seat and placed her palm against her cheek. "I'm glad you had someone, but you're mine, and I'm not good at sharing. Not when it comes to you."

"I'm all yours, baby. I love you and your heart is safe with me. I know it, and more importantly, so does Jacqueline. She really was just calling to check on us after that argument about the land."

"Sorry, I didn't mean to go all cavewoman on you, but I get a headache thinking of you with someone else." Reagan took a sip of her coffee and put her head down on Asher's shoulder.

"Trust me, I know that. Delmonico might be a big fan of bull riding, but if she touches you again, I might introduce her to the sport." That made Reagan laugh, and that's the reaction she wanted.

They sat and talked about nothing important until they boarded, and this time Asher did sleep for the short flight with Reagan's head on her shoulder again. It was late by the time they reached the hotel, and Reagan insisted they shower before going to bed.

They'd slept together for weeks, but this was the first night Asher didn't dream about anything. She'd drifted off, concentrating only on the warmth of Reagan against her, and knowing that's how it would be for the rest of their lives. Eight seconds of excitement couldn't compete with that.

❖

Their day of naked fun almost made Reagan forget what Asher was about to do. The crowd that night was wired for what they were about to see, and in a way, she couldn't blame them. If you loved bull riding, the best in the sport were here tonight for that one last chance to make a move in the rankings. She smiled, thinking of what her father would be thinking if he was here. Nights like this were electrifying for him, and he dug deep for that perfect score no matter how he felt.

Asher was making her way to her after finishing up her registration, and the sight of her made her clench her thighs together. The jeans, boots, hat, and plaid shirt made quite the sexy picture, and if she could get away with it, she'd peel those pants down and put her mouth on her lover. Lately, she was having a hard time controlling her sex drive.

"You okay?" Asher pressed up to her and put her hand on the small of her back.

"I'm fine, why?" The cologne and body heat weren't helping.

"You look like you're in pain." The way Asher rubbed her back, straying close to her ass with affection, made her slightly unravel.

"I'm in pain, but not the body ache kind. Stop touching me unless there's a competition for how you can make me come in eight seconds." She laughed when Asher's eyes widened. "You asked."

"Thanks for putting that in my head right before I climb on a bull." The chairs with Asher's name on the back were out in the open, and that was the safest place for them right now.

"I'm sorry, but you look good enough to…well, you know." She sat and took Asher's hand. They didn't have much time together before the rounds started, and she lost her smile when she saw Tyler Wheeler headed their way. "God, not this guy again."

"Asher," Tyler said in a tone that made her think he was actually calling Asher an asshole. "Miss Wilson, it's nice to see you again."

"Tyler, is there something we can help you with?" Asher asked. She didn't appear amused.

"I had a twinge right here, and I thought Miss Wilson could help me out," Jerry said, putting his hand on his inner thigh. "I hear she did wonders for you."

"You can kiss my—"

Asher squeezed her fingers to keep her from finishing. "If anyone is going to kiss your ass, darlin', it ain't gonna be Tyler Wheeler." The grammatically incorrect declaration made Reagan wetter than she already was. "And Tyler, did you know that most people can only concentrate on one pain at a time?"

"What do you mean?" Tyler went from annoying to confused.

"It means that if you need help with that twinge, I'll be happy to kick you in the groin to take your mind off the pain you'll have in your hand when Miss Wilson breaks all your fingers. She isn't interested in anything having to do with you."

Tyler smiled as if enjoying that he'd gotten under Asher's skin. "Shouldn't she decide that, or do you have her under lock and key?"

"What Asher means is, fuck off. Your legend-in-your-own-mind personality is about as sexy as monkey pox."

Tyler lost his smile and kept walking, and Asher twisted in her seat to watch him sulk away. "If I haven't mentioned how much I love you lately, I love you."

"I love you too, honey, and I need you to win me that buckle tonight." She was wearing the one Asher had won in New Orleans, needing something to show who she was with. The competition all those months ago had been her opening back into Asher's life, and Asher had gladly fitted it onto a wider belt she wore loosely around the dress she'd gotten for the occasion. "I need something to wear for Vegas."

"I'll see what I can do, my love, but right now, I've got to go."

The announcer was starting to whip up the crowd even more, and Asher had picked the number two slot from the lottery at registration. Reagan walked with her hand in Asher's back pocket until they reached the chutes, and the sound of the bulls inside them chilled her. Asher bent and threaded her fingers into her hair before she kissed her. How she'd survived this long without this kind of affection was beyond her.

"Good luck, honey. Try your best to stay in the shape you're in now." Reagan pressed one more kiss to Asher's lips with her fingers on her jaw. "Do that and I'll give you a special prize later."

"You got it." Asher smiled that beautiful smile before her expression turned serious.

She didn't understand why anyone would want to do this, but she forced herself to watch Asher's process from beginning to end. At the last three events, all she could do was watch. Once Asher had busted out of the chute, she hadn't even blinked until she was back by her side. The way Asher waited at the top of the chute as a rodeo hand guided her rope around the big tan bull's chest was the picture of total concentration. Asher jumped on, and it was like watching the truest definition of fearlessness. It scared the shit out of Reagan, but in a way it also brought a sense of calm. There was nothing that could happen that Asher wouldn't protect her from. Her father would be so proud of the job he'd done with Asher, and she vowed to take as good care of her in return for as long as she drew breath.

She watched the clock over Asher and it was frozen on zero. The bull was going wild as Asher ran her hand up and down the rope and moved forward before nodding her head. The chute door banged against the arena wall as Asher came out. Time felt suspended as Asher was jarred by the animal she was riding, but Reagan silently counted in her head. When she reached eight, Asher jumped clear and tipped her hat to the crowd.

Two more rides to go, and she knew it wouldn't get any easier, but Asher seemed to understand and simply held her once she was out and by her side. "You okay?" Asher whispered right into her ear and didn't let go until she sighed.

"My love, I think I'm supposed to be the one asking that question," she said as she ran her hands down Asher's body. It was solid, strong, and unharmed, making her knees weak. "Are you okay?"

"Bo and I have a history, so I have some experience to draw from. Let's go sit."

She took Asher's hand and followed her to the chairs, or at least that's where she thought they were going until Asher kept going. The arena offices were mostly devoid of life, and Asher led her to the first open space and closed the door. She had no idea how much she needed the kiss until Asher held her and did just that. Her scalp tingled, and she smiled against Asher's lips.

"You do know how to make a girl feel things, cowpoke." She laughed when Asher slapped her ass. "And I'm looking forward to this being over so I can tell you all about it."

"Come on before I stroll out of here walking funny."

Reagan chewed on her thumbnail for the next rides and waited for Asher right outside the gate. A first-place finish would have taken

Asher into the finals in that same position, but damn if Wheeler hadn't squeaked it out on the last ride by drawing a better bull. It didn't surprise her that Asher didn't seem upset by the outcome, so she was pissed on her behalf.

"Are you sure you want to leave tonight?" She held on to Asher after Asher opened the rented truck's door for her. "We can sleep in again tomorrow, and there's a flight at two in the afternoon."

"Wouldn't you rather sleep in tomorrow in our own bed? If we head home tonight, we can spend the day in our bed if you want." The last flight out that night was at midnight, so they wouldn't get home until early the next morning.

"How can I turn that offer down?"

They both slept through the first flight and were out again when they were wheels-up on the second. It was three in the morning when they landed in New Orleans, and Owen was one of the few people in the airport. He drove them home and caught Asher up on all the ranch business before dropping them off at the house. The place was dark except for the light over the desk in the kitchen.

Asher grabbed them each a bottle of water and carried their bags up to the bedroom. "How about a shower?"

"I'll be happy to wash your back, honey." She dropped her dress and stepped out of it. Asher had to be dead on her feet, but her pupils dilated at the sight of her in her underwear. This was why she'd missed Asher. There'd never been anyone else in her life who'd made her feel like the center of their world. "Close your mouth, sweetheart. We're taking a shower and going to bed. We both need some sleep, but in the morning you're going to have to lock yourself in the bathroom to get away from me."

"You should've rethought the underwear if you wanted me to keep my hands to myself." Asher took her shirt off and stood before her in jeans and boots. The view was good enough that she was about to offer to have Asher's baby if she let her touch.

"Who said anything about you keeping your hands to yourself?"

Chapter Twenty-one

Y ou know what you have to do," Wade said as he and Asher rode the back pastures.

Now that Reagan had agreed to Asher's leasing proposal, her hands were busy restructuring the fences so the herd of Pinzgauer cows could spread out. That way they could take advantage of the acreage Asher had purchased on the other side of Moon Touch. The new configuration would require a new road up to Wade's place, but she promised she'd take care of it.

"Stay on the bull?" Asher winked and he lifted his middle finger in her direction. "Okay, what do I need to do?"

"You need to show some good faith." Wade smiled at the ranch hand who opened the gate so they could check out the new acreage.

Asher waved to the guys putting in the last sections of black fence that matched the posts surrounding Pemberley. The grounds needed some work, like where the new barn construction was almost finished, and the new grass would have to be planted. This would take another four to five months before it was ready for livestock, but she could envision it.

"I sent the payment for the land, so I'd hope you see that as me acting in good faith. Take your half and buy Frida something on your trip and convince her to marry you." She glanced out at the road that dead-ended at the back of the property and wondered if she could convince the parish to close it farther up since there was nothing on the other side. It would make security a lot easier.

"I swear to God, you're as dense as a fence post sometimes." Wade tipped his hat back and stared at her.

"What exactly are you talking about, Uncle Wade?" They were

having two different conversations, and hers was the only one that made sense.

"I'm not talking about bulls or all this real estate, Asher. I'm talking about Reagan." He pointed his finger at her and stopped for what she thought was emphasis. "I'm proud of you for not only forgiving her, but for loving her. You two, in my opinion anyway, belong together. Always have."

"And you think I'm not going about this in good faith? I hope you know me better than that." Las Vegas and the championships were on the horizon, and there'd been a lot on her mind.

Wade laughed and shook his head. "Calm down, Buck, but I had a dream about Silas last night, and we need to have this talk." He took his hat off and combed his hair back. It was as wet with sweat as hers was. "You know how he felt about you, and he taught you about love and commitment for a reason."

"I know, Uncle Wade. He was training me to be a good spouse for the one person in the world he thought deserved one." She remembered all the stories he'd told her about Reagan's mother, Christine. If there was a woman who hadn't deserved to be a mother, it was Christine Wilson, but without her, she wouldn't have Reagan. "Do you think I'm falling short when it comes to Reagan? If you're comparing me to Christine, then get off the horse and put your fists up."

"You're nothing like Christine. I just want you to start showing Reagan that there's a future here for her. Paying us to use the land isn't what I had in mind." Wade as always was blunt and honest. "And before you tell me how fast this is, think about all the time you've both wasted so far."

"This might make me sound like a total wimp, but I'm not just scared, but terrified. If she decides a month or a year from now that this isn't for her, then it's going to gut me." She loved Reagan, there was no denying it, but she'd also experienced the dark side of loving Reagan. "It's not that she's given me a reason to be worried, but it's an unfortunate ingrained response."

"I'd think you were lying to me if you'd told me anything but that. If you want my two cents, then trust what you feel. Being scared is a natural response, especially after what happened. Think, though, how long life is going to be if you decide to pass on the one woman who's your match." Wade moved his horse closer and placed his hand on her arm. "Anyone else will be jamming a jigsaw puzzle piece where it doesn't go. It'll distort the picture you're trying to build."

"That's profound, old man." She wondered if Reagan had any idea how much Wade loved her. "We're talking and taking it slow. I want to get it right this time."

"I see," Wade said, and those two words conveyed a lot. He wasn't in agreement, he was pissed, and he was trying to keep from yelling at her.

"The thing to remember here is I wasn't the one who left." She didn't think she needed to mention that, but the relationship they were building seemed to have erased a lot of memories best forgotten.

"That's what you're going to go with?" Wade asked in the same tone, only now he'd let a little of his anger bleed through. "Seriously?"

"Come on, you know me." She pointed at him like he had when trying to make a point. "I love your niece. I'm planning to spend my life with her if she wants that." Saying that she understood what he was talking about. They'd wasted so much time already, and making some big gesture might be either the way to cement what they were or what finally broke them apart. Either way it was a way forward.

Wade seemed to notice something in her expression. "Do you get it now?"

"Okay, don't gloat," she said, returning the favor of the middle finger.

"One more thing, Buck."

"Did you practice all this last night?" She laughed and stopped at the end of the property. Beyond this point was the start of the mouth of the river along with the delta that was formed by the moving water now that the levee system was starting to taper off.

"Don't be an ass." He swatted her side with his hat. "No, all I need for you to remember is to stay on the damn bulls. You're close enough to win it all, so don't settle. Not for anything."

Her phone rang before she could give him more grief, and she smiled at Reagan's picture. She'd stayed behind to spend the day with Helki to talk about horses. Booker and Albert were now in the pasture behind the house since the big black stallion refused to leave his new love and their coming foal. Asher couldn't blame him when she gave herself permission to dream about her future with Reagan and the family they could have.

"Hey, baby." She laughed when Wade put his hand over his heart and sighed. "You okay?"

"Hi, love, just checking on you," Reagan said but the easy words didn't fit somehow. "Are you and Uncle Wade on your way back?"

"We are, but can you do me a favor?" She waited until Reagan made a grunt of agreement. "I need you to find the plate in the office."

"I'll be right back," Reagan told someone. Asher stayed quiet until she heard a door close.

"Who are you talking to?" She turned the horse around and started back toward the gates. Whatever was happening, she needed to get home.

"Christine is here. She went to Moon Touch first, but one of the hands told her I was here. She said she wanted to surprise me, but also brought some legal papers." Reagan sounded upset, and it made Asher's chest hurt. "Will you come?"

Damn, it was like talking about her had conjured the bitch up. Reagan's question, though, broke something in her. That Reagan felt like she had to ask if she'd come meant they had a ways to go. "Baby, I'm on my way. If you want, stay in the office until I get there. I'll be thirty minutes or so."

"Thanks, honey. I don't think I can handle it alone. She hasn't changed one bit."

Asher remembered when they were fourteen and they'd come home to find Christine in the kitchen. She was way too made up, and all Asher could think was *plastic*. Christine Wilson didn't look like a real person, but she was a black hole of need. She didn't have any idea what the hell Silas had ever seen in the woman, but it wasn't her place to question.

The only good thing Christine had done in her life was Reagan. She hadn't raised her, hadn't been interested, but that day even with only fourteen years of experience she'd known one thing. Christine would forever see Reagan one way, and that was as her meal ticket. Whatever Wade had given her the last time must have run out. It was time to repay Silas yet again by taking care of this, but only if that's what Reagan wanted.

Wade followed but at a slower pace, so she sped her horse to a gallop, not wanting to keep Reagan waiting. She pressed her hat down and jumped down in the front yard and handed her reins off to the young hand waiting for her. Christine was probably parked in the kitchen, so she headed into the office. She hung her hat on the hook by the door and entered to find Reagan behind the desk, gazing out the window.

"Just remember one thing." She came up behind Reagan and put her arms around her until she could flatten her hands over her abdomen.

"What?" Reagan seemed to have trouble getting the word out. She held on to her arm like she was trying to convince herself that Asher was really there.

"I love you, and you'll never have to face anything alone again." She pressed up against Reagan and put her head on her shoulder. "I'm not trying to run your life, but would you like me to take care of this?"

"I can't ask you to do that. She's my mother." Reagan didn't turn around but tightened her hands over hers and sounded on the verge of tears. "I hate to call her that, but that's what she is."

"You don't have to ask. The way forward is together, but sometimes it's nice for one of us to lead. Today, if you allow me, it'll be my turn." She kissed Reagan's neck and straightened up. Wade was making his way toward the house, and she stared at him and his horse moving at a canter.

"Is your plan to throw her into the manure pile?" Reagan turned and put her hands on Asher's neck.

"I've been waiting on her. I can't be sure, but I think Wade took care of her last time. He wouldn't tell me how much he gave her, but it must've been substantial if we haven't heard from her in all this time. Unless she contacted you in Seattle."

"Just once, but I didn't want to see her." Reagan didn't look at her when she said that, and she thought it was because of the situation now.

She offered Reagan her hand and led her to the back where Christine seemed to be taking inventory of her surroundings. It was probably a way to gauge how much to ask for. "Christine," she said, getting her attention. "What can we do for you?"

"Asher, look at you, all grown up and so handsome." Christine's eyes were on their joined hands, and her smile was coy. "You're doing well from what I can tell."

"I am, but I'm not sure why you're here." It was no use being nice to this woman. She didn't want to waste her time on someone who'd never change.

"Don't be hostile, darlin'. You know I've always had a soft spot for you, but I'm here to see my daughter. It's been way too long, and then there's the matter of you using Moon Touch land." Asher pressed her fingers to Reagan's palm to keep her from showing emotion. "I saw the new fences going up where I have a say. You're trespassing from what I can tell, and we need to talk about that."

"I don't think that's right." She let Reagan go and took a step forward. When Christine took a small step back, it made her want to keep leading her toward the back door. "Now that you've seen Reagan, how about you and me talk business?"

Christine followed her, after picking up an old messenger bag that she must've bought at a secondhand store. Her eyes widened a bit when they entered the office and Christine stared at the desk. She'd be amazed if Christine remembered where it had come from. Then again, Christine went through life like an appraiser at an auction. When it came to money and things, she was always aware only because it might benefit her.

"It's easy to see who raised you, and the moves he taught you to intimidate me." Christine laughed as she sat across from her and crossed her legs. "Your hero wasn't the big man you all thought he was."

"I was raised by three good men. They believed in family, loyalty, and commitment." She steepled her fingers in front of her. "We're not here to talk about that either, so let's cut to it. What do you want?"

"Half of everything. The way I see it, half this place and everything else is mine. If you're a good girl, I'll let you keep the desk. It's so you." For dramatic effect, Christine dropped a stack of papers in front of her. "It's all in there."

Whatever this was, each page was yellowed with age. She took her time and got the gist of what this was. It was a will supposedly written by Silas giving Christine half of everything he owned, which Christine obviously thought included Pemberley. It was creative, but she knew better.

"How much will it take to get you to walk out of here and not come back?" She dropped the pile back in front of Christine and leaned back. "Think carefully, because if you agree, I'll have you arrested for trespassing if you come back."

"You can't keep me from Reagan, and you know what it'll take. You aren't family, Asher, so you have no right to any of this." Christine's voice started to rise, and it made Asher laugh. "Half of everything is what it'll take."

Asher opened the bottom drawer of the desk and pulled out a file. "This is the certified copy of Silas's will. It leaves everything in the estate to Wade and Reagan. You have no right to anything, especially here. Pemberley is mine outright, and the only one I'm sharing it with is Reagan, so stop wasting my time with this bullshit." She slammed her hand down, and Christine flinched. "How much?"

"If I'm not getting anything, then why offer me anything?" Christine appeared to be getting comfortable. She was staying, and she seemed resolute in getting what she wanted. "I still have the option of going to court. Maybe I lose but maybe I don't. No one's heard my side of the story."

"I know your side of the fantasy you choose to believe. The truth is, you left your child and your husband once you figured out there was no big payday." She slammed her hand again, ready to be done with this. Outside she heard the front door open and close and guessed Wade had finally arrived.

"A million and you never see me again."

Asher just stared at Christine and finally laughed when she saw she was serious. "A million dollars?"

"You don't look like a fool, Asher, so pay attention. Silas is dead, so I'm all Reagan has. If you don't want me to talk her into turning her back on all this, cut the check." Christine smiled in a way that was like a brash billboard advertisement that she had a secret that was too good not to share. "I've done it before, and I'm sure I can pull it off again."

"What…?" It hit her like Albert sitting on her chest. Give it to Christine to make the pain she'd suffered make perfect sense in the time it would take to snap her fingers. Reagan had been angry with Silas, and she'd turned to the one person who was an expert in hating him. Never mind that Asher had been collateral damage. Christine was like living napalm, and that's who Reagan had used to burn her to the ground.

"See, you're not a fool. You're just like him, and I tried my best to make her see that. She was never going to be your first choice in life. It's this fucking place, the bulls, and the role of big man that'll always win out over her." Christine laughed, and Asher couldn't breathe being locked in this room with her. "How much is she worth to you?"

She pulled out her checkbook and with a shaking hand wrote until she signed her name and put the pen down. "Take it, and don't come back. Reagan is free to have whatever relationship she wants with you, but you're no longer welcome here."

Christine glanced down and snarled. "Fuck you, Asher. You asked for this."

The door opened and Reagan stood there with an unreadable expression. "Honey?"

"Give it your best shot, Christine, but there'll be no more." Everything Wade had said came back to her, and she tried to tamp down her anger. Blaming Reagan now for a weak moment when she was eighteen wasn't fair, but it did put a spotlight on why she was afraid.

She gave in to the need for fresh air and left. It was a cowardly thing to do, but it was impossible to be strong all the time. "Fuck." She waited until she was at the fence to scream that into the air, and her mood summoned Albert and Booker. Trying to recover from losing Reagan again wasn't going to be as easy the second time around, and the first time hadn't been such easy riding. "Fuck." It was the best way to summarize everything in her head. She'd deal with the fact her heart didn't agree later.

❖

The tension in the office ratcheted up after Asher left, and Reagan didn't want to waste time with the shitstorm her mother had started. She'd stood outside the door but wasn't quick enough to open it before Christine gave Asher a history lesson. The truth was that she should've been honest with the entire truth before now. That was harder to face than Asher would be once she got rid of Christine.

"You had to tell her, didn't you?" she asked, and Christine appeared unfazed.

"Sweetheart, you have to face the fact that I'm the best friend you got in this world. Did you see how fast she ran out of here?" Christine pointed in the direction Asher had gone. "She's not in it for the long haul. You and me can sell our share and start over somewhere better than this."

Reagan stepped forward and snatched the check from Christine's fingers and glanced down. This was from Asher's private account and not the ranch's. Asher was trying her best to make it right for her, and she'd let her down in spectacular fashion. Christine lunged at her when she tore the check in two and then tore it again, letting the pieces fall to the ground.

"Get out and don't come back. I'm not eighteen anymore, and I'm not falling for this again. What you don't understand is how much Asher loves me because you don't have the first clue what love is." She put her hand up when Christine started to move toward her. "It took me a month before I figured out what you did back then, before you disappeared again, I mean. Once Daddy's will had been read and there was nothing in it for you, it was a couple of years before I heard from you again."

"It wasn't like that. I was trying to keep down two jobs so I wouldn't be on the streets, not that you care." When all else failed, Christine could fabricate guilt out of nothing. "I'm your mother."

"You gave birth to me, I'm not denying that, but you're no one's mother. I live with the guilt of how my relationship with Daddy ended because of the lies you sold me. It was my fault for believing you, so that's not on you." She pointed to the door, and Christine shook her head. "Asher forgave me, though, and I am starting over," she said forcefully, "here with Asher, and she was right. You're not welcome here or at Moon Touch."

"You can't do that."

"Don't make me get one of the hands to come and remove you," she said, headed for the phone.

"I'll take care of it, Buckaroo," Uncle Wade said. "You heard her, Christine. There's nothing for you here, so get out." He slammed the door after Christine walked through it before facing Reagan. "Hell, little girl, I'm out there giving Asher a lecture and she comes home to this? Do whatever you need to, but fix this."

She walked out and found Asher at the fence like she had that first day they worked on her ankle together. This time, though, Booker had joined Albert in offering comfort. "Please let me explain before you throw me out along with Christine."

"She's why you left?" Asher asked without facing her.

"Please, honey, let me talk to you. When Daddy got hurt and was in the hospital, Christine somehow found out about it. She called the house and caught me at a bad moment," she said and sighed. "I was angry and I fell for her lies. I stayed angry because I didn't know how to let it go, and it cost me so much. When the anger subsided, all that was left was guilt over what I'd done to you, and how I ended it with Daddy. After a year went by, I didn't see a way out of what I'd done—there was no way to fix it."

"Reagan, I wrote to you for two years." Asher wasn't exactly yelling, but her voice had risen. "That should've proved to you I wasn't angry, and you had a way home." Asher faced her then, but she knew better than to come closer and touch her. "You put me through hell, and it was all because of Christine. I don't know what to say to that. That she's the one who told me is like a gut punch."

"Do you know how hard it's been to keep that from you? I'm a fool, and of all the things I could've done to lose you, I can't believe it's this." Jesus Christ, she couldn't stop the tears again, and the hurt would never completely fade. "You have to know how mad at Daddy I was when he decided to go to that last rodeo. When he died, Christine sounded so reasonable, and she agreed with me."

"How long did she stick around?" Asher sounded flat, and they'd known each other long enough for Reagan to recognize it was a way of protecting herself.

"When she found out there was nothing for her in the will. What I did, it's not forgivable. I know that, but sometimes you don't see a way out because of grief, anger, and sadness. It's not an excuse, but it's what happened."

"It's not a deal breaker, Reagan, but it's a lot to process. Why didn't you tell me?" Asher leaned back against the fence, and Albert rested his chin on her head.

"I was trying to find a way, but I was scared." She shook her head. "It was more like I was terrified. I'd already hurt you so much, and this would've ended my chance with you if I'd told you. At least that's what I convinced myself of."

"Uncle Wade and I just had a talk where I told him the same thing, about being afraid. I'm afraid that you'll get bored and leave again." Asher tilted her head back and took a deep breath. "I didn't understand it the first time, and I sure as hell wouldn't get it now."

"Honey, I did not just go through all this to leave. Granted, I'm sure you'll toss me out now, along with my degenerate mother, but I want to marry you, not leave you." She took a chance and put her arms around Asher and held on. There was no way she could admit it to herself, but if this was going to be the last time, she wanted to memorize everything about the feel of Asher.

"I'm beginning to think we're both fools, and because we are, we're a perfect match for each other." Asher's arms came up and held her.

She laughed through her tears and counted herself lucky that fate had thrown her so many chances to get it right. "Why do you think so?" Her tears wet Asher's T-shirt, and she took a deep breath to control her emotions.

"We've both run these what-if scenarios in our heads," Asher said, "and have been too chickenshit to talk about it like reasonable adults."

"I'd say that was insulting, but you've included yourself in that assessment of the situation. You're right, though." It was a good thing Asher was holding her because she was weak enough to fall to the ground from relief. "Listening to anything Christine had to say, no matter how old I was, makes me the biggest fool of all."

"You're right," Asher teased and squirmed when Reagan pinched her. "Let's make a promise that there'll be no more secrets, and we'll try to do better when it comes to talking about what's going on with both of us."

"I know I asked you this already, but it's that simple?" She was chanting *yes* over and over in her head, hoping Asher picked up on her mental hints.

"When you love someone, it's easy to not only forgive but to forget. My dad used to tell me that all the time when he talked about him and my mom. They weren't together long, but like Silas, once she was gone, he never sought out anyone else." Asher framed her face and kissed her. "The only thing that really chaps my ass is that I gave Christine fifty grand. It's like paying her off for the most miserable years of my life."

"Actually, honey, your check is sitting on the floor of the office. I might sound like a heartless bitch, but I told her to never come back." She took Asher's hand when she headed to the barn closest to the house. Asher led out one of the young horses and vaulted onto his back without a saddle.

Reagan didn't hesitate to take a hand up when Asher offered it to her and hung on as Asher got them moving. They rode in silence until late afternoon, and they checked on the dairy barn that only needed a few finishing touches. She listened to Asher talk about all the things left to do before production ramped up. It was then—not that she needed the proof—that she knew she'd be happy if only Asher loved her until death parted them. Love wasn't found in the big grandiose overtures, but in the minutiae of the everyday.

Listening to Asher talk about what they would build might have been the big sweeping picture of the future, but the small details of what they were working toward made her daydream about all the things she'd never contemplated. In her mind's eye she could see children running around the big barn, trying to hide from going to school. They would all look like Asher and grow to love the land and the animals as much as the mother who'd teach them to.

"I love you," she said, squeezing Asher's middle as they headed back to the house.

"I love you too, Buckaroo, and we're going to be okay." Asher's voice was soft and wistful, and she wanted to reconnect to assure herself that what Asher was saying was how she felt.

"Want to turn in early tonight?" she asked when Asher helped her down. "I'm exhausted."

"How about a bath first?" Asher gave her a piggyback ride to the house but put her down when she spotted Uncle Wade.

"Asher, a word please," he said, not getting up from the rocker he sat in.

"Tomorrow, Uncle Wade—then you can ask whatever you want to," Asher said.

"Thanks for earlier, though," Reagan told him. "And stop frowning. Everything is fine."

"It'd better be," Wade said and winked.

"Trust me, she's a keeper, and I love her." That she meant, and she hoped Asher knew her as well as she knew ranching.

Chapter Twenty-two

Asher waited for their bags in the Vegas airport as Reagan stood to the side, talking to the driver who'd been sent to bring them to the Bellagio. They'd spent the days since Christine had come by with her big revelations in a kind of silent limbo that she was growing tired of. Eggshells were meant for chickens, but even after their talk about being honest and open, they were still hesitant.

"You ready?" she asked, shaking her head when the driver went to grab the bags. Carrying something made her feel more useful than breathing next to Reagan.

"Stan here was telling me we might make the next fountain show, honey," Reagan said. She was talking, but she didn't sound the same to Asher. Reagan sounded as if she was choking the words out, and she was getting tired of trying to get her to open up. "It's been forever since I've been here."

"I don't usually do much but the championships while I'm here, but it might be nice to take a few days before I get started." Stan dumped everything in the trunk while Asher glanced out the car window as Reagan took her hand. "Maybe tonight we could go out somewhere and have dinner. You've been stuck in the kitchen so long that I think Rickie is going to start complaining."

"I like taking care of you." Reagan's voice had a way of tapering off lately as if she wasn't sure Asher wanted to hear what she had to say.

They both stayed quiet after that, and by the time they checked in Asher had about as much of this as she was willing to put up with. Going into a bull riding competition with the best in the sport with her head in a jumble was asking to get gored or worse. Once the bellman put their bags away she ushered him through the door before he started on his spiel about the room and the hotel's services.

"Do you want to try something new?" she asked once they were alone.

What she knew in her bones was that some people would say Reagan wasn't worth taking a chance on. All the history between them, good and bad, was too much of a risk to overcome. But she wasn't some people. She was in love with this flawed but wonderful person. The truth, as Wade explained it, was she could walk away but by doing so would punish herself as well as Reagan, and she wasn't into self-inflicted pain.

"Like what?" Reagan stepped closer and took her hands. There was an apprehensiveness in her movements that Asher had to fix before they got to a point of no return.

"Get naked with me." That got her a laugh and a slight blush. Intimacy was something else they'd shied away from these last few weeks. "Get naked with me right now, and then I'll do whatever you want."

Reagan reached behind her and unzipped her dress, letting it pool at her feet. One of the things about Reagan that she loved was her choice of underwear. Today's set was white silk trimmed in lace, and Asher could've stared all day. She stood still when Reagan started unbuttoning her shirt, yanking it out of her jeans when she reached the waistline. That made her take a small step forward. The belt and the buttons of her jeans came next before Reagan pushed her to sit on the bed to get her boots off.

She slid the pretty panties off when Reagan stood between her legs, and she kissed Reagan's abdomen right under her belly button. Before they could get carried away, she pointed to the chairs by the window. They were high enough that no one would see in, and she sat in a chair and smiled at Reagan to put her at ease.

"Don't you think it'd be better if we could touch?" Reagan asked, taking the other chair.

"I haven't lost my mind, so don't worry. The thing I wanted to do differently is to talk with no barriers between us." She waved a hand down her body. "Nothing between us and nowhere to hide."

"You're amazing, do you know that?" Reagan said, blinking back tears.

"I want you to tell me why you don't believe me when I tell you that I've forgiven you." It had to be that Reagan was still skittish. "You've forgiven me, haven't you?"

"You haven't done anything wrong, so there's no reason you need forgiveness." Reagan wiped her face and laughed, but it didn't sound like anything resembling joy or humor. "I'm the one who keeps screwing up."

"You're talking about the woman I love." She leaned closer and offered Reagan her hand. "I need you to believe that I love you. Whatever happened is history, and I'm only interested in keeping the parts that we both cherish." She got on her knees before Reagan and took over the job of wiping her face. "For me, that's the days we spent with our fathers, with Uncle Wade, and the moments we knew this was it for both of us. It's also all the things we have now."

"Are you sure? I don't think I could handle it if you changed your mind." Reagan fell into her with her arms around her neck. "I love you, and I knew once Christine told you the truth, you'd never see me the same."

"See, was that so hard to say?" She cupped Reagan's cheek and kissed her. "Listen to me—I love you, and nothing is going to change that. And I don't see you the same," she said, and Reagan turned from her as if in shame. "I see you as the woman I love. That love started when we were children, but it's grown into something deeper, something more special, and something to fight for. So of course I don't see you the same. When I look now, it's so much better."

"Do you promise?"

"I promise." Asher kissed her again, missing Reagan even though they'd spent most of their time together.

"I promise too." Reagan smiled against her lips, and it seemed like all the tension in her body gave way. "And it was smart of you to get us naked."

"It'd be a shame to waste it, right?" She smiled back when Reagan wrapped her legs around her waist and hung on for the walk to the bed. "Will you do something for me?"

"Anything," Reagan said, and Asher believed her. "Whatever you want is yours."

"I want you to feel me"—she put her hand over Reagan's chest—

"in here. Feel me and believe that I'm not going anywhere. I'm right here, and I'll stay for as long as you want me."

"That's going to be a long time," Reagan said holding her jaw with her index finger and thumb as if she didn't want her to look away. It was intimate, something no one else had a right to do, and it turned her on. "I'm never letting you go, not ever again."

"Good, I want you to hold on and believe that." She moved her hand to cup Reagan's breast and never lost eye contact with her. They needed the connection that was more than physical for Reagan to know what was in her heart.

"Show me," Reagan said as her nipple hardened under Asher's palm. "Show me that I belong to you. Show me you're not going to let me go."

The soft command was freeing, and she moved on top as she put her hand between Reagan's legs. Reagan was wet and moved her hips up to encourage her to go inside. This place was hers alone, and she knew Reagan was hers. She blinked as she slid her fingers in and stopped, wanting to enjoy the way Reagan held her.

"Baby, please, show me." Reagan moved her hips again, and she pulled almost completely out before sliding back in. This was a moment to savor, enjoy, and to remember as their true beginning. Accepting that Reagan would always stay wasn't something she'd waste time worrying about anymore.

"Yes," Reagan said, looking into her eyes. "It's so good." The way Reagan squeezed her shoulders as well as her fingers made Asher speed their pace. "Like that, just like that."

The sound of skin slapping on skin, the way Reagan moved under her, and the smell of Reagan's perfume drove Asher to give Reagan everything she wanted. Love might've been about a whole life together, but this was special. Touching and loving Reagan was a privilege she'd never take for granted, not ever again.

"Oh God," Reagan said loudly before bowing her body and stiffening. Asher figured she'd have bruises on her shoulders, but these she'd wear with pride. "God." She started to move off when Reagan almost melted into the bed, but Reagan held her in place. "Stay," Reagan said, her eyes wet.

"Hey." The tears alarmed her. "What's wrong?"

"Nothing," Reagan said with a lazy smile. "Right now, there's not a damn thing wrong in my world."

Asher laughed and moved not too far away, not wanting to put her whole weight on Reagan. "I understand how you feel."

"You know I love you, right?" Reagan whispered in her ear when she pressed closer.

"I do." She rubbed Reagan's back all the way to her butt. "And right back at you."

"I do, but damn if I don't crave you. All those massages before we could get naked together were torturous. That you stripped so easily was downright cruel." Reagan's hand roamed from her chest down to her stomach, then her thighs. "It's a good thing you don't seem to realize how spectacular you are."

"Stripping is one thing, Buckaroo, but having your hands on me, and not the way I wanted, is my definition of torture."

"It sounds like we were on this same page even back then," Reagan said, squeezing her thigh. "It's nice being able to touch whenever I want."

"That is nice." She slipped her tongue into Reagan's mouth when she kissed her and groaned when Reagan broke away. There was no complaining when Reagan kissed down her body until she was kneeling between her legs. "You are one beautiful woman, my love."

"Thank you, but I'd have to disagree on what's the better view." Reagan's eyes swept down from her head to her knees. "Do you belong to me?"

"Yes," she said without hesitation. Her breath caught in her throat when Reagan lay on her stomach and put her mouth on her. It was embarrassing sometimes how fast Reagan got her to the point of total mindlessness, but it couldn't be helped. Touching Reagan ramped up her desire, which left her no room for patience when Reagan was this relentless with her mouth. "Fuck," she said as she put her hand behind Reagan's head.

The orgasm hit, and she gripped Reagan's hair trying to get her to stop before she broke something. "I love you," Reagan said as she kissed the inside of her thigh.

"And you're really good at it," she said with a smile. A wave of exhaustion hit her, but she gathered the last of her energy and held

Reagan when she moved up and draped herself over her body. "I love you too." She combed Reagan's hair back and kissed her forehead. "Do you believe me now?"

"Your powers of persuasion are hard to resist." Reagan rested her chin on Asher's chest and gazed at her. "Is there some precompetition ritual we should be doing?"

"I usually get here the day before and try not to think about the crowd." She threaded her fingers with Reagan's when she took her hands.

"Why are we here early, then?"

"I wanted to enjoy the time with you away from our crew asking questions every five minutes." She enjoyed the way Reagan smiled at that truth. "I was also thinking of locking us in here until you talked to me if this didn't work."

"Really?" Reagan let her hands go and moved up to kiss her. "You're a romantic fool, Asher Evans, and I love that about you."

"I have my moments, but right now I'm starving."

Reagan bit her bottom lip and shook her head. "I like the locked-in-this-room idea better than going out."

"I was going to say room service since the only thing better than naked talking is naked eating."

❖

Reagan had never spent the better part of four days doing mostly nothing. They'd explored the city, and it was surreal to be surrounded by so many cowboys and cowgirls there for the rodeo. They were a polite crowd, for sure, but still a crowd. That wasn't as surreal as the number of people who stopped Asher and asked for either her autograph or a selfie. Her lover had a legion of adoring fans, some of whom, mostly women, weren't thrilled to meet her and find out her role in Asher's life.

She'd said yes to Asher's dinner invitation instead of room service, so she was locked in the bathroom getting ready. The next night was the start of the bull riding competition, and she wanted to get Asher home early and into bed. Their time here had healed both the deep and shallow wounds between them, and for that she had to thank Asher. That her love had taken the time to not only put her at ease, but forgive her terrible mistake was the best gift she could've thought to give.

Her plan now was to convince Asher that their partnership should be more than just cows, horses, and pastureland. There was so much wasted time, all because of her, but now she was impatient to prevent anyone from usurping her place. She stared at the black dress she'd brought with her as she put on mascara and thought about Asher's reaction to it. Whatever it was going to be, it would have to wait until the championships were over. There was no way she was going to let Asher exert herself before she got on a bull no matter how much she loved her hands on her.

"Honey," she said and smiled when Asher jumped up, "could you zip me, please?" The underwear she'd chosen for the outfit matched the dress, and she could tell Asher liked it from the way she caressed her back. She'd skipped the lipstick for now, wanting to kiss Asher without having to redo her face.

"You look beautiful." Asher was about to kiss her again when someone knocked.

"Who is that?" If it was some fan who'd figured out where they were staying, she'd get rid of them herself. Why some women thought it was okay to openly flirt with someone's partner was beyond her.

"Maybe Uncle Wade," Asher said, shrugging. "If not, I wasn't expecting anyone." Asher patted her butt before going to see who it was, so she took the opportunity to put on lipstick and slip into her heels. "Uh…hi," she heard Asher say, and for some reason it didn't sound right.

"Hey, I hope I'm not interrupting, but do you know where Reagan is?" Steph asked.

What in the hell was Steph doing in Las Vegas, and why was she bothering them? For that matter, how had she found them? Steph's suit was Italian, as were the shoes, and all of it was perfect. If there was a pageant for handsome butch women, the two top contenders were right in front of her. "Steph, what are you doing here?" No reason for small talk. She had a date and a life to get to.

"I wanted to see you," Steph said with that smile that had fooled her one too many times.

When Reagan reviewed all the mistakes she'd made in her life, the most glaring ones made her wonder if she had some undiagnosed allergy that warped her brain. "Why?" She wanted to add a few expletives after that. In the interests of time and Asher not messing up her hand when she punched Steph in the face, she tried short and to the point.

"You haven't called me back, and I was worried about you," Steph said. If Steph had recited the entire works of Shakespeare, it would've been less bizarre than the explanation she'd just given.

"So you flew to Las Vegas to check?" Asher asked, glancing back at her. "Did you just take a wild guess she was here?"

Reagan found Asher sexy all the time, but jealous Asher was in a different league of sexy. "She's right. How did you know I was here?"

"I called the clinic, and they told me. That might sound stalkerish, but I *needed* to talk to you." Steph squeezed by Asher and came in. "You look beautiful, by the way."

Reagan flinched when the door slammed a little louder than she thought was courteous to their neighbors.

"Okay," Asher said, "let me get this straight. You called Reagan's work, jumped on a plane, and somehow figured out where we were staying so you could show up here? You did all that because you had to talk to Reagan? Does that about sum it up?"

"When you say it like that, it sounds creepy, but I thought Reagan and I could go to the rodeo together." Steph seemed completely serious, and Reagan put her finger up.

"We have a reservation, so I can't talk to you right now." She opened the door and waved toward the exit, grateful Steph walked through it. Steph turned to say something, and she slammed the door this time. "I had no way of knowing, and she's way out of line."

"Okay." Asher sounded way too in control. "Ready?"

"Honey, please. If it takes getting naked to have this conversation, we'll skip dinner and do that, but you know I didn't invite Steph here." She put her arms around Asher's middle under her jacket and tried to get Asher's attention. "That was over way before I met you, even if the first time we saw each other, I was with Steph. I tried being friends with her, but if it's going to devolve into this, then forget it."

"Is her sudden interest something to do with me, you think? That whole wanting something only because someone else does?" Asher relaxed as Reagan rubbed her back.

"Do you want to stay in?"

"No, I want to take you out because you look beautiful." Asher kissed the tip of her nose and took her hand. "Will I sound childish if it pissed me off that she said that like she meant it?"

"It only counts when you say it, honey, so don't worry. I dressed for you and no one else." They made it into the lobby, and when they stepped off the elevator, she saw Steph standing there. "Would you mind waiting just a second? I need to set some things straight."

"Take your time. I'll head to the lobby bar and call to have them hold our reservations. Want something?"

"I'd like wine with dinner, so don't order anything for me. I won't be long." She kissed Asher before turning and thanking God she didn't have a pistol in her purse. Steph would've needed a tailor to repair the great suit. "What in the hell? I mean, what in the holy fuck were you thinking?"

"When I didn't hear from you for a couple days, weeks actually, I started to question my life and what an asshole I was to you. I mean, I'm seriously in love with you, and I couldn't wait another minute to tell you." Steph put her hands on her biceps and held her in place as she talked a mile a minute. "If you can forgive me, we can start over."

"Have you completely lost your mind?" This had to be some kind of joke. "I'm in love with Asher, and even if I wasn't in love with Asher, there would be no going back. We were old history way before the move, and I think we're both intelligent enough to realize that."

It was obvious Steph was not grasping her polite way of telling her to fuck off. Maybe the pollen count in the flower garden in the Bellagio's lobby was making Steph high, but she needed to get the hell away from her. "Whatever is going on with you, the way to handle it is to get on a plane and lie down when you get back to New Orleans. Once you're rested, seek medical help."

"Reagan, listen—"

Whatever else Steph had to say died in her throat when Asher put her hand on her shoulder really close to her neck. It must've hurt because Steph grimaced when Asher squeezed. "Listen to me," Asher said, and Reagan went back to rubbing circles underneath Asher's jacket. She didn't want her to miss the beginning of her competition because she was in jail for attacking Steph. "You might think this is some big romantic gesture that's going to win you the girl, but let me tell you something."

"I made a mistake." Steph gazed at her and not Asher, which

proved she wasn't in her right mind. Steph's eyes should've been on Asher, to preserve her health.

"There's making a mistake," Asher said, "and then there's making a mistake while your jaw heals if you don't leave Reagan alone."

"You don't speak for her," Steph responded.

"No, I don't, but I don't see a touching reunion in your future." Asher held her hand out and Reagan took it.

"I'm staying here, so when you change your mind, call me," Steph said, and both Reagan and Asher shook their heads.

"Unbelievable," Asher said. They walked to Prime without looking back.

The manager treated Asher like visiting royalty, which made her smile. "Friend of yours?" she asked as Asher pulled her chair out for her.

"Customers of mine," Asher said, kissing the back of her hand. "Or should I say *ours*?"

"Are you mad?" She was still trying to figure out what the last half hour of her life was all about. While she didn't love Steph making a complete ass of herself at her expense, she did enjoy Asher's reaction. In her heart she'd always believed that love sometimes wasn't expressed in pretty words, but in deeds and action. Asher's defense had nothing to do with proving ownership, but in caring she was okay.

"At you, no. I'm not sure about your friend, though. People like that make up stuff in their heads and act out on it, so be careful."

"Trust me, honey. Steph is more interested in winning than in me."

"I know that, love, but you need to promise me something." Asher held her hand on the table, and she nodded. "I know you can fight your own battles because you're a strong, capable woman. The thing is, you don't have to do that alone any longer. If that woman gives you trouble, I need you to tell me."

"God, I love you."

The rest of dinner was wonderful, and it helped them both get Steph out of their heads. Whatever bizarre reason Steph had for showing up and professing her love had seemingly burned out because they didn't see her on the way back up to their room. The strangest thing was Steph hadn't seemed unstable when they actually had been together, so she hadn't learned not to trust her.

In the elevator she pressed against Asher and put her hand over Asher's heart. The older couple sharing the space with them smiled when Asher kissed her until she had to pull away before it got too heated. All her plans to let Asher rest were forgotten when Asher undressed her and pressed up behind her. In front of the full-length mirror, Asher let her hands wander and never took her eyes off her as she touched.

"Fuck, you look good in these panties," Asher said, her finger just under the waistband. Reagan was about to beg when Asher unhooked her bra and dropped it to the floor.

Once she was naked from the waist up, Asher palmed her breast until both her nipples hardened enough that she felt it in her clit. The other hand went back to the panties, and Asher shook her head when she moved to take them off. All Asher had taken off was her jacket, so she felt the belt buckle pressed to her back, but all that didn't matter. Right now she wanted—no, needed—Asher to put her hand between her legs and make her come.

"Don't close your eyes," Asher said as her fingers slipped into Reagan's very wet sex.

She wanted to be lying down with Asher over her, but this very safe and warm cocoon was also a place she didn't want to lose. Asher held her up as she went inside, and she had to fight to keep her eyes open and gaze at Asher's reflection as she loved her. That's what she was doing in the most tender, slow, and possessive way ever, and Reagan loved it. It was plain to see how much Asher loved her, and she leaned her head back on Asher's chest and let go.

Her moan sped Asher up, and she wanted to collapse onto the floor, but she hooked her arm behind Asher's neck and moved her hips in time with Asher's hand. "It's so…so good. Please, baby, make me come." Her skin tingled as the orgasm started, and her knees gave out, but she trusted Asher to keep her upright. "Yes, yes, yes." She couldn't help but squeeze her eyes and thighs together, trapping Asher's hand between her legs. The orgasm was intense, and she would've fallen to the floor if Asher let her go.

Her tears fell despite her eyes being closed, and she hung on as Asher carried her to the bed and laid her down. Asher had overwhelmed her, and she rolled on her side in a silent request to be held. It was hard to describe how completely happy she was, but it only ramped up when she felt Asher's naked body press up to hers.

"You know I love you, right?" She had to be sure that Asher was aware of how deep her feelings were.

"I do, and I'm just as in love with you. I don't want to go all caveman on you, but you're mine. There's no doubt I'm all yours, but you're mine." Asher held her as she whispered that as if not wanting to disturb the peace in the room. Here all of the madness of Vegas was far away from them.

"I do know, and you're right. I'm all yours."

Chapter Twenty-three

"Win or lose tonight, Asher," Tyler said as he shook her hand, "you've been good for the sport, and a hell of an opponent."

It wasn't often Tyler was this sentimental, Asher thought as she smiled when he slapped her on the back. "Thanks."

"I'm going to kick your ass tonight, but I'm glad it's you and me in there. We're the best in the business, so no one can dispute I'm the top dog when I kick you to the curb."

So much for Tyler's sentimentality. "Maybe next time, pretty boy. This is my last rodeo, and I'm taking home the buckle that's missing from my collection. If anyone's getting their ass kicked, it's you."

"What the hell does that mean?" Tyler asked in stereo with Red, the promoter, when he walked up on their conversation.

"I'm retiring before my body makes the decision for me, so good luck." She shook hands with Tyler again before he walked off, still looking a little shell-shocked.

"Is it Reagan who made this decision for you?" Red asked, whipping his hat off. "I know how she felt about all this when her daddy was alive, and I can't imagine she's changed much on the subject."

"I decided at the beginning of the season." She appreciated all Red had done for her, but the guy was like a freight train when it came to pushing for what he wanted. "New Orleans, that event you threw at everyone, was the proof I needed that it's time to go. I have a business and a life to get back to."

"Dammit, Asher, you're at the top of your game. Quitting now is plain rotten timing."

"Good to see you, Red, but I have to go and get ready." She walked back toward the arena, wanting to check it out before the competition began. This time around she'd sent both Uncle Wade and Reagan up to the stands to enjoy the event. It's not that she wanted to be alone, but it made her happy to have them looking on instead of worrying at the fence. Not that they wouldn't worry up there, but watching from the stands gave a whole different perspective. The little bit of distance almost made it more tolerable for her family.

"You really quitting?" Tyler asked when he bent and scooped up a handful of dirt and poured a bit into her palm. They both scrubbed their hands with it and didn't make eye contact.

"I love doing this shit. I won't lie about that." She gripped the rail and nodded. "In the end, though, it has to stop sometime, and that's now for me. I have the girl I've always wanted, and she's worth more than all this."

"Do they give you a buckle for that?" Tyler slapped her on the back again. "Congratulations, and once this is over, I'm inviting myself over to train with that stable of bulls I keep hearing you have."

"Anytime, my friend, and you are that. Despite your overinflated ego, you've been a good friend, Tyler." They headed back to the holding area to wait for their lots to be pulled.

"Don't blow smoke up my ass, Evans. You know damn well I thought you didn't belong here when we first started, but you've proven me way wrong. I'm now an evolved member of the male dumbass species because of you. That should make you proud." They both laughed. "Next thing I know, I'll be wearing pink boots."

"Now who's blowing smoke."

They set the roster, and they were together at numbers six and seven. If she didn't know any better, she'd say that Red fixed the order to showcase the best four after starting off with the guys who had no chance at the buckle. She stood close to the chutes and watched Tyler waiting for the chance to get on the black bull that acted like someone had stuck a prod up his ass. Good old Bo III was getting loaded into the next chute, and she'd wait until Tyler was out before trying to get on. The two bulls seemed to feed off the other's bad mood, so she almost felt bad for Tyler.

The crowd roared at hearing Tyler's name, and it only got louder when he flew out of the chute like someone had gone for the prod again. His form was good, and she winced at the ninety-four he posted. He pointed at her and then the scoreboard before raising his fist. The high score was beatable, but only if she was on top of her game. She didn't think about waiting and jumped on Bo's back, hoping to get him somewhat under control.

He started bucking right away and seemed to have figured out that moving side to side would get the chute door to open faster since she didn't want a broken leg. She turned her feet in and laid them flat against his body as she tightened her rope. Bo let out a scream that she'd never heard a bull do, and in a way, it was a harbinger of this ride. The chute opened when she nodded, and Bo almost fell sideways he was in such a hurry to get out.

The first buck that moved her body backward made her shoulder hurt from the pull it took to keep her seat. It was like this damn animal remembered her and was trying his best to get her off and under his hooves. She closed her hand into a tighter fist and threw her arm back. Every lesson Silas taught her came back into her mind. Silas always told her to slow the ride down in her mind and remember the mechanics. It's what had won it for him, and that had been her way to the top.

She shook her head when she heard the buzzer and didn't take the chance to stay on Bo's back any longer than she had to—she jumped clear. He turned his head as if trying to find an angle of attack, so she made it through the gate as the score came up. Ninety-six put her in the lead, and she laughed when Tyler lifted his middle finger in her direction.

The next ride wouldn't be for a while, so she sat and accepted a water bottle from one of the attendants. She glanced at her phone and laughed at the emoji blowing a kiss from Reagan. She sent a response that she was taking it easy until she was up again. That her phone rang right after that didn't surprise her.

"Hey, love." She wiped her face with a towel.

"I'm terrified for you, but you were so good. Are you okay? Did the ankle hold up when you jumped off that monster?" Reagan's questions came fast and furious, but she was used to it.

"I'm okay, and it's insulting to my physical therapist to question my ankle." That made Reagan laugh. "Two more, and I'm all yours all the time."

"You're all mine all the time now," Reagan was quick to respond. "And I'll deny this until we're old and feeble, but you look hot doing that."

"See, got you there in the end." She laughed this time, and Reagan joined in.

"I just said I'd deny it, and Uncle Wade wants you to know you were almost perfect on that last run. According to him almost is for losers, so try harder." Reagan must've cupped her hand over the phone for the last part. "Now meditate, or whatever it is that helps you get ready, and know I'm right here and I'm proud of you. I love you, Buck."

Reagan's use of her nickname made her fingers twitch like they always did when she said it. Silas might've come up with it, but Reagan's use of it had a very different connotation, and it still had the same effect on her. "I love you too, and you own my heart. Whatever comes next, know that we'll get through it together."

"Remember to duck and weave or whatever gets you out of there in one piece."

"You got it, and when I'm done we'll have plenty to talk about."

❖

Reagan ended the call and slipped her phone into the back pocket of her jeans. She'd been biting her thumbnail from the moment she sat down, but Uncle Wade held her free hand and didn't talk. He was good at knowing when there were no words necessary. Hearing Asher's voice had helped, but she wouldn't relax until this was over and Asher was back in her arms.

"Reagan…" She heard her name, and she was instantly wary. "Just five minutes and I promise I'll leave you alone." Shit, maybe Asher was right and she should've been more concerned.

"Steph, come on. What in the hell is all this? We both know you aren't getting me back." She moved when Steph reached to touch her, and Uncle Wade's expression must've been enough to make Steph drop her hand. "How did you even get here?"

"I tipped the usher, and I'm not going to take long." Steph was at the railing, and Reagan didn't want Asher to glance up and see her there.

"Five minutes and then I'll have security carry you out."

"I did miss you, but I'm really here for the rodeo. I wanted to see Asher in action, and I do believe this will be her year." Steph spoke faster when she narrowed her eyes. "I know you hate me after last night, but I do care enough to make sure you're okay. She loves you, and I'm glad you finally found your happily ever after."

"I'm not sure if anyone's ever told you how full of shit you are, so let me be the first. What's all this about? You have yet to answer that question." She put her hand up. "And don't say it's because you love me, or I'll throw a punch."

Steph shrugged, which was never good. "I did call the clinic, and the receptionist told me you were here. That part was true." The speed of Steph's words meant whatever was coming should be quickly gotten out of the way. "It made me want to see you, and since my current relationship is as exciting as reading the phonebook, I thought you'd like to do dinner or something. You said you weren't interested in Asher. You and me don't have to be some big love affair, but we know each other. It could be fun."

"That I believe, and you really need professional help. Either that or a priest who can lead you in prayer to become a decent human being. You're really unbelievable."

"Come on, Reagan. You can't blame me for checking to see if you were interested. You used to love me."

"Love was something that never happened between us, and if you come around again, I'm taking Asher off her leash." She had to laugh at Steph's approach to life. In truth she'd once been a good friend, but not the woman for her.

"I thought you'd say that, so tell Asher she's one lucky bastard. You're in good hands if last night was any indication." Steph smiled, but that ploy wasn't getting her forgiveness this time.

"Did you stop by last night to get that reaction out of her?" Good God, her life was turning into some kind of reality television nonsense.

"I doubt you'll believe me, but I do care about you, and I wanted to make sure you'll be okay. Like I told you before, you were never mine because your heart has always been with Asher. That first night, though, made me question if she'd ever get there with you." Steph placed her hand over hers, and she didn't move away. "It was dicey last night because she was willing to fight for you, and to me, that means you're fine."

"You're a complete fool, but thank you. Now go find your seat, so I can go back to worrying about Asher."

She watched Asher sitting on the railing getting ready through the binoculars Uncle Wade had brought, and she held her breath studying Asher's expression. It was the kind of focus Reagan figured anyone needed if they were contemplating getting on an animal that did in no way want to be ridden. All she could focus on was that Asher was strong and knew what she was doing. And she knew there was only one ride after this.

"Who picked out that shirt?" Frida asked when she lowered the binoculars.

"She does look good in white," someone standing behind them said. "It's the tan, don't you think?"

Reagan turned and found a smiling Jacqueline Blanchard. She was even more gorgeous than the first time she'd seen her, and she could just image what Asher would be doing if she was stuck up here at the moment. If there had been a competition, Asher would be the winner for the ex category.

"Hi." It was all she could think to say.

"Hello, and congratulations. I'm thrilled you and Asher are together," Jacqueline said, sitting in the empty seat behind them, then moving over when a guy joined her. "When she called and said you were able to work it out, I was happy for both of you."

"Thank you, and thank you for being such a good friend to her." It was painful to say, but it's not like she hadn't given Jacqueline and a whole line of women an in.

"I know what you're thinking," Jacqueline said with a smile that spoke volumes. "Asher's memorable, not going to lie about that, but she's all yours. I knew it from the day I met her, only I didn't exactly know it was you."

"It's easy to see what she likes about you," Reagan said and laughed.

"Trust me, she loves my ability to pay for good steaks." Jacqueline winked and put her hands on Reagan's shoulders when they called Asher's name again.

She glanced up and saw Steph sitting a section up from them, but she was on her feet like everyone else who was a fan. Tyler had posted a ninety-six, so Asher had to post ninety-five or higher to keep the lead. The name of the bull came up on the large screens, and the oohs from the crowd tightened her shoulders and stomach. Diablo was a cliché name for a bull for sure, but the way Asher was moving in the chute, the bull was aptly named.

It was like she was standing alone in the arena when the chute opened and Asher came out. The sport was barbaric, but she remembered everything her father said to look for when watching a rider, and Asher's form was as close to perfect as she'd seen. Reagan had picked the white shirt Frida had mentioned and could see it was the perfect choice. Had Asher been a weaker rider, the white against the dirt of the arena would've highlighted every mistake, but in Asher's case it had the opposite effect.

Reagan counted in her head and saw Asher lean one way leading the bull before jumping off the other side. Her heels seemed to sink into the dirt once she was on her feet, but she started for the gate with a wave to the crowd. The clowns were trying their best to get the bull's attention, and it was working until the bull changed his mind. She screamed for Asher to turn around, but with the thousands around her, her voice was swallowed by the crowd. When the bull's right horn hooked Asher's leg, Reagan lost the strength in her legs, and she dropped into her seat.

"Come on," Uncle Wade said as Asher was helped through the gate.

It felt like an instant later that she was standing over Asher, whose face was a mask of pain. But all she could think was that, while it probably didn't feel great, Asher was fine. She'd be okay, and she tried to take comfort in that as she kissed her like she wanted to assure herself that would indeed be the outcome.

"I'm okay, baby. I promised I would be." Asher sat up and moved so Reagan could sit next to her. "It cut me, but it didn't hit bone."

"Asher, we have to stitch that up," the medic said.

"Man, I came so close," Asher said in as dejected a tone as she'd ever heard from her.

Reagan tightened her hold on Asher, wanting to take her to the hospital and agree that she'd come close, but it was over. That's not what Asher needed from her right now. "Honey, let them stitch you up, and then I'll wrap it. You have one more ride in you, so don't tell me you're done. You're done when you win."

"I'd listen to the lady," Tyler said, standing over them. "We're all tied up after that ride. There ain't no way I'm listening to how I won because you chickened out. Get the stitches and get the third ride over with, so I can kick your ass in a clutch finish."

"Come on, we'll do it in the bus," the medic said.

Reagan followed her in and helped get her jeans off. "Do you have an extra pair?"

Asher shook her head and rolled to her stomach. "I'll finish in these. They're not that ripped, are they?"

"You'll look badass," the other medic said.

"She's right," she whispered into Asher's ear. "You have one more. I don't want to hear later how you should've tried. You're going to, end of story."

Asher rolled her head to the side so she could look at her and appeared confused. "You want me to go back out there?"

"Listen, I was wrong. I've told you this a thousand times. The thing is, I know how much you want this, so unless you think you're physically incapable, it's either go back out there, or we go through another season to get back here. Daddy can't be the only one in the family with a championship to his name." She leaned in and kissed Asher again. It had taken so much to get to this point, not just for Asher, but also for the two of them. Asher didn't do this for ego or fame, but to prove to herself she could. Her father had done the same. That was the simple truth of it.

"I'm not putting you through that again. I promised, and I intend to keep it." Asher grimaced, and Reagan glanced back to see the medic starting to stitch.

"I know, Buck, but this is important."

Asher bit the tip of her index finger when she put it near her mouth. "Our future is important."

"Then go out there and win this for me. I need a new buckle, so start meditating the pain away." She pointed to the lidocaine, and the medic injected more around the wound. "Do you need something to drink?"

"Get me a water." When the woman was done, Asher stood and pulled up her pants. "And maybe an aspirin."

"No aspirin, my love, and pull your pants back down again."

"Not the time for that, baby." Asher laughed as she lowered her pants.

Reagan kissed her abdomen before accepting an ACE bandage from the medic. She wrapped Asher's leg tight enough to keep the pain at bay until she was done, but not tight enough to cause a problem. Asher allowed her to pull her jeans up and buckle her belt before bouncing on her feet as if testing her leg.

"How's that feel?" she asked as Asher put her arms around her.

"Good, thanks for taking care of me."

They kissed, and the tension in her stomach dissolved when Asher pressed their lips together. "I love you, so don't let me or your cheering section down. It's getting crowded."

"What's that mean?" Asher nodded to the medic when she gave them some privacy.

"With Steph, Jacqueline, and the family—it's crowded." She laughed at Asher's expression of…well, she couldn't figure out what exactly. "Don't worry—Steph's little act was a test for you, according to her, and Jacqueline does seem like a good friend."

"You want to head back up?" Asher slid her hands into her back pockets and kissed her again.

"This last ride, I want to watch it from down here. I don't think I can be that far away from you, especially since I know you're hurt." She stood on her toes and put her lips on Asher's forehead. They heard Tyler's name, so they didn't have a lot of time. "I love you, and I know Daddy is watching out for you, so don't hold anything back."

"Thanks, love, and for much more than for being here. You understand?"

She placed Asher's hat on her head and kissed her for luck. "When it comes to you, it'll always be my goal to understand you as well as love you with my whole heart."

CHAPTER TWENTY-FOUR

A sher put on Silas's gloves and climbed the side of the chute. The russet-colored bull named Lupo was one of the worst on the circuit, so of course he was the one up next for her. When life gave you shit, there were only two ways to deal with it. Walk away or slosh through it and say you survived it. That's what her father had taught her, and she wasn't about to walk away.

"You okay?" the rodeo worker asked when she got to the top.

"I need a patch job on my pants, but I'm ready to go." She waited for Tyler to finish his ride and wasn't surprised when he finished strong. A ninety-eight would've been hard to beat with no injury, but now it was slogging uphill for sure. "Do you have time to shave his horns down?" It was a joke, but she couldn't help but stare at the horns that appeared to be filed to sharp points.

They wrapped the rope around the bull's chest, and she took a deep breath before climbing on. Her leg hurt. She didn't know if the adrenaline in her system was overriding the numbing shots, but she was in pain. It couldn't matter right now. Right now she needed to get ready for the last ride of her career and make Silas, Wade, her father, and Reagan proud, win or lose. She'd give it all right now to get this done.

She ran her hand up and down the rope, thinking of Silas and the run he'd had when he won. He'd been so fluid on that ride, almost as if he'd trained the bull to move the way he wanted. It's what had gotten him the ultimate—the control and movements had been as perfect as the score. The worker pulled her hat down when she motioned for him to, then nodded before she could rethink the million little things that could go wrong.

Her arm went in the air from the moment the chute opened, and she gripped the big animal with her legs, ignoring the pain. She kept her eyes on the big head and tried to anticipate the way he was going to move and went with it. The best way to go with him was to relax as much as she could without falling off. Her mind was quiet, no old ghosts rattling around, and no second-guessing.

The bull's hooves sounded like a drum when they pounded the dirt, and he seemed to conserve his strength by not grunting. For once the roar of the crowd bled through a little until the buzzer sounded like a canon signaling the end of her battles. There was nothing else she needed to do in the arena, and she was happy with that decision. She lifted her right leg over and jumped free, dropping the rope and doffing her hat to the crowd.

"Asher Evans, everyone," the announcer said as she spotted Reagan. "Can you believe it?" He announced the score, and she thought for a moment he'd misspoken, but the roar of the crowd made it real.

Reagan smiled like she did when she was totally pleased with life. "A perfect score, honey." She threw her arms around Asher's neck, and her legs around her waist. "Daddy would've been out of his mind. I know I am."

She'd remember this moment for the rest of her life. The joy of winning was made better because Reagan was holding and kissing her for winning a bull riding competition. If that didn't prove they'd come full circle, nothing in life ever would. Now they could move forward, and it meant she'd won the best prize of all.

"This year's champion bull rider, everyone," the announcer said again as the gate opened. "Asher Evans!"

She lifted her hand and laughed when Tyler came out and shook her hand. "It's yours next year."

"Won't mean the same if I can't kick your ass, but that ride was something." He walked away to let her have her moment.

She glanced around until she found the section where Wade and Frida were seated. They both stood, and Frida blew her a kiss. She placed her hand over her heart and tapped her fingers over her chest. Now that one of her dreams had come to be, they had the freedom to go and enjoy the life they were still trying to build together. Right now, she loved them for the support they'd given unselfishly through the years to get her to the top.

"Come on," she said to Reagan when it came time to collect her winnings. The money would pay off the barn, and the other one she had planned for the other end of the property. Even with all that construction, there would be a good bit left for whatever else they had planned, making her promise to Silas a reality. Taking care of Reagan wouldn't be a problem, but he'd gotten that part wrong. They'd take care of each other.

She was exhausted and in pain by the time they got back to their room, so the thought of going to Blanchard's to eat was as appetizing as taking a shower with that last bull she'd ridden. Reagan sent her into the bathroom and she took her time scrubbing off the dirt of the arena. When she stepped out with a new bandage on her leg and a robe, there was a table set up in the middle of the room with dinner. There was a note in the flowers, and she recognized the handwriting.

Congratulations, cowpoke, and I don't mean for the title you walked away with tonight. She's lovely, so take care of her. J

"Are you ready to head home?" she asked Reagan as they sat down.

"Yes, and I've made up my mind about my condo." Reagan fed her a shrimp from her plate, and Asher couldn't help but notice the opening of her robe.

"I'm okay with whatever you want, love."

"I want to go home, put up a For Sale sign, and never leave Pemberley." Reagan undid the belt of her robe and pointed to her plate. "Now, eat up. You're going to need the energy."

It was hard not to think about how far they'd come. Pain was transforming, but it made you appreciate days like this. "I love you, and I think that's some great ideas."

"You, my love, are everything I ever dreamed of in a partner. Loving you will be the best thing in my life, so thank you for this life you've given me." Reagan leaned in and kissed her palm.

"I can't wait for what comes next."

❖

Reagan woke up and sighed when she found the bed empty. They'd been home for three weeks, and Asher had taken very few days off as the new barn came online and they worked out the kinks as they started producing milk. It was Saturday, though, dammit, and that should mean a day off, but she'd moved in with the worst workaholic on the planet.

Rickie was still in the kitchen when she made it downstairs, and she handed over a cup of coffee and a muffin. She was a lot like Frida—if you didn't make it down by six, you missed out on a hot breakfast. It was kind of funny, considering the kitchen was in essence hers, but she didn't feel like arguing.

"Hello, pretty," she said to the mare the hand brought out to her when she requested a horse. Booker was still pregnant, so she'd given her a break until the foal was born. "Is Asher at the barn?"

"No, ma'am." The young hand tipped his hat after giving her a hand up. "You might want to head over to the graveyard. She said she had to talk to your daddy this morning."

She set out and kept going when she didn't see Asher at the tombs. There were fresh flowers on each one, so she went to the one place she figured she'd find Asher. The small cabin's door was open, and the horse Asher had ridden was grazing off in the distance, so she dismounted and allowed hers to join it.

"Good morning," she said when she went in and found Asher in the small kitchen putting together a plate of something. "You could've stayed home and had whatever that is in bed."

"True, but if I had, I wouldn't have been able to lure you out here for the day," Asher said, putting the plate in the refrigerator. "Here I get you all to myself."

"I like the way your mind works, then," she said, hanging on when Asher hugged her hard enough to lift her off the floor. "Is it crazy to miss you when I see you all the time? Either way, I've missed you."

"Sorry about that, love, but now that we're milking, it should get easier. That's why I wanted to spend the day with you." Asher moved them to the couch and kept her arms around her. "There was something I wanted to give you, and I didn't need an audience."

She got goose bumps when she thought about what it could be. There was something she wanted from Asher, but there was no way she'd push. "What?" Asher grabbed a box from the bottom of the couch and handed it over. She tried her best not to show disappointment. The box was way too big for what she had in mind. "What's this?"

"Open it." She lifted the top off and found the buckle Asher had just won. Asher had handed it over the night she'd won it, but she'd given it back.

"Honey, you should wear this. How about I have it put on a nice belt, and you wear it for special occasions? It's too nice to hang on the wall."

"I have one of those already. Your dad gave it to me." Asher pointed down to the belt she was wearing. It was her dad's championship buckle.

"Thank you." She held the buckle and smiled at Asher, just noticing something about her. "Is there some reason you're all dressed up?" The dark jeans paired nicely with the white shirt and great boots. It was a variation of what Asher wore when they went to Uncle Wade's on Sundays. Frida insisted no one look like they were about to round up cattle.

"I thought I'd put in the effort even if our date is out here where only you'll see me." Asher sat on the coffee table across from her.

She put the gift aside and took Asher's hands. It was things like this that warmed her. That same Asher who would voluntarily get on a bull was also this sweet and romantic, and that made the naive young fool she'd once been still live on in her memories. There was lucky, and then there was having Asher Evans love her.

"You have a way of making me feel special." That got her a smile, followed by a kiss that made her unbutton the top two buttons of Asher's shirt.

"We'll get to that, but there's one more thing before we get naked." Asher moved until she was on one knee. "We've been through a lot, but the best thing that's ever happened to me is that we found our way back to each other." Asher took her hand and it felt clammy. Nervous was a state Asher didn't do often.

"That's because of you, honey."

Asher smiled again and pressed a finger to her lips. "No knocking yourself, so please let me finish." They kissed again, and Asher cocked her right eyebrow as if to keep her from talking, and she nodded. "It might've been painful for both of us, but I'd live through it again if I ended up here with you."

"That's sappy, baby, and I love it."

Asher pinched her side and laughed. "Stop talking so I can get to the proposal part of this."

Those words froze her brain. She'd wanted it, prayed for it, and wished but never thought Asher would ask so soon. "Really?"

"Reagan, I love you. Hell, I want to spend a lifetime loving you, and I want the world to know it." Asher took something from her front pocket and palmed it. "That might be sappy, but I don't know how else to tell you." She opened the box to a beautiful square-cut diamond in what appeared to be a platinum band. "In this life and all the others to come, there will only be you for me. You're my perfect match, and I don't want to wait another moment not telling you how much I want a life with you. Will you marry me?"

She'd started nodding the second Asher said *proposal*, but she was having a hard time getting the word out of her mouth. To ground herself, she pulled Asher forward and kissed her passionately. She took a deep breath and closed her eyes for a moment. "Yes, a thousand times yes."

Asher placed the ring on her finger and held her when Reagan fell into her. "If you want something different, we'll go shopping together."

The ring caught the morning light through the front window, and she couldn't imagine it not being on her finger. It was gorgeous and exactly what she would've picked for herself. "You gave it to me, and it's not coming off."

"Then it's you and me, a wedding, and forever." Everything Asher had said that morning was perfect, and that only added to the emotions building in her.

"I love you, and that sounds perfect." She kissed Asher again and smiled. "You are perfect for me."

EPILOGUE

Three years later

Reagan sat in the grass at the back of the house nursing her and Asher's five-month-old daughter Wynn while their two-year-old daughter Dustin got a riding lesson from Asher. It had taken some convincing for Asher to go along with naming their firstborn after her father, but the name fit perfectly. Dustin, like her late grandfather, loved every animal on the ranch from the moment she could walk, and like her mother, showed no fear.

That at times drove Reagan wild with worry, but she'd suspected when they'd agreed to start trying for babies that they'd all act and look like Asher, especially since they'd used Asher's eggs both times. It's what she'd wanted, and she'd gotten that in two tiny Asher clones who had her wife wrapped around their little fingers.

She watched the two together and smiled at how Dustin concentrated on what Asher was telling her. They were both in jeans and white T-shirts, and Dustin's hat was a smaller version of Asher's. The belt around Dustin's waist had a small duplicate of Asher's championship buckle, and she'd never heard their kid squeal as loud as the day Asher gave it to her. Reagan had a sinking feeling she had another bull rider in the making, but she had time to get Dustin interested in other things.

"Keep your knees close to the pony's body," Asher said as she led the pony through the yard.

Two was kind of young for this, but Asher had held Dustin at bay as long as she could before giving in to the kid's wishes. Asher kept telling Reagan that saying no to their kid was as hard as telling her no when it came to something she really wanted. It wasn't in her.

"Honey," Reagan called out, startling Wynn into releasing her nipple. Dustin had stood up on the pony's back with perfect balance when Asher turned around. "That kid is going to kill me before the year is out."

She got Wynn situated again and watched Dustin jump from the pony into Asher's arms laughing the entire time. She loved her children, but watching them grow up was giving her a better understanding of her father and what it had been like raising them as children. Granted, she'd never been as wired as Asher, but they'd gotten into their fair share of trouble.

Asher handed over the reins and let Dustin lead the horse around the yard. She watched her for a moment as she squatted close to the fence with her hat low on her head. Her wife really was the best-looking thing she'd ever laid eyes on, and on most days she had a hard time not dragging her off somewhere to get a better view of that handsome face.

"Come over here, Buck," she said, wanting that better view now.

Asher came and sat next to her once she seemed convinced Dustin wasn't going to take up trick riding if she took her eyes off her. She kissed the bottom of Wynn's foot, getting a kick to the mouth for her trouble, but it only made her laugh. "You doing okay?" She kissed Reagan next, and she loved how Asher lingered. "Any morning sickness today?"

"You know that only happens in the afternoon," she teased and kissed Asher again. They'd decided on one more and were waiting to tell anyone until she was at least past the nine-week mark, but she couldn't wait to add to their family.

The baby got fussy between them, so she leaned back and let her finish. Albert and Booker ran to the fence, obviously having spotted Dustin. Their horses were obsessed with their kid and were much gentler than Reagan would've guessed. The strange thing was that they were saddled, but she'd ask questions later. Asher was vigilant as the big animals lowered their heads so Dustin could reach. She burped Wynn and laid her on the blanket she'd put next to her for the baby's nap.

"What's your afternoon looking like?" Asher asked as she stretched out.

"I'm going with Helki to check out some horses later, but I trust her to go alone if you have something in mind." She rested her head on

Asher's chest and watched Dustin feed Albert and Booker buttercups. "*Did* you have something in mind?"

"They finished the new hay barn at the southern tip, and I thought you might like to ride out and check it out with me. We can pack a lunch and see if the loft is up to the job." Asher combed her fingers through her hair and laughed. Pregnancy had been a lot of fun, especially in those months when she thought she'd kill Asher with her demands. If great sex was a prerequisite to a happy marriage, theirs would last a thousand years.

"Are you up for the job?" She slid her fingers just under the waistband of Asher's jeans and gently bit her shoulder.

"Always, my love, always."

"Mommy, look," Dustin yelled. "Albert's kissing me." Albert was lipping Dustin's hair, and their kid was loving it.

"He loves you," she yelled back, making Asher laugh. "What? He does, and you should be happy it's the horse. Wait until she's sixteen, and you find her in the hayloft with some nice cowgirl or cowboy."

"Don't even say that." Asher covered her eyes with her hand and moaned.

"I don't know. It turned out pretty good for me." She chuckled at Asher's discomfort.

"We were doing more than kissing at sixteen in that loft," Asher reminded her. She rolled over when Asher prompted her to and gazed up into those eyes that fueled every dream she'd ever had.

"True." She lifted her head and kissed Asher like they were alone. "But I'll warn her about one important thing."

"What's that, my love?"

"Never kiss a cowgirl unless you're prepared to be swept off your feet. They do wild things like ride bulls and get along better with cows than most people, but they're loyal for life."

"I love you and this life you've given me," Asher said, cupping her cheek.

"Me too, Buck. Me too."

About the Author

Ali Vali is the author of the long-running Cain Casey "Devil" series and the Genesis Clan "Forces" series, as well as numerous standalone romances including two Lambda Literary Award finalists, *Calling the Dead* and *Love Match*.

Originally from Cuba, Ali has retained much of her family's traditions and language and uses them frequently in her stories. Having her father read her stories and poetry before bed every night as a child infused her with a love of reading, which she carries till today. Ali currently lives outside New Orleans, where she cuts grass, cheers on LSU in all things, and is always on the hunt for the perfect old-fashioned. The best part, she says, is writing about the people and places around the city.

Books Available From Bold Strokes Books

The Accidental Bride by Jane Walsh. Spinsters Miss Grace Linfield and Miss Thea Martin travel to Gretna Green to prevent a wedding, only to discover a scandalous passion—for each other. (978-1-63679-345-0)

Broken Fences by Jo Hemmingwood. Former army sergeant Seneca Twist has difficulty adjusting to civilian life until she meets psychologist Robyn Mason and has a place to call home. (978-1-63679-414-3)

Never Kiss a Cowgirl by Ali Vali. Asher Evans dreams of winning the National Finals Rodeo in Vegas, and Reagan Wilson wants no part of something that brings back the memory of what killed her father. (978-1-63679-106-7)

Pantheon Girls by Jean Copeland. Cassie Burke never anticipated the detour life is about to take when a meeting with a prospective client reunites her with a past love and reignites the star-crossed passion they shared twenty years earlier. (978-1-63679-337-5)

Roux for Two by Aurora Rey. For TV chef Chelsea Boudreaux and hometown boy Bryce Cormier, love proves as tricky as making a good pot of gumbo. (978-1-63679-376-4)

Starting Over by Nance Sparks. Jennifer has no idea if she can mend Sam's broken soul after the sudden loss of her wife, but it's never too late for starting over. (978-1-63679-409-9)

Three Wishes by Anne Shade. A magic lamp, a beautiful Jinni, and a cursed princess make for one unbelievable story. (978-1-63679-349-8)

Undiscovered Treasures by MJ Williamz. For Cyl and her friends Luna and Martinique, life's best treasures often appear when they're not looking. (978-1-63679-449-5)

Curse of the Gorgon by Tanai Walker. Cass will do anything to ensure Elle's safety, but is she willing to embrace the curse of the Gorgon? (978-1-63679-395-5)

Dance with Me by Georgia Beers. Scottie Templeton mixes it up on and off the dance floor with sexy salsa instructor Marisa Reyes. But can Scottie get past Marisa's connection to her ex? (978-1-63679-359-7)

Gin and Bear It by Joy Argento. Opposites really can attract, and as Kelly and Logan work together to create a loving home for rescue cat Bear, they just might find one for themselves as well. (978-1-63679-351-1)

Harvest Dreams by Jacqueline Fein-Zachary. Planting the vineyard of their dreams, Kate Bauer and Sydney Barrett must resist their attraction while battling nature and their families, who oppose both the venture and their relationship. (978-1-63679-380-1)

The No Kiss Contract by Nan Campbell. Workaholic Davy believes she can get the top spot at her firm if the senior partners think she's settling down and about to start a family, but she needs the delightful yet dubious Anna to help by pretending to be her fiancée. (978-1-63679-372-6)

Outside the Lines by Melissa Sky. If you had the chance to live forever, would you take it? Amara Rodriguez did, and it sets her on a journey to find her missing mother and unravel the mystery of her own heart. (978-1-63679-403-7)

The Value of Sylver and Gold by Michelle Larkin. When word gets out that former Boston homicide detective Reid Sylver can talk to the dead, the FBI solicits her help on a serial murder case, prompting Reid to assemble forces once again with Detective London Gold. (978-1-63679-093-0)

When It Feels Right by Tagan Shepard. Freshly out of the closet Marlene hasn't been lucky in love, but when it comes to her quirky new roommate Abby, everything just feels right. (978-1-63679-367-2)

The Fall Line by Kelly Wacker. When Jordan Burroughs arrives in the Deep South to paint a local endangered aquatic flower, she doesn't expect to become friends with a mischievous gin-drinking ghost who complicates her budding romance and leads her to an awful discovery and danger. (978-1-63679-205-7)

Lucky in Lace by Melissa Brayden. Straitlaced stationery store owner Juliette Jennings's predictable life unravels when a sexy lingerie shop and its alluring owner move in next door. (978-1-63679-434-1)

Made for Her by Carsen Taite. Neal Walsh is a newly made member of the Mancuso crime family, but will her undeniable attraction to Anastasia Petrov, the wife of her boss's sworn enemy, be the ultimate test of her loyalty? (978-1-63679-265-1)

Off the Menu by Alaina Erdell. Reality TV sensation Restaurant Redo and its gorgeous host Erin Rasmussen will arrive to film in chef Taylor Mobley's kitchen. As the cameras roll, will they make the jump from enemies to lovers? (978-1-63679-295-8)

Pack of Her Own by Elena Abbott. When things heat up in a small town, steamy secrets are revealed between Alpha werewolf Wren Carne and her human mate, Natalie Donovan. (978-1-63679-370-2)

Return to McCall by Patricia Evans. Lily isn't looking for romance—not until she meets Alex, the gorgeous Cuban dance instructor at La Haven, a newly opened lesbian retreat. (978-1-63679-386-3)

So It Went Like This by C. Spencer. A candid and deeply personal exploration of fate, chosen family, and the vulnerability intrinsic in life's uncertainties. (978-1-63555-971-2)

Stolen Kiss by Spencer Greene. Anna and Louise share a stolen kiss, only to discover that Louise is dating Anna's brother. Surely, one kiss can't change everything…Can it? (978-1-63679-364-1)

To Meet Again by Kadyan. When the stark reality of WW II separates cabaret singer Evelyn and Australian doctor Joan in Singapore, they must overcome all odds to find one another again. (978-1-63679-398-6)